Happily Ever After

Marylyle Rogers

St. Martin's Paperbacks

HAPPILY EVER AFTER

ISBN: 0-312-96046-8

Printed in the United States of America

St. Martin's Paperbacks edition/December 1996

St. Martin's Paperbacks are published by St. Martin's Press, 175 Fifth Avenue, New York, NY 10010.

10 9 8 7 6 5 4 3 2 1

HAPPILY EVER AFTER is Dedicated
in Loving Memory of My Father,
Lyle M. Knutson,
Who lent solace with his earnest belief
in that better place
waiting beyond mortal life . . . .

PROLOGUE

May 1, 1900

A slight breeze teased the mass of golden curls and skirts of a white-gowned woman gazing up an Irish hillside. Lissan's attention rested on beloved parents nearing its crest, bathed in the bright pastels of dawn. Her father, remarkably fit for all his years, climbed a few paces ahead and carried her fragile mother without the slightest sign of strain.

Clearly this was the moment she and her siblings—two brothers and two sisters—had been warned to expect. Each, on their twentieth birthdays, were called into the study for a private talk during which their parents requested a solemn promise. When their mother's failing health made it clear that the end was near, her children and grandchildren were to bid her their last good-byes. Lord Comlan of Doncaully was then to be left in peace to carry his wife into the Irish hills unchallenged.

Serious oaths had been given to neither follow nor question their father's action. The four older siblings, married and with families of their own, had curiously discussed this odd command but never argued against the wishes of a father both loved and respected. However, Lissan took pride in an indepen-

dent nature, and her curiosity was not so easily
quelled.

Days earlier, as his frail Amy began sinking into
an unmistakable decline while visiting a cherished
retreat, the small Irish home known as Daffy's Cottage, Lord Comlan had summoned their descen-
dants to her bedside. Seeing the inevitable looming
near, five adult children hadn't been surprised when
during the dark hours of night their father announced his intent. Though her brothers and sisters
accepted this decision with deep sorrow, Lissan, a
decade younger than the next older child, had
begged that she be permitted to accompany her parents at least as far as the first slope's summit. A
frowning Lord Comlan had agreed only after his
gravely ill wife added a whispered entreaty to their
daughter's plea.

When her parents halted at the brow of a rise beyond which lay others progressively steeper, Lissan
assumed that they had paused to wish her a final
farewell. She would then be expected to keep a
promise by returning to the family members waiting
in the quaint, ivy-covered cottage below.

"This can't be the last time I see you, not yet, not
now. . . ." Lissan huskily whispered, embracing both
her father and the woman he cradled near.

"But it is either *now* or never," Lord Comlan
firmly stated although love softened an emerald
gaze caressing the golden hair that framed his youngest daughter's captivating face. He loved all of their
children but shared a special bond with the ever-
curious, often impetuous Lissan.

Lissan bent to press a kiss against her mother's
papery cheek before letting her arms drop and beginning to retreat. Lady Amethyst's fragile hand restrained her.

Eyes clouding against the prospect of never seeing

her parents again, Lissan glanced down to find unsteady fingers affixing a beautiful brooch to the tucked and daintily embroidered dimity of her bodice.

"Wear my amulet *always*." This was an earnest appeal, which their speaker prayed Lissan would heed. "Wear it and you'll be protected from harm."

"But Mama—" Lissan started to protest this gift of her mother's most treasured piece of jewelry—an exquisitely carved ivory unicorn, gold-horned and rearing inside an onyx circle.

"Hush now, my baby, my fairy-child," Lady Amethyst gently rebuked. "Do as your mama says this one last time."

Firmly biting lips to block useless pleas that the lump in her throat would strangle anyway, Lissan stepped back. Yet, rather than depart completely, she froze a short distance away, waiting to watch her parents continue the foretold journey through Irish hills.

The sight of small white teeth mistreating a full lower lip brought a sad half-smile to Comlan's mouth. Despite carrying his youngest sister's name and having inherited both his fair coloring and emerald eyes, this willful daughter was very much her beloved mother's child—likely a further reason that she held a special place in his heart.

Lissan was puzzled when, rather than continuing the journey, her father stepped into the ring of beautiful flowers encircling an ancient oak and paused.

She'd been told that her name came from this site known since the distant past as Lissan's Fairy Ring. It was her favorite place in all the world, and she had long thought that fact the likely reason her mother called her a fairy-child.

As a youngster Lissan had begged again and again to be told the magical tale of the dainty fairy

damsel who'd fallen in love with a mortal warrior.
To share his life in the human world, the ethereal
princess allowed her mystical powers to drain into
the earth and at that moment around her feet a circle
of perfect flowers had sprung up—and bloomed
still. During the magical days of childhood Lissan
had often wished that fairies were real and fanta-
sized about the wondrous adventures she would
have if only she were one. Then, inevitably, she'd
grown up. . . .

Her attention abruptly returning to the present,
Lissan was horrified at having allowed foolish memories to claim her thoughts in the midst of this serious and sorrowful event. Guilt joined guilt as she
closely watched her white-haired father lower his
frail burden's feet to the ground. Holding the weak
woman barely able to stand close against his side,
he started to walk counterclockwise around the ring
of flowers. With each pace forward the woman's
steps became firmer while an aura of ever-brighter
light wrapped about them. Lissan's eyes widened as
every completed circuit seemed to strip years from
the luminous couple until they abruptly fell into the
circle's center . . . and disappeared completely!

Where were they? Lissan started forward but
stopped. Clearly this was exactly what they hadn't
wanted their children to see. But *how* had they done
it? What did it mean?

"Worse yet," Lissan murmured aloud—a regrettable habit she'd yet to tame. "How in sweet heav-
en's name can I possibly go back to the cottage and
explain?"

Bewildered, Lissan sank to ground padded by
thick grasses. She had long since outgrown fairy
tales and didn't believe in magic. But if what she'd
just seen wasn't magic, then what . . . ? How could
she explain the impossible? She couldn't return to

her waiting siblings and simply tell them that their parents hadn't died but instead miraculously grown young again? And then vanished.

No, that truth certainly wouldn't satisfy either her scientifically minded oldest brother, Garnet, or David, a well-respected clergyman. As for Opal and Pearl, her two sisters who were determined to see her as happily wed as they were and thus were preoccupied with finding a husband for her, well—Lissan grimaced, green eyes darkening to a forest hue while gazing morosely into the fairy ring.

Her family was certain to think that grief had weakened their little sister's hold on sanity and driven her back into childhood's wild tales of fairy magic. No, she couldn't rationally expect them to accept the truth for truth. But neither would she lie and say their father had simply carried his gravely ill wife ever farther into the hills. But if not that, then what?

Lissan's eyes narrowed. Perhaps she would discover a rational explanation by following her parents' path? Folly, utter folly. But still—

Yielding to the impetuous spirit that had so horrified past governesses but always earned a secret smile from her father, Lissan rose with innate grace. She unhesitatingly moved to the very point at which her father had lowered her mother's feet and began retracing their footsteps.

Before completing a first circuit Lissan wished she'd counted how many times her parents had gone around the circle before falling into its center, but by the time she'd made the second lap it no longer mattered. As if unseen hands were pushing from behind, she stumbled onward at an ever-increasing pace until, as if caught by centrifugal force, she was swept along at a terrifying speed. Panicking, she

summoned every shred of strength and threw herself free.

Lissan landed on her back—hard! Even the
ground's thick green padding was no protection.
Her head bounced but her eyes stayed open . . . and
widened against the flash of a double-bladed broadsword slashing straight down with deadly force!

CHAPTER 1

May 1, 1115

Rory O'Connor silently led his band of warriors through the ebbing shadows of night and up a heavily wooded hillside. They had tracked O'Brien's bloodthirsty raiders from the burned-out shell of an aging farmer's cottage and meant to wreak vengeance upon the vile curs.

Despite his men's desire to see the deed immediately done Rory had convinced them of the wisdom in banking the fires of anger the better to see greater punishment inflicted with smallest cost. At his direction, they'd circled around their foes to wait in wooded shadows surrounding an ancient fairy ring in the glade at the hill's summit.

With deceptive calm Rory stood motionless, broad back resting against one strong tree trunk while awaiting the propitious moment to strike back. As lord of the most important among a ring of fortresses protecting Connaught, he was honor bound to his young cousin, King Turlough, and must defend not only his own holdings but the whole kingdom against forces commanded by the too proud and ambitious king of Munster.

King Muirtrecht of Munster had long claimed the high-kingship of all Ireland, but Turlough, coming into manhood and ever rising in power, presented a danger to that ambition. Intending to weaken his threat, men from Munster harried the borders of Connaught by terrorizing inhabitants, burning farms, and stealing precious livestock.

A snapped twig, a muffled voice, earned Rory's immediate attention. He leaned forward, peering through thick leaves and down the slope to where men climbed toward the fairy ring single file. The rising sun spread its brilliant shades across a morning sky forming an appropriate backdrop for the violence erupting at Rory's signal.

Warriors with raised swords closed in on the summit's newcomers from all sides. Gasps of surprise ending in harsh curses accompanied the fierce clash of blade meeting blade. But as time passed uncounted the skirmish's initial taunts and blasphemous oaths settled into either grunts of exertion or groans of pain.

Caught in a prolonged and brutal fight with the strong leader of Munster's raiders, Rory lightly whirled to avoid the downward slash of the other's broadsword . . . and froze as it sliced through a beautiful, golden woman inexplicably tumbling at their feet.

Lissan glimpsed blood on the terrifying blade lifting from its deadly attack. That ominous sight jolted her out of shock and into horrified recognition of peril all around. In this glade gone eerily quiet, she was surrounded by men dressed as warriors from a distant past and, despite their broadswords, spears, and daggers, apparently terrorstruck to stone.

Too startled for either deep fear or sensible thought, Lissan automatically pushed her skirts demurely down while struggling to sit up. She knew exactly where she'd fallen and yet this long-familiar scene had changed. The ancient oak suddenly seemed half as old while dense forest and thick undergrowth covered ground where there'd never been more than lush grasses and a sprinkling of trees.

"The White Witch. . . ."

Lissan's emerald eyes instantly flew up to the source of gasped words—the stocky man still standing above and clutching a blade stained with blood as red as his hair. A chorus of fearful voices echoed his epithet even as their frightened sources whirled and deserted the battlefield to flee into woodland shadows. Although clearly the master of one side engaged in this conflict, her assailant followed their lead.

Disconcerted by these extremely odd doings and unaccountably altered surroundings, Lissan struggled to restore some measure of calm and make rational plans. She ought to dash away and rejoin the family waiting in a cottage below . . . but with everything so changed she didn't truthfully know what path would lead her there.

A deep voice like rough velvet intruded. "Are you unharmed?"

"Indeed, yes." Further befuddled to discover herself not so alone as she'd believed, Lissan instantly responded to the Gaelic question in that ancient language learned as a child at her father's knee. "My fall will leave bruises, but it's only my pride that truly suffers."

With the words, Lissan glanced up to meet a penetrating gaze so dark as to seem all of black. It belonged to the raven-haired, stunningly handsome man towering above—taller than any she knew save her golden father and brothers.

While the maiden of sun-gilded hair gaped at him, Rory studied her so long and so well that a wild blush rosed her cheeks. She was dressed in a pecu-

liar gown of amazingly fine cloth such as he'd never
seen before. But, despite courageously uptilted chin,
it was plainly apprehension that widened emerald
eyes of amazing clarity. Surely the White Witch
couldn't, wouldn't, be afraid of him?

"Once well struck—" Rory calmly probed for a
more satisfying response. "Mael O'Brien's blade
rarely fails to mortally harm its target."

Cheeks rosy an instant earlier went pale. The
broadsword! Sweet heaven! That it had well and
truly struck her was proven by the blood she'd
glimpsed on its blade. But how could that be? Heart
pounding erratically, Lissan glanced down to a mid-
riff so completely untouched that even the delicate
cloth of her morning gown remained whole and un-
bloodied. No wonder her attacker and the other men
had fled in fear.

"Can you account for your deliverance?" Having
learned through hard experience that little was as it
seemed, Rory was annoyed with himself for instinctively sympathizing with the beauty doubtless en-
acting a well-practiced charade.

Lissan blinked rapidly against panic roused by the
unspoken disdain flowing from a powerfully built
interrogator clearly growing impatient. Absently
slipping into an action habitually used to busy nervous hands during times of tension, she brushed a
cloud of bright tresses back with slow deliberation.
Unfortunately, she could no more explain this miracle than she could solve the puzzle of the many
abrupt changes in her surroundings or her parents'
disappearance.

Suspecting the golden maid's silence was a further
feminine ploy to win indulgence by feigning helplessness, Rory flatly demanded, "Who are you?"

"Lissan." She immediately responded, pleased
that this question, at least, had a simple answer.

"Like the fairy responsible for those forever-blooming flowers?" As Rory O'Connor nodded toward the circle of blossoms, the sunlight that gleamed over black hair was the antithesis of his dark frown. Having long scoffed at the superstitious tales and foolish portents accepted by too many fools, even this mention of otherworldly magic made him uneasy—particularly after this woman's extraordinary arrival.

Lissan's attention flew to the fairy ring she could nearly swear had been trampled by fighting men but now looked fresh and as untouched as she was, despite the broadsword's blow.

"Yes." Lissan's sharp nod sent golden tresses again tumbling over slender shoulders. "I was named for the fairy in that tale."

Rory's frown deepened. "And from whence do you hail?"

"My home is in London." Uncomfortable beneath a masculine disapproval rarely encountered and never so long sustained, Lissan smiled winsomely at this man unreasonably displeased by answers given as promptly and honestly as she could.

Those responses, however, left Rory more thoroughly and, he was certain, justifiably annoyed with the beauty so confident in her vanity that she blandly confessed what she must know he'd view as a crime. And this she did even while boldly enticing him with an alluring smile to forgo his own honor.

"I assume, then"—ice coated Rory's deep voice—"that you were sent by King Henry."

Lissan rightly heard this statement for the accusation it was. These words, however, merely added another layer of alarming bewilderment. After all, Queen Victoria had ruled the British Empire for decades and there hadn't been a royal Henry in a very, very long time.

As a first step toward solving this daunting riddle, but wary of the answer, Lissan quietly asked, "What year is this?"

Disgust for so blatant and foolish an attempt to cloud dangerous issues further deepened Rory's voice as he growled, "The year of our Lord, 1115."

1115? It couldn't be and yet—The image of the broadsword slicing through her body echoed in her mind. She lifted her eyes to meet the stern gaze of the strangely dressed man towering above her.

"Then—" The word caught in Lissan's throat and her forlorn gaze dropped to the hands tightly clasped in her lap. Drawing a deep breath, she forced more words through stiff lips: "Then I have no home in this world."

Rory's black brows drew together in a fierce scowl. What did this beauty, this stranger, mean to suggest? That by virtue of her mere presence on his land he was responsible for her? Hands curling into fists, he backed two steps away fully intending to leave the intruder to fend for herself . . . but . . .

The forlorn droop of slender shoulders cloaked in hair like spun gold stabbed Rory with a sharp pang of guilt. And though he had no qualms about dispatching foes, he'd be a soulless ogre to abandon such tender prey to the vicious beasts of the forest. This admission only deepened his frustration with the muddle Lissan's inexplicable arrival had made of his morn's carefully laid battle plans. That fight had ended not only without a clear winner but with his warriors fleeing as readily as their opponents— a poor position from which to repel the next assault. And he knew all too well that further assaults were inevitable.

Lissan was lost in a glum haze of questions impossible to answer—the greatest of which were how, why, and could she ever return to her own time?

Thus preoccupied, she was caught unprepared when a strong hand suddenly seized one of her smaller ones, pulling her up to stand facing its tall, dark owner. Too startled to reason clearly, her wary gaze locked with Rory O'Connor's. At this close view, she realized that his eyes were not truly black but deepest blue and so penetrating it seemed disturbingly possible that he could read her soul.

Rory, in turn, felt himself drawn into fathomless green crystal depths but, as a warrior of courage, fought the lures of a woman who must be either witch or spy. An instant later his skill as tactician reminded him that the best defense was offense.

Swept suddenly full against a broad, muscular frame and held there by arms that seemed bands of steel, Lissan gasped. But even that faint sound was muted by a kiss rough at the outset which gentled into a persuasion stealing her breath and dropping her into a blaze of unfamiliar sensations. Hands uselessly balled into fists failed to land a single blow of protest before she was unceremoniously thrust aside.

Gazing into eyes of green mist, Rory stepped back while self-disgust hardened his handsome face into a mask of cool cynicism. He had intended to disarm her snares by exercising his own considerable skills as a ladycharmer, but she'd defeated him with lips that tasted of innocence and the stunned expression of a virgin seduced to reckless passion. It was an act. It must be an act—but with it she'd won.

"Follow me," Rory coldly snapped.

"Follow you?" Horrified by her own responsiveness, Lissan glared at the man. "First you assault me and then you have the gall to think I'll obey your orders. I think *not!*"

"The forest is a dangerous place even for an armed man and deadly for a woman alone. There are wolves in these woods. Wolves and wild boar with vicious tusks. And, of course, bands of desperate outlaws and outcasts. All of whom will find you sweet meat for a feast—of one kind or another. That is if you're witless enough to linger here alone and unprotected."

"But if I am the witch you believe me to be, what have I to fear?" Even as Lissan demanded this, her thoughts filled with visions of the fangs she'd seen on wolves in the London Zoo. And, too, she remembered the crude drawing of a wild boar ravaging its kill. It had been reproduced in the same history book where she'd read about how roving gangs of the angry dispossessed joined dangerous outlaws to make traveling hazardous during the early centuries of this millennium.

For the first time, it occurred to Lissan that her interest in ages gone by, her ongoing attempts to satisfy an endless curiosity about everything from ancient art to the newest scientific discoveries, might have a negative side. The next instant she scolded herself for being foolish when surely every morsel of knowledge would be useful in navigating her way through the unfamiliar territory of an ancient past.

"So be it," Rory responded after a long pause. While she'd fumed, he had conducted a leisurely examination of the scowling maid. His scrutiny had taken in the full length of her from the mass of gilded hair framing a heart-shaped face down slender, white-gowned form to the dainty slippers as unusual as the rest of her. Now with a sardonic glitter in dark eyes and a mirthless smile, he turned and began striding away.

"No-o-o." Lissan hadn't expected her formidable opponent to capitulate so easily. No gentleman of her day would leave a well-born woman stranded. "I'll follow . . . for now. . . ."

Hearing in her own words an echo of the type of fainthearted, determinedly frail females she most despised, Lissan cringed. To make matters worse, the wickedly attractive and far too arrogant Mr. O'Connor didn't bother to turn and face her again. Clearly he expected her to be grateful when his pace slowed sufficiently for her to follow through the dense woodland. Annoyance deepened by the fact that gratitude was owed, Lissan indignantly picked up delicate dimity skirts and petticoats to trail behind, ducking under low-hanging branches and stepping over fallen trunks.

When not glancing down to secure firm footing, Lissan pinned her gaze to the tip ends of raven-black hair falling just below the Irishman's broad shoulders. All the while she was fully aware of the towering trees and thick undergrowth making a path known since childhood suddenly unrecognizable. It was the unfamiliarity and new dangers of terrain encompassing the fairy ring that forced Lissan to reluctantly acknowledge she had no choice but to follow the formidable Rory O'Connor's lead.

Yet even as Lissan tagged after a reluctant rescuer, it felt as if she'd been dropped into some childhood fairy tale come to life—and feared her destined role was truly that of the apparently wicked witch she'd already been named.

This couldn't be happening! She again refused to accept this impossible situation. It must be a dream brought on by the grief of her mother's imminent death. No, not a dream but a *nightmare* from which she would surely soon awake.

Lissan instinctively dug the nails of one hand into the palm of the other . . . and winced at the pain. Was it possible to experience such sharp discomfort without waking? Or—horrors—was this reality?

Still irritated at having failed to prevail against the

beauty's surely feigned purity, Rory remained as emotionless as if carved of stone when he stopped at the edge of a clearing.

"This abode has been unused since the death of the woman who last lived here."

At these words, Lissan glanced up to find a tiny thatched building nestled against the base of a hill—in, it seemed fairly certain, precisely the same spot as the one she'd left this morning. And yet this structure had but one level and was even smaller than Daffy's Cottage, something she'd have sworn impossible only the previous day. This was not a dream nor even a nightmare. This was *real!* Lissan struggled to maintain an outward composure while her heart plunged into a sea of panic.

Rory continued while Lissan gaped. "It contains sufficient amenities to shelter you—all save food-stuffs. Those I'll bring on the morrow."

When without a further word the man turned to leave, a fountain of questions burst from Lissan.

"Wait! Tell me who you were fighting . . . and why . . . and will they have followed us here? Am I safe?"

Dark brows arched inquiringly as Rory answered with a mocking question. "Was it not you who claimed that the witch you are is always safe?"

As the irritating Irishman strode away Lissan whirled to stomp toward the small, deserted building with green fires snapping in her eyes and fanning a burning determination to find the way home.

Rory refused to glance back toward the beauty he could almost believe born of an otherworldly fairy breed but whose questions were surely those of a spy. He couldn't consign her to the dubious mercy of a wolf pack but neither would he allow her to intrude so far into his sphere that she might learn enough to be of interest to King Henry and a danger to his own.

During the depths of night a hulking figure of far more power than grace was admitted into a heavily guarded and sturdy wooden keep. Fergil promptly approached the dais with its high table where his red-haired master impatiently waited. After the requisite bow he delivered his report with a confidence shaken when, at its end, his master's expression had changed not one whit. Fergil was left to fear his work was a disappointment and his words were doubted—something for which a high price might be called forfeit.

" 'Struth, my lord." As a proud warrior still clad in garb stained during the honorable battle aborted now nearly a day past, the nervous Fergil leaned closer to his seated lord and earnestly defended his report. "O'Connor led the strange lady to Tuatha Cottage and left her there . . . alone."

"And why not?" Contemptuous of his dull-witted minion, sarcasm dripped from Mael O'Brien's words.

"O'Connor is a fool!" Fergil heatedly asserted. "After our many successful raids across his border, how can the great tactician he is reputed to be fail to see that a woman unguarded is easily captured?"

"O'Connor is many things I despise," Mael growled. "But a fool he is *not!* 'Tis obvious he sees what you've either overlooked or aren't clever enough to perceive without an explanation reduced to simple terms."

Fergil cringed beneath his lord's disdain but listened carefully as from between gritted teeth Mael spat out his meaning in clear words.

"A witch has little reason to fear anything or anyone and even less while cradled within those spell-becharmed walls."

Fergil's mud-brown eyes lost their rare spark, returning to a more usual opaque dullness. In an alarm-strained voice, he tentatively asked, "Then you believe the woman to truly be a witch?"

A sneer twisted Mael's thick lips but his nearly colorless gaze was hard. "You were a part of the bitter battle and saw my broadsword slice cleanly through her. You saw, too, that the blade dripped with blood while the pristine purity of her odd gown went unsullied."

In frustration, thick hands slammed palm flat against tabletop, sloshing ale from the drinking cup planted directly in front of the speaker.

"Oh, aye," Mael thundered. "She is a witch!"

The two guardsmen posted on either side of the door lost their grip on cloaks of impassivity and joined Fergil in cowering before their master's rage.

Rather than feeling shame for having caused this response, Mael was pleased. It was his view that inspiring fear, even terror, was the most effective measure for keeping underlings in line.

"Aye, a witch," Mael added in softer, darker tones. "The White Witch of ominous legend."

Though Fergil admitted his master might be right in thinking him weak-witted, he took pride in his courage and it was with courage that he stood straighter and dared pose another question.

"What then can we mere mortal warriors do to defeat one of her powers?"

While an uncomfortable silence lengthened, Mael's strange eyes seemed to freeze Fergil into a motionless statue. It was an illusion supported by the strong shiver that passed through Fergil once Mael glanced away and began to speak.

"Even a witch can be trapped—or eliminated."

Earned by the wariness in his followers' expression, a cruel grin lacking any hint of warmth spread across Mael's lips. "With the right materials and aid of one even more powerful, she will be! Then after we've neutralized the White Witch's threat, O'Connor will submit and lead his royal cousin in yielding to the power of our sovereign, Muirtrecht O'Brien, King of Munster and High King of all Erin."

CHAPTER 2

Dawn's light crept through a crack between the slats of one shutter and fell in a narrow band whose path slowly lengthened across the sleeping Lissan's creamy cheek. Under this minor annoyance the journey to wakefulness began with hope for surfacing from strange dreams. Thick lashes fluttered open to disappointment of finding herself not only still in the past but the focus of another's steady gaze.

A young girl of perhaps six or seven sat cross-legged at the far end of a crude bed—no more than a simple straw-filled pallet. With chin resting between cupped hands the child looked like a lost waif of unwavering eyes so dark a blue as to appear nearly black. Was that a common trait to inhabitants of this area? Or was this child in some way related to the powerful man who'd left Lissan here?

"Good morrow," the dark-haired child said softly.

"And to you," Lissan responded, practical enough to know that since bemoaning an impossible situation would be useless, she must deal with *this* reality. While continuing to meet the child's unblinking stare directly, she slowly sat upright, an action that sent a golden mass of sleep-tousled hair tumbling over her shoulders. "Have you been here long?"

With a slight shake of her head, the solemn child
smiled at last, warming her serious face and lending
a soft gleam to her eyes.

"Won't your mother be missing you?" Though
surely a logical next question, Lissan immediately
regretted the words that extinguished the light in her
young companion's expression.

"She's gone to sing with the angels." Thick black
lashes blinked rapidly in a brave attempt to restrain
too ready tears. "Though Morag says 'tis silly, Liam
says it's because Mama's voice was so beautiful that
God summoned her to sing in his heavenly choir."

Lissan wanted to ask who and where was this
Morag, but the somber child's lingering grief stilled
the words. Rather, she forced a warm tone to her
voice and brightly said, "I'm Lissan, what's your
name?"

"Lissan?" Abruptly straightening, the plainly
awestruck girl gasped, "Are you the fairy princess
from the magical ring of flowers?"

Amazed that the little one was familiar with this
apparently very old fairy tale and the fantasy figure
at its heart, Lissan ruefully shook her head.

"Mama always said that we are descended from
her . . . and the mortal warrior she loved," the waif
announced lifting her chin defiantly as if expecting
her claim to be ridiculed.

"Then you must be very special indeed. . . ." With
brows raised in a show of admiration, Lissan
promptly allayed the young girl's concern. "I was
merely named after that fairy princess."

Pleased by the words of her new acquaintance, the
child's shy smile returned. "Mama said it was true
but Morag swears she only made it up to please
me."

Lissan was appalled. This Morag must be heartless to crush the shining dream of a grieving child.

The girl unintentionally prevented her from asking more about the unpleasant Morag by uncurling thin limbs and scrambling to stand.

"Are you hungry?"

Lissan grimaced. She hadn't eaten since sharing rolls and tea with family members in the predawn hours of the previous day (how odd—the sun wouldn't rise on that day until hundreds of years had passed). She gave her head a brief shake to clear her thoughts of strange facts and the sad memory of trailing her parents up the hillside.

Hungry? Yes, Lissan admitted she was very hungry but . . . .

"Before leaving, the gentleman who led the way to this cottage warned me that there's no food here. However, he promised to bring provisions today." Lissan hoped for the child's sake that Rory O'Connor would keep his promise even while stifling the regrettable leap of senses caused by the mere mention of the devastating rescuer nearer to being captor.

Unfazed by either the woman's announcement or use of the unfamiliar term "gentleman," the waif leaned forward and with an impish grin loudly whispered, "*He* doesn't know everything about this cottage." She `sat back and gleefully clapped her hands. "Leastways he doesn't know about the cellar that Mama and I dug last autumn to stock with supplies enough to see us through even a hard winter."

Although Lissan continued to smile, she was surprised. Clearly this child knew the man who'd deposited her here. But how? The stern Mr. O'Connor hardly seemed the sort to indiscriminately spread news of his activities.

"Come—" The girl held out an inviting hand. "They don't snap when you bite into them anymore but the apples are still tasty. And there's at least one unopened barrel of salt pork and near a whole side of smoked venison."

Lissan rose, rewarding the arch grin of this solemn waif transformed into a mischievous elfling with a radiant smile. She ached from head to toe but knew her discomfort resulted more from a preceding day spent tramping up and down hillsides than a night lying atop the strange and much less than comfortable straw-filled mattress.

"Then this is your home?" Lissan asked, openly curious and gently probing to learn more about her unexpected companion.

"It was until Mama . . ."

"Went to sing with the angels." Finishing the sentence which an again solemn speaker let fade into silence, Lissan rued the question that had thrust the child back into unhappy thoughts.

"Come—" the girl repeated. Plainly determined to suppress hurt and move onward, she seized Lissan's hand and began tugging her toward the cottage's entry. "I'll need your help to open the cellar's hidden door."

"Wait—" Lissan held back, atoning for the delay with another warm smile. "That you are a fairy child I've no doubt, but while I dress pray tell me your name and where you live today."

Pale cheeks rosing with delight over this lovely lady's pleasing description, the child released Lissan's hand and willingly complied.

"I'm Hildie," she announced. "In truth, Hilda after the first Abbess of Whitby . . . but I've always been called Hildie." With a winsome smile, she added, "And I live with my papa in the keep."

Keep? Lissan reached out to retrieve the dimity gown she'd hung from one among a row of pegs that ran along one wall, all likely put there to accommodate an inhabitant's wardrobe. Mentally search-

ing for all she could remember of events during this
general area of Irish history, Lissan called to mind
several famous keeps—all fortified structures hous-
ing important defenders of the various kingdoms in
Ireland. Was Hildie's father a warrior in the garrison
or a servant?

As fine-spun, snowy fabric drifted down over the
dainty chemise in which Lissan had slept, Hildie's
eyes widened. But it was when a heavy swathe of
golden hair was lifted to flow freely over slender
shoulders that the girl gasped.

"You *are* the White Witch."

Lissan's first instinct was to deny this label as
quickly as she had refuted the suggestion that she
might be the fairy princess . . . but hesitated. Hadn't
that false identity held her safe earlier by putting
even armed men to flight? Perhaps permitting this
erroneous designation to stand would be her best
protection amid a society filled with unfamiliar people and strange practices—at least until she found
some way to make sense out of extremely odd recent
events. And how better to learn more of this apparently alarming mythical figure than from the innocent Hildie?

"What do you know of the White Witch?" Lissan
gently inquired.

"Same as everyone does." Hildie peered at her
companion suspiciously.

"Won't you retell the tale for me?" Lissan softly
pleaded with a smile of amazing sweetness.

Why would the White Witch ask such a thing?
Hildie frowned. Was it a test of worthiness? No matter. While the golden beauty patiently listened, Hildie launched into an earnest restating of the very old
tale, careful to use exactly the same phrases with
which it had been repeated throughout many generations.

"Long, long ago and cradled in the mists of a distant past, Elesa, the great seeress, foretold a time of turmoil. Connaught dangerously hovers between the depths of ruin and the pinnacle of power. During this bleak and desolate period the White Witch will appear—suddenly as if dropped from the sky. 'Tis her destiny that from amid a bog of perilous foes and deceitful friends she shall point Connaught's way—" As Hildie paused a shadow crossed her face. "Either to generations of slavery or over a thorny path to safety within the golden light of victory."

"But which?" The question inadvertently slipped from Lissan's lips.

Several dark tendrils fell forward as Hildie slowly shook her head. "That answer not even the powerful seeress knew . . . but surely you do?"

Meeting the wistful hope in deep blue eyes, Lissan recognized the depth of responsibility she'd unknowingly accepted with her foolish plan for self-defense. Now, faced with the sort of amazing actions her new acquaintances expected of her fantasy alter ego, she would've firmly, even vehemently denied (albeit belatedly) any connection with this White Witch . . . were the opportunity not already lost.

"So this is where you've gotten off to, Hildie." Rory had opened the portal so quietly that neither of the two inside heard a sound.

Once the door swung wide, the golden vision inside caught Rory's breath. He instantly fought to regain command of his own responses—a chore rarely difficult before the beguiling stranger's arrival. *A fool I've suddenly become,* Rory berated himself. *And no woman makes of me a fool!* Filled with self-disgust, he reminded himself that this woman's stunning beauty was certain to be either a weapon honed by King Henry of England for the sake of working her dan-

gerous wiles on him or a mask constructed by magic
and thus more dangerous still.

"Morag cautioned me to look for you here but I
refused." Rory forced his gaze and thoughts back to
the first matter at hand . . . an errant child. "I swore
you knew it wasn't safe and wouldn't flee to this
cottage again. No, not *again*." He sternly scowled.
"But it seems my trust was misplaced."

"I am sorry, Papa," Hildie apologized, dark head
bowed.

"I dare say you are, poppet." An instant's fear that
he'd taken his own frustrations out on the child gentled Rory's tone as he directed, "Go, wait in the cart
until I'm ready for the return to Ailm Keep." Ignoring the lure of green-fire eyes, he kept his attention
on the penitent child until she slowly disappeared,
pulling the door closed behind.

"Are you her father?" Lissan asked, letting disapproval tinge her voice. Apparently Hildie and her
mother had lived in this tiny hovel while the alarm-
ingly attractive man now stepping two paces closer
resided in a keep that doubtless provided more comfort and assuredly greater safety.

"That's what they say." With this enigmatic response Rory steadily met the challenge in emerald
eyes and turned the question back on a golden inquisitor too impossibly lovely for her appearance to
be natural. "Are you the White Witch?"

Though having wished only moments past to refute this claim, Lissan held the dark, penetrating
gaze without blinking and promptly echoed his answer, "That's what they say."

Grateful for the concealing dimness of a room in-
adequately lit by the few sunbeams slipping through
a poorly shuttered window, Lissan fought to stand
braced against the unwavering force of blue granite
eyes. At the same time she struggled even more val-

iantly to restore a normal pattern to oddly shortened breaths and calm a pounding heart, both instinctive but unwelcome physical responses to the devastating Irishman too near.

"Are you hungry?" A warrior renowned for his skillful use of tactical surprises, Rory purposely startled his inexperienced opponent with an abrupt shift of focus.

Lissan's lashes fluttered. Though initially bewildered by the unexpected concern of one who'd relentlessly held her in an unbroken visual duel, in the next instant she was grateful. His question had, after all, disrupted an intense awareness of the intriguing man that she feared embarrassingly obvious to him.

Lissan straightened to her full height and, hoping to cover the awkward pause, boldly answered, "Very!"

Though refusing to quail before the intimidating warrior warily viewing her as a likely enemy, Lissan hoped a winsome smile would mask her uneasiness with him and all else contained in this world with its strange mix of things both comfortingly familiar and terrifyingly alien.

Rory was impressed equally by the maid's undaunted response to his verbal assault and the power of a smile so sweet it seemed certain to flow from the bright magic of the fairy whose name she bore rather than the dark forces of witchery. Rory's handsome face froze into an expressionless mask. He was irritated with himself for dumbly gazing like a moonling adolescent at the beauty whose arrival was suspicious and intentions were in serious doubt. Seldom had he met a member of the frailer gender interesting enough to claim his attention uninvited or hold it for more than a few hours' pleasure. It was disconcerting that within the span of a single day he now found himself constantly drawn to this

possible adversary whose own responses were as
much a mystery as was her purpose for coming.

"Outside I've a cartload of provisions," Rory
coldly announced. "Along with garb more practical
for you to wear."

Welcoming any distraction to ease the strain of
this meeting, Lissan ignored his implied insult for
her taste in clothing and started for the door despite
feet protected only by the stocking she'd worn to
bed. The intimidating man's abruptly upraised hand
halted her in mid-step.

"Though you may possess mystical powers, I have
none able to divine whether you've come for the
good or ill of Connaught. Until that question has an
unequivocal answer, I dare not allow you to roam
freely through my lands. Thus, along with the promised supplies I've brought a companion who will
provide protection both for . . . and against you."

Lissan scowled. This rapid shifting from antago-
nism to apparent concern and then back to antago-
nism again was disconcerting. Annoying, too. With
that admission came an unpleasant realization. If
Mr. O'Connor could command another to guard her,
then he was more than the humble servant or even
the simple warrior she'd speculated that Hildie's father would prove to be—far more.

"Liam—" Rory called through the door he'd
thrown open.

In an instant the doorway was filled by a young
man of stocky build and sun-streaked blond hair.

"This is Lissan, your new mistress," Rory announced, waving toward the woman in the room's
center without glancing her way. "I charge you to
guard her from harm with the same diligence you
are to employ in ensuring that she wreak no ill
amongst the people of Connaught."

Warily Lissan watched as the newcomer stepped

nearer and planted a tall oak stave squarely in front of himself. While securely clasping the primitive weapon in both hands, he nodded so deeply his forehead momentarily touched the thick, use-smoothed pole in silent acknowledgment.

Lissan responded to this example of ancient courtesy with a brilliant smile of such intense sweetness that it widened the hazel-green eyes of a recipient already dazed by the beauty gilded by rays of sunshine streaming through the open portal.

Despite the instinctive tightening of his jaw, Rory was unwilling to admit, even to himself, an uneasiness in seeing the ethereal damsel share such close association with another male. He told himself his concern was for Liam, the earnest boy he would never willingly see subjected to temptations that might lead to disloyalty and the staining of honor. Had he made a mistake in choosing to act as guard this impressionable youngster at nineteen barely more than half his own age of thirty-four? No! Rory's eyes snapped with blue lightning as he vehemently answered his own question. Liam was as worthy of trust as any man in his garrison. Still, to both break the younger pair's visual bond and divert his own unwelcome thoughts, he brusquely spoke.

"Lest you think either Liam's youth or rustic weapon might render him unequal to his task, let me assure you that I've seen the boy lay low many a skilled, sword-wielding man."

Disgusted with himself for his unnecessary emphasis of Liam's youth, Rory was quick to add, "And should limited space threaten the effectiveness of his stave, he possesses yet another useful ability." Never shifting a penetrating gaze of black ice from the damsel, Rory motioned toward the younger man.

Lissan gasped as an instantaneous silver flash of

honed metal sliced through the air. The dagger pierced one wall with a loud thwack after neatly splitting the same wooden peg that had earlier supported her dimity dress.

As the peg's two useless halves fell into rushes scattered across a dirt floor, Lissan inwardly conceded this young man's skill with a dagger and had no doubt but that he was equally adept with his stave. Both were barbarous, deadly arts utterly unthinkable amidst the inflexible class boundaries, rigorous courtesy, and tight restraints ruling the world to which she'd been born. More importantly, Liam's talents were a fierce reminder of the forethought she must carefully give before either speaking or taking action amid these unfamiliar and likely hostile surroundings.

Standing on bare earth just outside the cottage door, Lissan's eyes narrowed on the cart carrying Hildie and her father away until it joined a previously unnoticed track and disappeared into the thick cover of trees on the cottage's left side.

Between them Rory and Liam had efficiently emptied the cart of its provisions in a remarkably brief time. While they worked Lissan had tried not to stare at the dark, fascinating man like some besotted fool. But it seemed as if it were *he* who possessed magical skills enabling him to summon the attention of any other at will, and, despite a worthy fight to refuse his call, her gaze had repeatedly turned toward the one certain to dominate any scene.

Sháme over her failure to remain impervious had been increased severalfold by one simple fact. So far as she knew—and as her eyes had rarely left him, she was certain she would know—the devastating Irishman hadn't glanced toward her even once after motioning his young cohort to throw the dagger. It was a remarkably bleak fact. . . .

Don't be a silly goose! Lissan immediately chided herself. *You hardly know the man so what earthly reason is there for you to care?* She only wished the logic of that statement made a ha'porth of difference.

Desperate to restore rational thinking, Lissan gave her head a sharp shake only to realize that her newly assigned companion was speaking to her. She concentrated on his words, anxiously trying to catch up with the gist of his conversation.

"So, you see how our bridge is the gateway between Munster and Connaught." Liam waved Lissan's attention toward the portion of encompassing forest that seemed to stretch endlessly beyond the unplanted fields outside the cottage's front door.

"Were Mael O'Brien to succeed in capturing that span, the whole of this kingdom would be in grave danger of falling under the control of another." Hazel eyes gleamed with the fervor of a warrior prepared for defense.

Bridge? Lissan's thoughts immediately flew to where a railspan crossed far above a river often rain-bloated into a torrent flowed down a deep ravine not far from the Tuatha Cottage which in 1900 stood on this very spot. An endless curiosity had led Lissan to "borrow" her older brother's binoculars and study the span's design. Knowing how intricate was its making, she was certain that here in 1115 they didn't possess the technology for so advanced a structure. Liam's next words easily reclaimed her attention.

" 'Tis why King Turlough entrusted the whole of this pivotal area to the guardianship of Lord Rory, his favorite cousin and greatest warrior."

"Lord Rory . . . the king's cousin," Lissan mused aloud, hardly surprised by this statement of the ar-

rogant man's importance. Her slight smile tilted
awry. Clearly, as learned earlier, she had been foolish to worry that Hildie's father might be some non-
descript warrior or lowly servant.

" 'Struth," Liam proudly confirmed, obviously his
leader's wholehearted admirer. "Cousin and mentor.
More than five years Turlough's senior, Lord Rory
taught our then young, fatherless king to fight and
how to devise the winning strategies that hold Connaught safe."

Munster and Connaught; O'Brien and O'Connor.
Delicate brows furrowed while Lissan absently nibbled her lower lip. She loved history, particularly
that of Ireland. But, despite having avidly studied
the subject as a whole, she could remember few con-
crete details about events during this early period. *If
only I could delve through books in the library at home
in London—if only I could simply be home!* But, no,
until she could figure out *how* she'd fallen through
time it would be impossible to return. And that
meant she must make the best of her current situation. That bleak admission perversely renewed her
wish for the library's benefits . . . longing for even
the beloved books covering a wide assortment of
subjects from history to science that were carefully
packed in the large trunk resting at the foot of her
bed in the London town house.

But that library didn't exist and the books both on
its shelves and in her trunk wouldn't even be written
for hundreds of years. Lissan's heart sank with the
undeniable truth that at least three centuries, perhaps more, would have to pass before the mechanics
for a printing press were invented.

Liam saw the dark expression cloud the fair damsel's face and worried that he'd said something to
offend. But then, if she were the White Witch—His
immediate scowl was far deeper than her faint

frown. Of course this woman *was* that legendary figure. Her unworldly beauty made it a certainty. That
being the case, a more serious question arose. Had
his unguarded tongue revealed more than a loyal
man of Connaught ought honorably share?

"Mistress—" he hesitantly began, uncertain what
next to say.

"Please—" Lissan was aware that Liam feared
having misspoken and sought to soothe his concerns
by diverting his attention. "Call me Lissan."

Along with the request Lissan's soft, pink lips
curled into a gentle smile of exceptional warmth. She
could hardly explain to her young guard how in her
world the term "mistress" meant something quite
different and far less honorable.

Wanting to please, the young man guileless by nature responded with a nod and shy grin, happy to
absolve her of possible ill intent . . . unless and until
solid proof to the contrary presented itself.

With quiet words and soft smiles—all part of
every debutante's arsenal of social talents Lissan
soon coaxed Liam into fondly recalling the family
and farm where he'd been raised. She learned that
as an only son amidst a bevy of sisters, his father—
a farmer but freeborn—had struck a bargain with
Lord Rory. In exchange for an additional measure of
each harvest, the lord would take Liam into training
as guardsman for the keep.

From this Lissan clearly saw that the position was
a coveted one and likely not often given to only sons
of farmers who needed help to work the land. But
she was curious about more beyond that issue.
Could a farmer's small plot of tillable land possibly
produce enough to repay the surely considerable ex-
pense of training, in addition to the cost of room and
board?

By maintaining an expression of deep interest and

murmuring occasional words of encouragement, Lissan soon had Liam regaling her with tales of his younger siblings' mischievous acts and his parents' loving ways. His journey through memory lane also provided her with the opportunity to lend a portion of her attention to more important matters.

Unfortunately the harvest of Lissan's mental exertions yielded only the pitifully few facts learned from people met during the past twenty-four hours along with what little she remembered from the scant written records of this time into which she'd quite literally fallen.

Historically, O'Connor's Connaught and O'Brien's Munster had been locked in a deadly struggle —that much was certain. And, horror of horrors, that was just what the seeress had foretold in Hildie's tale of the White Witch!

Lissan desperately hoped her face looked more natural than the stiff mask it seemed to have become the instant full comprehension struck, that moment when she'd recognized the alarming depth of this tangled morass into which she'd blindly wandered! Lissan longed for the always wise advice of her beloved father. He would know what to do . . . but he wasn't here. . . . She was alone now when, truly, incredible feats would be expected of her. Yes, expected of *her*—someone who couldn't even explain how she'd fallen through time and was far less able to point the way to see anyone safely free of this bog more likely to drag her into its deadly abyss!

Of a sudden, Lissan was aghast at the realization that she'd subconsciously begun thinking of herself as the White Witch. But more frightening still was not knowing whether her fated actions were destined for the good or ill of Connaught!

CHAPTER 3

The shutter creaked as Lissan tugged it open and looked outside. A low ground mist hid the cleared land stretching out toward the dark silhouette of forest beyond. In the sky above, a thick layer of clouds obscured dawn's pastel shades, save for the faint rosy glow outlining the eastern horizon.

Lissan had spent a second night sleeping fitfully, plagued by unsettling dreams haphazardly strung like black pearls on the twined strands of anxiety spun by recent inexplicable events and the looming prospect of a dubious future.

Thankfully this onset of a new day, albeit gloomy, cast one fact into sharp focus: The enchanted fairy ring was the clasp which joined past to future and must hold the secret for finding her way home. It was to that circle of forever-blooming flowers she must return—if only she knew which path to climb to reach that destination.

Behind? Her first instinct was to circle around this structure and climb the slope rising there. The fairy ring of her youth rested upon a hilltop directly behind the cottage from which, only two mornings past, she'd followed her parents. This abode did seem to rest on the same site but . . .

Curling her palms over the crude wooden windowsill, Lissan leaned forward to peer intently at the hazy shapes of surrounding terrain. Did her present shelter even face the same direction as Daffy's Cottage? The answer to that question must be the determining factor in choosing which hill to climb. Select the wrong path and likely her quest would end in a wretched, ill-advised jaunt through the uncharted forest she'd been warned harbored wolves, wild boar, and all manner of desperate men.

A slight scowl settled over the green crystal gaze darkened by inner clouds as Lissan blindly studied the shadowy scene. Only days past she'd looked toward the future with joyous anticipation and taken pride in being an independent woman boldly entering the twentieth century. But now, inexplicably finding herself in a *much* earlier time, her confidence wobbled.

"Don't be a goose," Lissan muttered, scolding herself for faltering. "I am still me, still intelligent enough to make decisions . . . and still prudent enough to take sane precautions."

And the wisest, most prudent decision was to tame the impetuous desire for immediate action. She wouldn't go haring off into perils best avoided by finding the *right* path. But how? The answer was clear and close to hand: Liam. Surely Liam knew the way and could resolve this problem.

Swinging the shutter closed, Lissan stepped back and nearly tripped over shoes foolishly left at the site where she'd pulled her toes free—in the middle of this small structure's severely limited open space.

Still wearing the chemise and stockings in which she'd slept, Lissan absently settled her feet into supple leather. It was fortunate that before leaving Daffy's Cottage she'd chosen this simple pair easy to put on or remove. A buttonhook was required to deal with the walking shoes that were the current Season's favored style and likely the ones her mother would've recommended. Had she fallen through time wearing them, her options would've been severely limited: remain trapped in them forever or destroy them by cutting herself free. Neither was a pleasant prospect but she'd have been doomed to bare feet by the latter. And that, in turn, would've effectively prevented her from reaching the fairy ring by climbing a hillside blanketed in close-grown trees and dense undergrowth.

"Fairy ring!" Lissan gasped aloud as remorse for permitting even a momentary distraction sent errant thoughts back to that important goal. Her amiable guard must know the path and, if discreetly asked amid a casual conversation, would surely motion toward the right direction. Liam had spent the night in the same lean-to built against the cottage's outside wall where his horse was tethered. Once dressed, she . . . No, she couldn't blithely go to her guard but rather must wait for him to come and check on her— a disheartening delay.

Despite frustration over the need for idle waiting, Lissan comforted herself that at least she'd identified one small step to take on a first, shamefully belated plan of action to deal with this (it must be admitted) bizarre experience.

Praying she could drop back into her own era as suddenly as she'd tumbled into this one, Lissan moved toward the basket resting atop a trestle table of planks roughhewn but worn smooth, doubtless by repeated scrubbings. From the wicker container she pulled folds of mud-brown homespun and shook them out to reveal a simple gown.

Lissan apprehensively eyed the garment so plain it must've come from the wardrobe of a servant. No, she corrected herself, in this time period not a ser-

vant but a serf. This new garb wasn't pretty but
would do. She could hardly wear her dimity gown
every day for heaven knew how many more to come.

Giving a sharp shake to her golden cloud of untamed hair, she tried to scatter useless, bleak
thoughts. Lissan chided herself instead to be grateful
for this apparel able to disguise her actions while she
moved through the forest and ascended a waiting
hillside. Her own dress would almost certainly act
as a beacon demanding attention.

Pulling on cloth rougher than any she'd ever
worn, Lissan silently thanked Liam again for the
buckets of icy water he'd hauled from the well and
emptied into a large vat the previous night—providing her with a bath welcome despite its chill. After
tightening the gown's front laces and tying them at
the base of her throat, she held arms out on either
side to inspect the cuff ends of raglan sleeves. They
were nearly the perfect length, ruching only slightly
about each wrist. However, either the garment was
entirely too long or there must be a belt enabling her
to adjust it by pulling the excess up and over. . . .

Lissan lifted the seemingly empty basket. After
tipping it upside down, the hoped-for item fell softly
unto the table—a simple length of braided leather
thongs apparently meant to be tied, as there was no
buckle or slide to hold it in place.

Adjusting crude belt and excess cloth, Lissan
glanced down wanting to be sure skirts settled at the
right length—and grinned. Shoes perfect for a young
lady of fashion in 1900 were utterly ridiculous with
the rustic garb of a serf in 1115! *But alas,* she thought,
suppressing a laugh, *what is a poor, lost damsel in distress to do?*

At that moment a soft knock brushed the door and
her giggle slipped free. Plainly, the hesitant one tap-

ping so gently was no bold knight come to rescue
her.

"Enter, Liam," Lissan called, inwardly scolding
herself for mocking this anticipated arrival. "And
please forgive my laughter. I—" She couldn't explain and apparently needn't try. Liam's hazel eyes
were steadily trained on strange shoes exposed by
an uneven hem.

"I wish I could explain, Liam." He wouldn't believe a truth she was struggling to comprehend herself. "I really do."

"No, mistress." As Liam bowed slightly sunbeams
flowing through the open door gilded the lighter
streaks in his dark honey hair. "I am here to serve."

"Not mistress," Lissan was quick to correct, "but
rather Lissan."

"Aye." Liam obediently nodded, Adam's Apple
bobbing as he gulped before adding, "Lissan."

"Are you hungry?" Plainly anxious to leave an
uncomfortable subject, Liam held up a stick from
which hung the two freshly caught fish that had
brought him to her door so early.

"Fillet of—is that trout?—would be most welcome." Lissan rewarded her companion with a smile
of amazing sweetness. "You must have gone out to
snare them even before dawn."

Cheeks warming with a faint rose glow, Liam
beamed and nodded again. "If you'll stir the embers,
I'll go and clean our meal."

Lissan watched as the young man already proven
an amiable companion spun on his heel and rapidly
walked out. She then returned her attention to more
somber matters. Picking up the same supple branch
that Liam had stripped of bark and leaves to use for
this purpose the previous evening, she jabbed at
banked coals in the central firepit until flames again
took hold.

Alone with her thoughts, Lissan threw a new chunk of wood in to feed the fire's revived hunger, and for the first time in her life wished that she'd followed the example of her older sisters. They had learned *how* to prepare meals even though raised to expect a future in which they'd occupy a position where household chores would always be managed by a cook and full staff of servants.

A wry smile lifted one corner of Lissan's mouth. Rather than cookery, she had been blessed with education in a variety of areas rarely open to females. Between an indulgent father and the tutoring of an older brother, currently a professor of science at Oxford, she had learned not merely how to speak and read several languages but had been led through the mysteries of scientific progress and was competent in various areas of advanced mathematics. All useless in the year 1115. Here in this time period it was certain that a woman, *every* woman, must master not only culinary arts but the skill to prepare food over an open fire!

Lissan's crooked smile faded beneath the weight of a harsher truth. The fact that she was so ill prepared for life in this era made it all the more important that she find the way back to her own world.

"My papa went off in Uncle Donal's company before dawn to patrol the border shared with Munster." This soft statement disturbed the room's silence as effectively as a thrown pebble would breach a mountain lake's calm surface. " 'Tis likely they hope to thwart further raids by the marauders who in recent weeks, even months, have wreaked much damage."

These simply stated facts startled Lissan from a dismal analysis of her predicament. She glanced up to find Hildie's silhouette in the bright rectangle of sunlight falling through a still open door. She straightened from the finished chore and sent her guest a welcoming smile untainted by hidden regret for plans now of necessity postponed.

To achieve and maintain this desired aplomb, Lissan focused on the curious fact that for someone of her youth, Hildie's language skills were really quite remarkable. But then, it was probable that—as when telling the White Witch's story—the girl merely repeated terms and phrases heard from others.

"Papa and Uncle Donal patrol near every morn but today even Morag has gone out . . . no doubt on one of the many errands of charity in which she takes such unnatural pride." The disgust in Hildie's last words made her contempt for this claimed purpose clear. "So I am free to spend the whole day as I please."

The delight lending sparkle to dark eyes effectively dissipated the last of Lissan's initial regret for a lost opportunity.

"And in return for your hospitality," Hildie brightly continued, "I've brought loaves of bread just pulled from the oven's heat."

"Too bad they'll be cold," Lissan unintentionally murmured while her mind filled with visions of steaming, newly baked bread, a prospect even more appetizing than the fish Liam had caught. And under these circumstances the promise of both seemed the offer of a feast even finer than those in hazy memories of the overabundance of choices and courses at every function during each social Season in her world.

"Tsk, tsk." Hildie playfully rebuked the hostess whose incredible beauty was in no way lessened by the garb of a serf. "Ailm Keep is not so far away that careful wrapping will've failed to hold their heat—so long as we eat them posthaste."

Lissan blinked when the scene before her changed.

As if summoned by her vision of his fish, Liam appeared behind the child blocking the doorway.

"So, Elfling, you've brought fresh bread to go with my fish?" Grinning, Liam fondly tapped the top of a dark head with the forefinger of one hand while the other dangled fish ready for frying a scant distance from her nose.

"You've been fishing in the lord's stream—again?" Hildie whirled to glare up at Liam with fists firmly planted on her hips.

"Me? Tempt my master's wrath?" A deeper hue than the hair atop his head, Liam's eyebrows arched in exaggerated affront. His gentle teasing of this fiery imp often provided the few spots of light-hearted enjoyment that brightened days otherwise devoted to serious duties.

"I'll have you know that I've your Lord Father's leave to pull from his stream as many of these tasty little morsels as will take my lures." With the proud claim, Liam lifted his trophies higher and closely inspected them, sparks of silent laughter dancing in changeable eyes.

Watching the friendly banter between this young man and the fragile girl-child, Lissan saw the fine strands of their unspoken alliance. Her attention was diverted when a second later Hildie reached up to snatch the "tasty morsels" from unsuspecting hands.

"Then," Hildie gaily announced, "I'll put them on the fire to see them properly grilled while you go down to the cellar and fetch up a round of cheese."

"Ah, that I gladly would—" Liam began while sorrowfully shaking his head in mock regret for the child's plainly addled wits. "*If* a cellar there was in this place."

"Though you might claim that you do, you *don't* know everything there is to know." Hildie's grin robbed the insult of any possible sting. "Outside and in back of this cottage you'll find the latch to open a cellar door. It waits beneath the few split pieces of firewood seemingly tumbled from the left side of an elsewise tidy stack.''

Hesitating only long enough to see a flat metal sheet placed squarely atop the iron grating laid over open flames, Liam slipped out and made his way around to the woodpile protected by a makeshift roof. Wasting no time in doubt of Hildie's directions, he tossed stray chunks atop a neat stack before kneeling to brush aside loose dirt and the remnants of dead leaves. Once done with this task the promised latch was revealed.

Liam used that simple loop of rope to lift a door no doubt discarded after it had warped and developed deep cracks, thus becoming useless as defense against intruders.

Liam was impressed that his young friend had held this matter in silence—even after being resettled in Ailm Keep. Impressed but not surprised. After all, for inhabitants of a cottage so close to the border crossed too often by dangerous marauders, it was prudent to hold private the existence and position of either stored supplies or concealed caches of valuables. He wondered only that Hildie had so easily, so quickly revealed the secret to a woman others, including her father, declared the White Witch. An instant later, Liam realized that with the artless instincts of a child it was likely that she'd almost immediately sensed Lissan's honest heart.

When Liam began descending a ladder nearly as decrepit as the door, his shadowy path was lightened by pleasure over Hildie's unspoken confirmation of his own view of their hostess.

During the time that the young man toiled to win entrance to the cellar, Lissan watched the deftness with which Hildie smeared lard across quickly heat-

ing metal doubtless used as a frying pan. Her feelings of inadequacy deepened when the youngster
efficiently spread trout atop rapidly sizzling grease
before turning to brightly direct their next action.

"Let's go fetch the loaves and have them waiting
when Liam returns with the cheese."

The child's guileless pleasure was infectious, and
Lissan found herself grinning as she followed to the
site where a small pony patiently waited beyond and
to one side of the cottage door.

Carefully delving into a sack formed of coarse ma-
terial, Hildie drew out several bundles, each neatly
swaddled in cloth.

Curious, Lissan watched the girl unwrap and
proudly display one of her trophies. Flat, round, and
dark brown—where not charred black—this was a
peculiar "loaf" bearing little resemblance to the
white, fine-grained bread to which she was accustomed.

Before Hildie could glance up and see her companion's reaction, a loud crash signaled the sudden,
unpleasant detour on their day's intended tranquil
path. The door to the cellar had abruptly banged
shut. Liam punctuated his lengthy bellow of protest
by banging noisily against rotting timber until it
eventually shattered . . . but too late.

At near the same instant that the initial resounding crash was heard, cruel arms trapped Lissan inside their tight circle. Though lifted completely off
the ground she struggled, kicking wildly and
screaming until breath was driven from her lungs
by being thrown roughly across the back of a horse.

Lissan's hands were jerked up and tied against the
base of her spine, but she lifted her head and caught
a glimpse of Hildie. The spirited child fought val-
iantly against the rawboned man who tossed her
over one shoulder and hauled her into the cottage.

Helpless and frustrated, Lissan could only pray the innocent girl would be left without serious injury.

While the steed carrying an uncooperative woman, as well as her captor, plodded ever deeper into forest gloom the former began to tire. Having little other choice, Lissan opted for a reverse strategy. She let herself go so utterly limp that others might mistakenly think her unconscious—or even dead. It was a decision she felt amply rewarded when during the relative silence of ensuing moments her two captors' self-congratulatory words could be clearly heard.

"The White Witch can be no further danger," said the captor all too near. "Leastwise not once we have our seized prize securely imprisoned somewhere deep inside Munster territory."

"'Struth!" This second voice was fainter for coming from behind but audible still. "Better yet, we succeeded without the fearsome machinations of Mael's sorceress. Hopefully, now he'll recognize how unnecessary are her unsavory skills and allow us to see our strategies cleansed of her sordid touch."

"Mayhap . . ." The first speaker sounded none too convinced. "But I've a suspicion he's got grander schemes for the future, schemes that will require the wielding of her dark powers."

As complete silence descended, Lissan realized that the last bleak statement had stolen not only pride in their feat but confidence in the future. It was difficult but she maintained her limp and motionless pose until, as they passed too close, a bramble bush caught one golden lock of unrestrained hair.

"Ouch!" Knowing that with this inadvertent exclamation the charade was lost, Lissan arched her back and twisted, hoping to free hair with as little discomfort as possible. Her hopes were dashed

when the captor whose face she had yet to see accomplished the task with a vicious jerk. It was her
useless attempt, however, which was responsible for
a different painful stab that renewed awareness of
the brooch still pinned to the inside of her chemise.

Her mother's beautiful brooch. Even with eyes
wide open Lissan could visualize its delicate ivory
carving of a gold-horned unicorn rearing inside an
ebony ring as clearly as if she held it in her hand.
Sudden memories of her mother wearing the piece
while wrapped safely in the crook of her father's
arm swamped Lissan with loneliness and brought
the silver sheen of tears to her eyes. Trapped in an
unfamiliar age and captured by dangerous strangers, Lissan gazed blindly down at the forest floor.
She fervently wished for both her mother's encouraging embrace for support in the face of incredible
events and her father's wise counsel on what to do.

"Sweet Mary's Blood!" The strangled panic in
gasped words acted as an invisible hand jerking Lissan's head up to take in a shocking sight.

Bearing down on her assailants were a horde of
golden warriors riding magnificent steeds whose
hooves struck the earth without making a sound.
Though amazed by this spectacle, it was another el-
ement that truly stunned Lissan. Their leader was
the young version of her father that she'd last seen
falling into the center of the fairy ring three days
past with her mother held close in his embrace.

Cruel arms again assaulted Lissan, roughly scoop-
ing up and tossing her free. She landed with bruis-
ing force on the ground in an inelegant heap.
Gasping for breath and sharply shaking her head to
scatter a disorienting haze, Lissan glanced up in time
to catch a glimpse of her adversaries disappearing
into green shadows as completely as soon did the
pursuing army riding at her father's command.

CHAPTER 4

Sprawled on ground remarkably hard despite its thick layer of vegetation, Lissan gazed up into green eyes the mirror image of her own. Unwilling to question a wish granted, she gladly yielded as her father reached down and lifted her from an awkward position.

It wasn't until lowered to stand that Lissan became fully aware of discomforts left by the injuries caused during her spirited struggle for freedom. Unprepared for the sharp pain in putting weight on bruised soles, she would've lost her balance but for the father fondly cradling her close and tucking her face into the crook of his neck. She welcomed the embrace until . . .

Considering the peculiar twists her life had taken in recent days, Lissan had hoped to become inured against what were proving to be inevitable surprises—but wasn't yet. A fact well proven when she suddenly realized that they'd somehow been transported to a wooded glade, one she would swear to never before having seen. It certainly wasn't the spot beside a narrow pathway where only brief moments past she'd landed after being rudely pushed from a horse's back.

"What are you doing here?" Lord Comlan's question was a deep, disapproving growl. "And how was the journey accomplished?"

Attention called from a quick inspection of this small clearing in the midst of towering trees and thick undergrowth remarkably undisturbed by encroaching humans, Lissan stepped back. Head tilted to one side, she stared dubiously at her inquisitor. The answer to her father's first question was precisely what she wanted to learn from him. After all, he was here, too. And he surely must know more than she. For as long as Lissan could remember her father had always provided the answer to her every question. With this reassuring memory soft lips parted, but before she could speak, the sound of approaching horses intruded.

"We will talk again—*soon*." Comlan rued the impatience lending a rough edge to his words and belatedly tried to curb the underlying cause—his frustration with the mortal world. Having quickly reacclimatized to his Faerie Realm, this return and the need to deal with humankind's limitations was annoying. Yet, not for a moment would he ever hesitate to do this and likely a great deal more for the beloved daughter bravely struggling to restore firm footing after tumbling into a baffling chaos of matters which she could no way comprehend alone.

That her father's second statement implied as much disapproval as his initial question was not lost on Lissan, merely overshadowed by amazement for the impossible feat performed right before her eyes. She'd been watching her father. Truly she had. And yet, although literally within hand's reach one instant, in the next he had vanished!

Really, this was more than any sane person could be expected to calmly tolerate. Was that the answer?

Was she going mad—living in some delusional world?

"What are you doing here?" These words were growled from behind by a familiar voice deep like distant thunder.

That question—again? Lissan spun around to face Lord Rory. Time seemed to halt while she stood motionless as if struck to stone, boldly scrutinizing him with the same unsparing intensity with which his dark gaze raked over her.

But behind the façade of brave defiance whose regrettable flimsiness, pray God, only she knew, Lissan found herself caught in a strength-stealing awareness of his near physical perfection. And his ability to affect her responses was not the only danger. No, despite their brief acquaintance, further complications were threatened by what she'd observed of his relationship with others.

Lissan had watched him use gentle firmness to deal with the errant Hildie and later stand as encouraging mentor to Liam. Both actions showed him to be an honorable man, and clearly a man host to such admirable traits must deem her a dangerous threat to be so habitually rude. Not that his suspicions were a surprise, couldn't be after he'd alluded to them that first morning before leading her away from the fairy ring and then bluntly stated his concern when assigning Liam to act as guard.

Although the utterly inappropriate bubble of laughter slipping from Lissan's throat was as startling to her as to him, she couldn't regret being perversely pleased by the harsh greeting delivering proof that she wasn't mad. This truth shone as clear as the light of a beacon through the storm of thoughts muddled by rapidly shifting emotions, events, and locations. Her inexplicable experience wasn't merely a demented person's fantasy, couldn't

be when any imaginary world created in her mind
would have this devastating man courting with soft
words rather than verbally attacking at every meeting.

Shocked by her own shameful but regrettably accurate admission, Lissan felt a fire of color creeping
up to overwhelm ivory cheeks while the belief in her
sanity firm an instant before wavered dangerously.
Had she truly gone mad? After all, how could her
father have appeared and disappeared, both in an
instant's time? He couldn't. Furthermore, he
wouldn't have come without her mother. Delicate
brows furrowed. This was nonsense, she scolded
herself. But then little or nothing had made sense
since the moment she'd thrown herself from the
fairy ring. Frightened by strange visions and self-
doubts, Lissan was even more determined to find
her way to the fairy ring and from there return to
her own time.

"What are you doing here?" Rory demanded again
while swinging down from his horse, irritation aggravated by the beguiling beauty's too innocent expression of confusion. This wrong he added to the
initial offense in finding a grudgingly welcomed
guest meandering aimlessly through dangerous
lands. Aimless? Not bloody likely. Not when the
path Mael's marauders used most often to breach
the border lay suspiciously near.

Lissan was proud that, unlike the simpering deb-
utantes of her time, she didn't blush—ever. That she
was blushing now was an embarrassment for which
he was responsible. And yet it was self-disgust that
ignited green flames in eyes that glared at her protagonist.

"I escaped two men who carried me as hostage
from the cottage where you said I'd be safe!" Lissan
knew this echoed more of a defensive ill-humor than

a truthful explanation likely to win acceptance. But this too was his fault. Surely even in this barbaric age, he couldn't expect her to stand meek beneath a roared demand so rife with unspoken criticism.

"Took you hostage?" Rory nearly hooted his disbelief even while striving to smother a flicker of admiration for the valiant spirit refusing to falter. "Liam could easily defeat any two opponents foolish enough to challenge his prowess."

"And no doubt Liam would have—" Lissan responded with a false smile of sickening sweetness. "Had he not first been trapped in the cellar."

Cellar? Rory's expression hardened. Here was too bold a lie and with it likely verification of his suspicion that the purpose behind her walk was to meet with allies from Munster, perhaps even to cede her mission as a lost cause and retreat with them.

Beneath the penetrating gaze of a man who apparently refused to respond, Lissan inwardly trembled yet refused to cringe. Within moments of explaining the reason for Liam's lack of defense, she remembered Hildie's proud claim that even her father didn't know about the cellar, but was loath to tell the arrogant lord something he wouldn't believe anyway. Rather, with motionless, unblinking silence she boldly resumed the same defiant stance with which their confrontation had begun.

Time crawled forward at the pace of a snail but neither yielded, not even to investigate the crashing sounds of someone or something breaking through vegetation and drawing ever nearer.

A mounted Liam burst into the glade and abruptly halted. He was shocked to find his master, a man much envied for his skills as ladycharmer, in open conflict—with a woman. The very air seemed to crackle with the ever-increasing tension between them.

"Praise God and all his Saints!" Liam rushed into speech hoping to sunder their hazardous bond before it exploded with likely regrettable consequences. "You've rescued Lissan."

The visual duel ended with a draw when in the same instant both participants turned toward Liam.

"A rescue was needed?" Silver sparks of reproach glittered in Rory's dark gaze. "Despite the guard I posted to hold her safe?"

Liam grimaced sheepishly. "I failed to either look or listen for intruders before climbing down into Hildie's new cellar." After an awkward search for words, he forced a further admission through his tight throat. "I was caught unprepared for defense against the blackguards who shut me inside."

There *was* a cellar! The magical creature hadn't lied! Rory felt as if the power of bright sunlight had just vanquished a gloomy storm. However, his moment of relief was immediately tempered by reality. Neither the cellar nor an abduction was sufficient evidence of innocence. Could even be that a sham capture was part of some plan to fool him into granting unearned trust.

But although Rory sought to deal fairly with everyone, his trust was neither easily earned nor given. From his experience with a not inconsiderable number of females, he'd learned that far more often than not the degree of their beauty was matched by the depth of their untrustworthiness. By that criterion, this stunning creature must be the most treacherous of all. Because of this Rory was certain that, no matter her purpose for coming, life would be infinitely easier were she proven part of an infiltrating enemy. Confirmation of such an offense would allow the freedom to rid himself of the beguiling damsel's temptations simply by arranging for her expulsion from Connaught.

To Liam the lengthening silence seemed weighted
with justified reproach. He'd fallen far short in the
honorable performance of Lord Rory's charge to
protect and felt lower than an unrepentant sinner
come to judgment. Head bowed in shame, he failed
to sense his lord's shift of focus and continued with
aching sincerity.

"I will be forever grateful that you were in the
area and able to intervene on Lissan's behalf."

Foul mood intensified by the fact that Liam had
now twice referred to their guest simply as Lissan,
a muscle clenched in Rory's cheek. It was true that
her status in the world couldn't be verified, but by
bearing and the quality of strange clothing worn
when first encountered, she was obviously wellborn.
That being so it was inappropriate for Liam to so
familiarly address her. And the next time they were
alone Rory would assuredly take time to ensure that
this was clearly understood by his young guardsman.

"It wasn't your fault." Lissan moved forward to
consolingly pat Liam's tension-clenched forearm, an
action that further and more dangerously provoked
Rory's displeasure.

Lissan purposely ignored the bad temper fairly radiating from the frighteningly attractive lord and focused on an injustice. She wouldn't willingly see
Liam blamed for matters beyond his control. It was
unreasonable for Lord Rory to expect a single warrior, no matter how skilled, to guard against invaders at an isolated site so near the border. Even less
should he expect it from one barely more than a boy.

"Come—" Rory's voice was as sharp as honed
steel. He'd had enough and would stand for no
more! "We'll go to Ailm Keep."

At this prospect, Lissan was immediately flooded
with anxiety for the young girl last seen roughly

hauled into a raided cottage. She would've questioned the lord's decision had Liam not intervened,
concisely providing sufficient information to both
calm her unspoken concern and restrain her from
further aggravating his master's ire.

" 'Tis much closer than a Tuatha Cottage now
empty."

Lissan heard and rightly interpreted Liam's emphasis on the word "empty" as assurance of Hildie's
safety. But it was another part of his message that
briefly widened green eyes—*Tuatha* Cottage. How
was it that the cottage had been named for the fairy
folk?

Done with waiting and watching the two young
companions he couldn't bear to think of as a pair,
Rory took Lissan's elbow in a firm but not cruel grip
and led her to where his mighty black stallion
waited.

As the powerfully built man exercised incredible
masculine grace in swinging up into his saddle, Lissan could neither avert her attention nor banish the
helpless appreciation glowing in her eyes.

Her involuntary admiration roused Rory's sardonic humor. Though far from the first female to
react to him this way, Lissan was the first to fight
him at near every turn. And he found it pleasing that
she could no more block awareness of him than he
could prevent images of this intriguing beauty from
stealing uninvited into his thoughts and even his
dreams. He refused to investigate why.

Lissan was horrified by her inability to look away
from the man, big, dark, and frankly threatening, but
even more so by the helpless fascination she couldn't
hide from its mocking source. When, with a bone-
melting smile of such potency as she'd never before
encountered, he extended an inviting hand toward
her, she stepped back. Having stood strong against

his scowl, Lissan had surprised them both by instinctively retreating from a smile.

Self-derision chilled Rory's expression as, unwilling to appear even more the fool before a frankly gaping Liam, he bent to wrap one arm about an incredibly soft waist near buried in homespun and swept Lissan up to sit sideways in front of him.

Lissan was shocked. In her world never would such intimate proximity be permitted between a couple unwed. Indeed, even married couples would be more circumspect and, at least publicly, exercise prudent restraint. Her world would never allow this to happen, she uselessly reiterated, but here in this time and place she found herself sharing a man's steed for the second time in a single day. Twice she had ridden with a man seated behind, but each had won drastically different responses. The first she had fought with all the strength she could muster. But this second, despite an impersonal hold, was undeniably the more perilous.

Lightly held close to a powerful form, Lissan was far too aware of the steely strength of muscles moving as he urged their steed from the glade. Breath grown embarrassingly short, she surreptitiously peeked up at the disturbingly handsome face resolutely averted. She couldn't abolish wild wonderings—if he were again to cradle her fully against his massive chest and put that hard, cruel mouth over hers, would the kiss be as devastating as the one shared the morning he'd rescued her? It was a shameful memory yet with it she could almost taste his mouth again and went hot all over, soft lips parting on a silent gasp.

Exercising considerable control, Rory fought to tamp down his natural response to the sensual tension he felt building within this seemingly curious little virgin. He recognized a faint hunger in the

brush of green eyes across his mouth while lips
whose honey-sweetness he intimately remembered
parted slightly, as if in anticipation of a lover's kiss.

Black, shoulder-length hair barely stirred with the
infinitesimal shake of Rory's head. Surely these practiced wiles supported his initial assessment of her as
a spy.

*Don't fall victim to such beguilements, don't allow her
to make a fool of you.* Rory ridiculed himself for finding it so difficult to banish thoughts of Lissan to the
same dark corridor in his mind where resided the
uncounted, nameless women who in the past had
held his attention for a limited span of time.

Feeling as if the man beside her had turned into
frost-covered granite, a shiver passed through Lissan. It seemed they would never find common
ground. But what else could be expected of two from
pasts so vastly different?

While the powerful black stallion steadily continued their journey, Rory's face hardened into grim
lines and Lissan stared without seeing into green
shadows on one side of their path.

Liam trailed well behind the self-involved pair
who likely had forgotten his company. Nearly
everything had been restored to its proper place.
Hildie was safe and Lissan had been saved by his
master. Only one niggling question was left. What
had happened to Donal, Lord Rory's brother and
daily companion on patrol?

"An army, you say?" Mael scoffed at the speaker
who, with another, stood again below the dais in his
keep to report the results of an assigned duty. "A
golden army that throttled you both and then vanished?" Never had Mael heard a more far-fetched
tale, and he found it an affront that Fergil dared use
it in trying to justify failure.

" 'Struth." Fergil nearly pleaded for acceptance although he'd known at the outset that this truth would be heard at best as a poor excuse unlikely to see them absolved of their wrong in returning without the intended captive.

"They pursued us into the forest." The second man facing an irritated lord shifted the weight of his angular frame uneasily from one foot to the other while with an expanded account of the event adding his appeal. "That they did we know because their bright light almost overtook us."

"But it didn't?" Disgust thickened Mael's words and soured the sidelong glance he cast the woman sitting next to him at the high table.

"No," a resigned Fergil promptly answered, knowing any further arguments not merely unlikely to be accepted but apt to further vex their naturally ill-tempered lord. "They disappeared as suddenly as they'd come."

"But surely—" Younger and having yet to learn the value of cautious silence, Paddy foolishly continued to plead. "You must understand how, to escape their unearthly powers, we had no choice but to flee?"

"What I see is that the pair of you have imaginations fired by shame for being bested by a lone boy with only his stave." Though soft, Mael's words were the hiss of a poisonous snake coiling to strike. "Either that or you actually expect me to believe the White Witch able to conjure forth from the devil's host an entire army to fight on her behalf."

Since it was Mael who had assured him that the female who'd arrived so shockingly was truly the White Witch, Fergil thought it odd that the man now mocked the suggestion of a witch's spell. Despite often being named dullard by his lord, as Fergil studied the pair seated behind a table laid with cloth of pristine white he realized Mael was likely the one most humiliated by their thwarted plan. Particularly when beside him sat the sorceress he'd intended to impress with the success of his own schemes.

Resenting a lesser's scrutiny and believing his anger justified by the folly of these two men witless enough to provoke it, Mael's fiery brows crashed together in disapproval.

Fergil cringed but his lanky cohort actually turned as if to make a too hasty retreat. His hand immediately shot out to restrain Paddy from taking an addlepate's action. Any display of cowardice could only confirm Mael's conclusions and increase the price they'd have to pay.

"Or—" Mael's humorless smile was frightening. "Perhaps you think the uninvited newcomer able to summon a cavalcade of luminous warriors from the Faerie Realm?" The acid fair sizzling in this suggestion made it clear that he deemed it by far the most improbable.

"Nay, Lord Mael," a deep but feminine voice spoke in calming, dulcet tones. "I much doubt you'd entrust so serious a task to men likely to harbor such absurd notions."

Slowly and by effort of will Mael relaxed fists clenched atop the table and shifted his gaze to the dark-haired woman leaning intimately closer.

"I wonder only why you unnecessarily put two valuable warriors at risk?" Although posed as a question, she made it clear no response was sought by immediately continuing. "Even while forewarning you of coming danger, I promised to neutralize it without harm to you or yours."

"And had you prevented that female danger from becoming so public a pawn," Mael testily responded, "I would gladly have left her to you." Pale eyes glowing with poorly repressed anger threatened to sear the annoyingly unruffled woman at his side.

Mael nearly snarled, "But instead she appeared not merely in the midst of a crowd but in the thick heat of battle! Worse, despite a blow that would kill or leastways maim any mortal man, she went unharmed."

"I concede that the timing was unfortunate, but not fatal." Though the woman's words were soothing, she erred by failing to keep her tone free of the condescension so common to her voice.

"Hah!" Temper bursting the last of its bonds, Mael slammed his hands palm flat on the table so hard the table rocked. " 'Twas enough to make it plain that *I must* be seen to overcome her threat. Her simple disappearance will *not* be sufficient, not after a great many saw her survive my mightiest blow unscathed."

CHAPTER 5

"Ailm Keep," Rory announced, pride ringing in terse words issued seconds after breaking through the edge of a forest encircling the base of a steep rise.

The muscles of the broad chest against which Lissan had unthinkingly relaxed flexed and when with a sweeping gesture Rory waved toward their destination his black cloak rippled in the breeze like a raven's wing. Lissan's attention followed the motion up to the summit guarded by a staunch palisade of upended logs closely joined together with the top end of each sharpened into a dangerous point.

Although a curious sight, more interesting still was the *stone* keep soaring upward from its midst. It was not a square Norman tower, squat but nearly indestructible. No, this was an ancient and distinctly Irish structure—circular, slender, and amazingly tall. But then Lissan reminded herself that in the year 1115, if memory served, the Normans had yet to make appreciable incursions into Ireland. Thus, a Norman tower would rightly be a far less likely sight than this graceful keep seeming to ascend into heaven itself.

Pay heed, a quiet inner voice warned Lissan. *If truly you are destined to play a role in coming events, you may be grateful for knowing even the smallest detail.*

Despite uncertainty about where her future lay—
here or in the world into which she'd been born—
Lissan accepted this silent admonition. The folly of
doing elsewise was clear. Anxious to miss nothing
that might later prove important, she continued an
intent examination of their destination as they approached the gate through its palisade . . . a wall of
wood and therefore vulnerable.

"Hold and speak." The gruff demand came from
a guardsman peering suspiciously down at the small
approaching party through a vee between the
pointed tips of two logs.

That this warrior was well trained and worthy of
trust was made clear by a dedication to duty that
would exact a response from even the man he must
recognize as his lord.

"The Lord of Ailm Keep returns." Rory's answer
was as formal as the call for it. "With me I bring
your comrade in arms, Liam, and one guest who
comes for a brief visit."

When the guardsman dropped from sight only to
quickly reappear while swinging half of the massive
double gate wide, Lissan was certain that he must
have stood atop a ledge of some description on the
wall's far side. As Rory urged his stallion into the
courtyard beyond, she wasn't surprised to discover
the guardsman's perch merely part of the wooden
path constructed near the palisade's sharp-toothed
rim. Beginning on one side of the gate, it traveled all
the way around to end on the gate's far edge.

Even while faithfully noting that this parapet
walkway would be a fine position from which to
repel any advancing assault, Lissan was uncomfortably aware of curious eyes assessing her. And not
those of the guardsmen alone but the many others
less evident yet surreptitiously peering at her. It was

an uncomfortable sensation which left her feeling adrift in a stormy sea of uneasiness through which flowed clashing currents of hope and distrust.

"Niall, take Midnight to his stall." After swinging down from his stallion with the graceful ease of one well used to hours ahorse, Rory gave this order to a lad promptly emerging from the stable's gloom.

"I won't need him again but I will later require the cart harnessed and readied to escort our visitor back to Tuatha Cottage."

While Rory issued instructions to the earnest young boy of perhaps ten years who was plainly anxious to please his lord, Lissan took close stock of the keep's inner courtyard. An assortment of crowded buildings encircled the open space at the foot of a steep stairway leading at least one level up to the keep's entrance.

Lissan gladly dropped her attention from the intimidating sight to focus on the rest of the courtyard. Not only was there a stable (the largest building save keep) and a three-sided structure containing the metalsmith's forge but others as well. Doubtless they housed the many trades and workers necessary to maintain the smooth running of this demesne and assist neighboring farms.

No, Lissan chided herself, in Ireland the lord's land wouldn't be called a demesne. She struggled to recall the proper term but her memory was annoyingly muddled by too close proximity with Ailm Keep's master. Then before she found its answer, her question was lost beneath the shock of being effortlessly lifted by two strong hands wrapped about her waist.

Lissan gasped and reached out to clasp broad shoulders as the only firm anchor in a suddenly tilting world. Though merely seeking stability while held aloft with apparent ease, the feel of hard muscle

beneath her touch trapped breath somewhere between lungs and a tight throat. An inner voice
shrieked warnings, scolding Lissan to break her visual bond with the stunning, midnight deep eyes directly below. She earnestly tried . . . but couldn't.

While keeping her deliciously soft form a mere
hand's span above for far too long, Rory unwillingly
acknowledged that although likely not what she
seemed in many ways, Lissan truly was light as a
dream and temptingly sweet to have so near. He
found himself helplessly beguiled by a gaze darkening from the bright shade of fresh clover to the
seductive green of a shadowy forest.

Irritated by the unwelcome success of her wiles,
Rory's face went as hard and emotionless as stone.
The White Witch she might be but in this moment
seemed more the elusive siren of myth, luring un-
wary men to sacrifice themselves against treachery's
cruel rocks for want of her. Silver sparks like ice
crystals chilled dark eyes with an unspoken warning
while he slowly, deliberately lowered her feet to the
earth.

Though shaken by the sudden coldness of Rory's
expression, once Lissan stood again on solid ground
free of his disturbing hold, even that discomfort was
overwhelmed by the returned sensation of myriad
watching eyes. Doubtless her faceless observers had
drawn the wrong conclusion from the prolonged
and seemingly intimate exchange just passed. Lissan's face immediately flamed with what she had no
doubt must be the brightest blush ever seen—certainly a record for someone who had on many oc-
casions proudly claimed herself not susceptible to
such absurd displays.

The soft rose tinting cheeks he knew to be petal
soft struck Rory with an unexpected urge to lessen
the self-conscious beauty's uneasiness. The next in-

stant he named himself a fool for again falling prey
to Lissan's wiles when he had no doubt that she
merely feigned this disarming mask of innocence
and timidity.

When her intimidating escort motioned for her to
begin ascending the steep stairway, Lissan felt as if
she'd been ordered to climb the scaffold for her own
execution. She took a deep breath to bolster the bravery she had for so long and—it now seemed—so
erroneously thought strong. While forcing herself to
put one foot on the bottom step and the other foot
on the next, she gazed apprehensively up a stairway
that turned on itself twice before reaching any doorway.

Hoping to divert courage-stealing awareness of
both the man following too close behind and the
horde of strangers waiting above, she fought to
clearly recall even dim details from books she'd read
about methods of defense during this era.

Lissan's next step dislodged a pebble, sending it
down to land far below and clatter across earth
hardened by the passing of many feet. Its impossible
path reminded her of one tactic likely to be taken in
defense of this soaring tower. If Ailm Keep were attacked, its inhabitants would surely prevent their
foes entry by seeing these wooden stairs reduced to
ashes.

"Of course," Lissan muttered wryly to herself,
"they'd find themselves under siege. And by waiting
out their enemies would be caught by their own
drastic measures. Trapped, they would perish unable to get down so long and daunting a drop to the
ground." She shivered against the chill of this unpleasant possibility even as she gave it voice.

" 'Tis an insult for you to think us such simple-
minded dolts." Rory's hearing was excellent and he
had not only heard every word but knew precisely

to what Lissan referred. Still, what galled him the most was that out of all the females he knew, this lone woman whom he dare not pursue and yet unwillingly wanted most to impress thought so little of either his wits or skills.

"None among us would be so foolish as to stand unprepared for so obvious a danger." Rory glared at the mid-point of a golden cloud of hair flowing down a slender back unrestrained as no wellborn lady of his acquaintance would publicly permit.

"A hidden postern door offers safe escape. And should that secret exit be blocked it would require little exertion for any man with a stout rope and firm anchor to hastily lower himself to the ground."

Oh, horrors! Lissan was careful to keep this comment silent. Who'd have thought the wretched man would hear thoughts unintentionally murmured aloud? She hadn't meant to disparage anyone! And if only the language of her thoughts and even dreams hadn't so quickly shifted from the English of her world to the Gaelic common here, he'd have been none the wiser. Gratefully Lissan recognized and held tight to one small blessing—Rory followed behind and couldn't see the fresh shade of red burning her cheeks.

Lissan bit her lip as an additional bar against further release of unfortunate words even while spontaneously increasing her pace to such an extent that by the time she reached the last few steps her breath came in gasps. Halfway up the first angle of stairs, Lissan unexpectedly glimpsed a pleasant sight. All the trials were lightened when she found a small welcoming party of one waiting in the now open portal.

"I'm so glad Liam caught up in time to rescue you!" Hildie wrapped thin arms tight around Lissan's waist and enthusiastically hugged.

"No, Hildie." Liam spoke from some distance down the stairway. "It wasn't my feat but your father's."

A stab of shame struck as Lissan realized she hadn't merely been unaware that the young man was trailing after his lord but had forgotten him completely. And yet it was Liam's claim that sent her gaze over one shoulder not to him but to the powerful lord now unexpectedly close. Would Rory also deny he'd had any part in that deed?

Were Rory to disavow such a role here in front of the crowd Lissan sensed hovering beyond Hildie, it would seem she'd freed herself—an unlikely feat doubtless damning her in the eyes of a good many already suspicious observers.

"Hildie." Rory quietly spoke while Lissan held her breath. "Pray consider your duties as the hostess of Ailm Keep. Don't keep your lord and his guest lingering outside hungry and thirsty, too."

With a guilty grimace the girl instantly stepped back, clearing the way for the three outside to enter.

Thankful for the heartening presence of one friend at least, Lissan gave a brave smile and tilted her chin upward as she followed Hildie well into the center of a surprisingly small hall.

"Ah, so here we have the flesh-and-blood reality of the witch from ancient legend. The very one inspiring such a multitude of whispers and rumors that one hardly hears the mention of anything else." Although lightly spoken, these words were heavy with an offensive skepticism.

Lissan's spine straightened against this insult addressed to her back but refused to give its source the satisfaction of seeing her spun about in awkward haste by the taunt. Lissan might doubt this supernatural identity herself, but she'd be damned before meekly faltering beneath a condescending arrogance even more despicable than any shown by her host who, as lord, arguably had the right.

"Lissan—" Rory's terse voice was granite hard but for once its animosity wasn't directed toward the tender beauty. "Meet here my younger brother Donal."

Although sensing a gulf of unpleasant tension between the two men and certain others nearby must also, Lissan knew she had no option but to turn. While slowly shifting to face her insulter, she tempered annoyance over the unavoidable action by telling herself it was just as well since only this way could she appease curiosity about this second party in a deeply strained dissension.

As both brothers had dark hair and amazing eyes of deepest blue Lissan wasn't surprised by how very much alike they were. However, as Donal was at least a decade younger, slightly shorter, slightly heavier, and with features softened by self-indulgence, he seemed merely a dim reflection of Rory.

Once the target of his verbal assault had trained her unblinking eyes of green fire on him, Donal stumbled several steps back. Here because of his much-resented brother's introduction Donal was forced to squarely meet confirmation of an ominous warning. But share a meal with her he would not!

Before the servants could finish spreading pristine cloth over long trestle tables, Lissan saw Donal slip away—to no one's apparent regret. But while it seemed her disdainer wasn't hungry, as someone who'd eaten precious little since tumbling into this world, she would be grateful for edibles of almost any description.

As dusk settled over the hilltop tower, Lissan joined Rory at the high table for the evening meal. A large variety of dishes were presented and she

sampled them all but found few tasty enough to accept a larger portion. They were oddly prepared and
even more oddly spiced yet by dinner's end her hunger had been replaced by the discomfort of having
overeaten.

Through it all Rory was an attentive host, ensuring the trencher they shared was constantly replen-
ished with items Lissan seemed most to enjoy and
making certain her wine glass was never less than
half full. Surreptitiously watching the powerful man,
relaxed amongst his own, Lissan observed enough
to believe her initial impressions verified. He was
clearly a man of honor concerned about each person
under his care, no matter their station, and as generous with praise for things well done as with his
hospitality. It was equally clear that he was not
merely respected but held in affection and admiration by those who called him lord, whether warriors
supping on his bounty or servers prompt to answer
his call.

After the removal of huge platters so emptied of
roasted meats that only stripped bones remained, a
final course of fruit, nuts, and deep yellow cheese
was delivered. Like twilight deepening into night, as
the evening progressed people at tables below consumed ale in great quantities and the atmosphere
grew increasingly rowdy.

Intensely aware of the beauty too near and constantly casting him sidelong glances, Rory couldn't
help but sense her growing uneasiness with ever
bawdier language and coarser actions. Though naming himself a fool for caring, he gently offered the
only certain relief for her distress.

"Are you ready now for a return to the peace of
your cottage?"

Lissan warned herself to quash an immediate yet
irrational and doubtless fleeting hope that Rory's

words naming the cottage hers suggested a wish for her to remain nearby. Beneath the thrilling weight of a dark gaze, Lissan nibbled a full lower lip to berry brightness, restraining the winsome smile likely to expose too fully her pleasure in his company.

Rory completely mistook Lissan's wordless response for apprehension. That she could fear him so dishonorable as to ravish the clearly nobleborn woman he had provided—no matter how reluctantly—with home, provisions, and even a personal guard was both irritating and perversely amusing. His chair scraped as he pushed it back. With a wry smile Rory rose to his feet and gallantly proffered his forearm to a still-seated golden colleen.

Charmed by this very old and courtly gesture, Lissan laid dainty fingertips atop the fine wool of his sleeve, accepting his support to aid her in standing. Many eyes followed as they crossed the hall, but with Rory a willing escort Lissan found withstanding their uncertain threat much easier. Then, having long since wished a sleepy Hildie good night and as Liam had departed for the cottage before the last course was served, it was in relative privacy that Lissan cautiously preceded Rory down narrow, twisting stairs.

Niall stood waiting in the courtyard holding the reins of the sturdy plowhorse harnessed to a cart. However, before the couple could move more than a few steps from the stairway another spoke.

"Ah, brother, you're home?" a sultry feminine voice called from the shadows. "I assume then that my husband is, as well."

Fingers once more resting lightly on the arm Rory had again offered after reaching the bottom step, Lissan felt him go tense—but against the words or the speaker herself? Lissan's narrowed green eyes peered toward the tall, slender figure gliding forward from where she vaguely remembered seeing the stable.

"Lissan." Rory's voice crackled with ice. "This is my brother's wife, Morag."

Before Lissan could nod an acknowledgment, in a voice gone chill the dark-haired beauty offered an apology so patently insincere that it was obviously meant to be as much of an insult as her husband's earlier attack.

"I am so sorry to have missed your visit." Grey eyes hard and cold as granite, Morag twisted her lips into something far nearer to a sneer than smile. "But a difficult birth on a farm some distance away prevented my earlier return."

Having endured several social Seasons in London where she'd been subjected to every variation of subtle snub and survived unscathed repeated bouts of quelling repartee, Lissan was unaffected by the slight. In truth, she suspected herself far more experienced in such arts than Morag would ever be. The arrogant woman had, nonetheless, achieved one goal by making it absurdly clear that she chose to see herself as the lady of Ailm Keep, staking her claim with the mention of having performed a mistress's duty in lending aid to someone in need.

Lissan told herself that after taming the wild assault launched by this woman's husband, she ought to find Morag's defensiveness amusing. More so considering the woman's resentments couldn't be less necessary, not since Lissan had begun to suspect herself prey to a disconcerting lack of courage where the devastating lord was concerned. She already doubted that, even if unable to return to her own time, she would be either brave or foolish enough to seek his too-potent attentions.

"I'm certain *my* guest sees no reason for fault in

your absence." With these words, Rory firmly reminded the dark woman that she was *not* the lady
of Ailm Keep. The pity was that this wasn't the first
nor, he feared, was it likely to be the last time he'd
have to make so simple a fact clear to Morag, his
brother, and all the people of his lands. Allowing no
further delays, Rory led Lissan to the cart.

Still feeling the other woman's lingering glare, Lissan gasped when without warning strong hands
again lifted her from the ground. She instinctively
reached out to clasp broad shoulders but the instant
Rory settled her on the driver's seat she jerked her
hands back as if burned by the contact.

Rory's mood was not improved by Lissan's hasty
action. Not after having his patience severely
strained by Morag's posturings and endless pursuit
of what he'd refused to share years earlier and had
since been forced to repel furtive attempts to usurp.

Climbing up to sit at Lissan's side, Rory took the
reins from a gawking Niall with ill humor. Inwardly
declaring a pox on all females, he urged the plowhorse on its way.

While an uncomfortable silence reigned Lissan sat
motionless, all too aware of the powerful man scowling down a night path further darkened by the
branches of massive trees entwined overhead which
blocked all but a few intrepid rays of moonlight.
What a nasty end to a surprisingly pleasant visit.
Prior to that ghastly woman's intrusion, Lissan had
harbored a faint spark of hope that Rory had begun
to realize she would do nothing to harm him or his
cause—at least not willingly. Now it seemed Morag's barbs had succeeded in reminding the man of
Lissan's dubious position as a foreigner.

"No, I wouldn't, couldn't harm either you or
yours." Lissan was so intent on asserting her posi-

tion in defiance of Morag that she didn't hear herself
murmur it aloud.

Intending to ward off the subtle tendrils of attraction he'd begun to fear this dangerous siren able to
weave too easily about him, Rory immediately chal-
lenged a quiet claim barely understood above the
steady thudding of the horse's gait.

"So you'd do harm to neither me nor mine?" By
the cynicism in his question it was plain that Rory
doubted every word.

A renewed flood of embarrassing color washed
Lissan's cheeks. The deeply regretted habit of thinking aloud had betrayed her again and at a moment
when she'd far rather have bitten her tongue in two
than be heard. But what was done was done—leaving her to defend that position. Her talent for quick
thinking came to the rescue. Plainly, there was no
defense other than attack—hadn't Rory used the
same tactic on her after she asked if he was Hildie's
father?

"How can you think I might be a danger to you
when I was the one assaulted and forcibly hauled
away?"

"Were you? Were you really?" Dark brows arched
while Rory drawled questions whose answers he felt
certain could never be proven. "Then how was it
that I found you free and alone in the forest?"

Through effort of will Lissan maintained a serene
expression despite the sheer panic driving her heart-
beats into a wildly erratic pace. How could she possibly explain to this skeptic something she didn't
understand herself?

Don't flounder now! Lissan's pride silently scolded.
*Stay calm, use the logic you cultivated once but which by
recent disuse has begun to atrophy.*

Lissan took comfort in the fact that she had instinctively recalled and properly used the term "at-

rophy." Confidence bolstered and happy she hadn't permitted anxiety to show, in a mild tone Lissan added true though possibly distracting details to her narration of the capture. "I was taken by two men I vaguely remember being involved in the battle which my arrival interrupted."

Rory's brows dropped into a scowl like black thunder clouds over the silver streaks of lightning flashing from his dark eyes. Two forces and many warriors had been involved in that fight which meant she had named the perfect culprits—men whose identities would be almost impossible to verify.

"I heard them talking—" Lissan enticed with another morsel of information, one Rory was apt to find the most interesting. "The man whose horse also carried me told the other he hoped my taking would convince Mael that *his* terrifying witch was unnecessary."

Mael? Rory stared steadily into the distance while an inner cold seemed to freeze his impassive face into pure ice. Yes, he could easily believe his adversary of long standing would stoop low enough to take a woman hostage. It wasn't, however, the only or even most likely explanation. Lissan could as easily have invented false tales to win sympathy and trick him into giving unmerited trust. Still, such a possibility couldn't excuse him from the duty of considering others. If Mael had forged an alliance with a witch of his own, might not that faceless female be the actual figure of ominous legend while this beguiling creature was innocent of all the wrongs in which he'd suspected her guilty?

"*You* stated it was Mael's broadsword which struck me that first morn." Confidence faltering against Rory's chill silence, Lissan tried to revive it with a further rational argument. "Now he's tried to capture me. Surely this is sufficient to prove that I am *not* your enemy?''

A sardonic smile did nothing to warm Rory's expression. He saw no need to point out another possibility. Perhaps collusion between Lissan and Mael had tricked warriors into accepting as fact a mere illusion that his blade had passed through her. Rory's one-sided smile deepened. Her true relationship with Mael mattered little one way or the other. The greatest danger came not from Mael but from across the Irish Sea—the place Lissan had already admitted was her home.

''You claim me to be a witch from the fires of Hades—'' Lashed by his continued silence, sparks of temper burst from the frayed edges of Lissan's nerves. ''But how could that be when a man of ice sits beside me impervious to the heat?''

This argument jolted Rory from the examination of bleak potentials. His gaze immediately shifted to meet the defiant green eyes dominating a tender face of apparent innocence. Was this spirited damsel an experienced temptress or a naïve fool? Did Lissan even know what manner of retribution she risked with this dare so blithely thrown? No matter, he would accept.

The slow, sensuous smile warming his face with potent charm alarmed Lissan, and she most heartily rued her too ready temper. Fearing this devastating man would see how thoroughly and with what appalling haste her defenses had fallen, Lissan's thick lashes fluttered and yet she was unable to break from the thrall of his midnight gaze. She tumbled into depths where molten silver flashed while this incredible man's attraction wrapped around her, drawing her nearer.

Lost in the power of longings never before suspected, Lissan barely felt the hand sliding beneath a flow of silk-soft hair to cup the back of her neck and hold her face steady while his mouth moved gently, enticingly across smooth cheeks to nibble at the corners of beguiling lips.

Briefly lifting his head, Rory read Lissan's unwilling and surely honest fascination in a gaze gone soft with passion's mists. Then, trusting the plodding horse to continue down a path bordered on either side by dense trees and thick vegetation, he swept the ethereal beauty from where she sat to lie across his hard thighs. His mouth returned to sear hers with the tender heat of joining.

While their kiss became long and slow and hard, Lissan's world seemed to become a dizzying whirlwind of fiery sensations. She instinctively wrapped her arms around its center, tangling fingers into a black mane, and savoring the power of his broad back.

Even while Rory deepened the kiss, his finely honed conscience intruded. Again he pulled back to gaze down at the tender damsel, golden head tilted back, eyes drowsy with new desires, and lips a deep rose—moist and softly swollen. If she were the sweet virgin she appeared, honor demanded he leave her chaste. His chest rose and fell in deep, uneven breaths. It would be extremely difficult and require his every shred of control. Were she later proven naught but another example of treacherous womankind, he'd never forgive himself—or her. And yet he dared not take the chance of sullying so tender a damsel and would soon leave her undefiled. Soon. Yes, soon but not yet.

The melding of their mouths seemed to drain strength from Lissan's body. Held close and ever closer against Rory, for her all logical thought ceased, lost in the hungry fires he stoked. Shudders of wild excitement shook her until another more jarring motion jolted them both from the grip of irrational need.

Dazed, when Rory pulled away, Lissan glanced to the side and struggled to focus on the scene.

Home. Lissan saw that the horse had come to an abrupt halt with muzzle nearly pressed to the front door of Tuatha Cottage. No. Lissan shook her head in mild self-disgust. This wasn't London. It wasn't home . . . or was it?

CHAPTER 6

Lissan jerked the coarse homespun blanket up tight below her chin then destroyed its warming effect by rolling to lie facedown. This had been a very, very long day, and she needed the sleep proving disgustingly elusive.

Capture . . . rescue . . . Rory . . . Donal . . . Morag . . . Rory . . .

Throwing herself again to her back and glaring into the dark overhead, Lissan fervently wished for some means to switch off an endless review of events as easily as Mr. Edison's electric lights could be darkened.

Although the pallet that served as bed was never comfortable, tonight it seemed as if straw poked through ticking to jab her from every angle. She wouldn't be surprised to find scratches in the morning to match all the aches that came with each dawn.

But, Lissan ruefully admitted, complaints about both the bed's discomfort and the day's dizzying whirl of happenings were mere distractions encouraged to free her mind from persistent images, even fantasies about a devastating Irish lord and the thrill of his arms, the taste of his kiss. . . .

By biting her lip hard enough to be painful, she

reminded herself yet again that she and Rory O'Connor had nothing in common. Nothing! They didn't even share the same century and barely the same millennium. Oh, if only she'd been able to ask her father . . .

Her father! Lissan softly moaned, a sound half plaintive regret and half frustration. How had she allowed *anything* to distract her from the miracle of his rescue, and what wicked imp had led Rory to come upon them at just that moment? Her fingers absently sought the precious brooch still pinned to her chemise. If only she'd had time to seek her father's counsel. Surely he could explain, could remedy whatever blunder had landed her here.

"Daughter, what would you have of me?" Affection warmed Comlan's wry question. After frightening her abductors into fleeing, he'd promised to return as soon as possible and now he had.

Amazed by the twice granting of this same wish, Lissan abruptly sat up. Turning toward the source of a soft glow, she met the amused gaze of her inexplicably luminous father. As he lowered himself to sit on the pallet beside her, she fought to whip the sharp wits she was so proud of back into sensible order. Despite having no firm notion of the best place to begin, her soft lips parted only to have sound repressed by a long finger lightly pressed against them.

"I know you're alone in this cottage but I also know another is near enough that our talk might be overheard—and misunderstood. So, come, put your face against my shoulder as you did when I lifted you from your fall."

Though still dazed by his unexpected arrival, Lissan instinctively trusted this suddenly young version of her father and gladly yielded as he gathered her into his arms and tucked her face into the crook of his shoulder. Seemed she'd no sooner closed her eyes in the cottage's seclusion than she felt a fresh breeze brush her cheek.

Pulling back, Lissan gazed up into the far reaches of a star-speckled sky. Again she'd been transported in the briefest of instants and glanced down to meet her father's amused half-smile.

"How did you do that?" After this first demand for an explanation dropped from her lips, several others more important immediately followed. "How did you get *here?* No, how did *I* get here? And where's Mother?"

His beloved daughter's bewilderment struck Comlan with the deep pang of a response rare to one of his nature—remorse. And not for Lissan's present quandary alone but also for a human lifetime of secrets he'd carefully guarded.

"I am your father, Lord Comlan of Doncaully." Mercurial moods a part of his true nature, he nearly laughed when Lissan sent him an impatient look of disgust for this sharing of facts hardly in question. "But since long before I adopted that name, I have also been Comlan, king of the Tuatha de Danann."

Tuatha de Danann? King of the Faerie Realm? Dumbfounded, Lissan slowly shook her head. Must she pay for a childhood love of fairy tales with her sanity?

"It is important that you recognize my statement for the truth it is," Comlan said coaxing his apparently reluctant offspring. "You asked how we moved so swiftly from the cottage to this fairy ring—'tis my ancient identity that provides both the answer to your question and a sweet haven for your mother, my darling Amy."

Gaze probing night shadows, Lissan acknowledged undeniable proof of his wondrous ability. The crude pallet they'd been sitting on in the cottage had

truly been replaced by the lush grasses that cushioned the ground inside the fairy ring. Doubts scattered, Lissan was left to accept the impossible as fact.

"But if you're the king of the Faerie Realm, that
would make me...."

Comlan quietly completed her unfinished statement. "Half human and half fairy—a split blood."

By the strain in her father's tone while uttering the
last two words, Lissan assumed this description a
derogatory one and wasn't surprised when he continued almost without pause.

"You were meant, as your mother wished, to live
a mortal life in her world ... but it seems we mis-
calculated." Steadily meeting eyes that even in the
gloom of night were as bright a green as his own,
Comlan fought to control nagging impatience. "I've
answered your first question, now you owe me an
answer to one of mine. How did you get here?"

"What?" Lissan's incredulous gasp ended on a despairing wail that she immediately rued for a milk-
sop's weakness.

By his daughter's honest astonishment Comlan realized that her presence in an age not her own could
only have occurred by a likely accidental but distinctly unfortunate exercise of powers she could nowise have understood. This admission brought
further reason to question his wisdom in preventing
her from earlier learning what now he would have
to explain. Though normally good-natured, Comlan
didn't like even the mere possibility that he'd been
wrong—a thing he rarely was—and his next question was unusually cool.

"Tell me, what were you doing the last moment
before you found yourself here?"

Knowing that the time had come for confessing
the transgression she already suspected responsible

for all that had come after, Lissan took a deep breath for courage to begin.

"Although I promised that if allowed to accompany you and Mama to the brow of the first hill, I would make my way straight back to our waiting family—" Lissan stopped. This had to be one of . . . no, *the* most difficult thing she'd ever done.

A deep scowl formed between Comlan's dark gold brows. His daughter had done just what he'd feared on finding her lost so far from her own time. He tersely stated, "You followed."

Hearing in her father's voice an anger never before turned on her, Lissan straightened with false bravado and nodded. "After you carried Mother around the fairy ring, I followed."

To Comlan that scene was chillingly clear. Carefully blanking his face into an unemotional mask, he flatly spoke his thoughts aloud. "And you fell *out* of rather than *into* the ring."

Again Lissan nodded. "And somehow dropped through time to land in this place where they immediately took me to be some legendary White Witch."

Comlan momentarily clenched his eyes shut. He'd been a fool to think matters could get no worse. Hands cupping slender shoulders, he held his errant child steady while his serious gaze probed.

"Aye," Comlan eventually and reluctantly conceded. " 'Tis possible that you *are* the one foretold." A moment later, with the mercurial moods of his kind, he grinned.

First witches and now fairies; first people from this past and now her own father suggested she might be a creature of supernatural powers. Lissan felt herself sinking ever deeper into a bog of confusion, dangerously near to drowning in murky depths.

"Father, I am not a witch." Lissan scowled at the abruptly smiling man before deliberately scoffing, "And as I'm only half fairy what could I possibly do to solve anyone's problems, even less defeat a force of brutal warriors?"

"Think on it." Yielding to the soon-rued urge to gently tease Lissan with truths, Comlan answered her question without a moment's hesitation. "You know a great deal that humanity will not learn for many lifetimes to come." The next moment he regretted words opening the door to actions that must never be taken.

"But—" Lissan almost wailed. "I intended to return here earlier today." Fighting to stay clear-headed, she drew a deep breath before continuing. "I hoped to find both logical answers for too many questions and a guidepost pointing the way home."

Comlan answered with a faint smile and serious words. "The return to your own time is a wise goal to pursue; one I'm glad you desire." The next instant his emerald eyes danced with unaccountable laughter. "But," he said wryly explaining the reason for his amusement, "in my Faerie Realm things of a certainty one way or another are an anathema." Though prevented by the laws governing contact between his realm and the mortal world from offering information unasked, to her implied question he could respond. "Thus, my sister's fairy ring is the last place to come seeking practical answers."

Long familiar with her father's preference for the unexpected, Lissan's attention quickly settled on another matter. "Your sister?"

"Yes." Comlan was pleased with his daughter's sharp wits and how rapidly her thoughts had leapt to question to his statement. It boded well for a quick and satisfying end to their problem. "Now I can confess that the first Lissan was my beloved younger and still-missed sister."

"But that was hundreds and hundreds of years ago, meaning that you must be—"

Comlan lifted a hand, signaling Lissan not to pursue an issue he was less anxious to discuss. "Fairy time is not measured in mortal years and our lifespans are considerably longer." His forbidding grimace settled into stern lines while he lent full attention to the goal of nudging his daughter's line of questioning toward the all-important issue of correcting the wrong that had allowed her to fall through time. "But surely there are other matters more important . . . questions you would have me answer, explanations you seek?"

A slight frown drew Lissan's brows together while through her mind, as clear as the chimes of Big Ben, rang an odd fact she'd never before thought to investigate. Although it was undeniable that she'd learned far more from her father than from any tutor or school, he had never offered answers unasked.

"Are you saying that you can tell me nothing unless I've posed the question?"

Comlan's answer was a brilliant smile.

"That being the case, can you tell me how I survived despite the blow of a broadsword that sliced completely through me?" With the remembered action came a faint tremor while her hand unconsciously traced the blade's downward motion.

"You must have been wearing your mother's amulet," Comlan simply stated. Then, to clear the puzzlement lingering in her expression, clarified his meaning. "Her brooch."

Lissan automatically laid one palm over the mentioned item concealed inside her chemise. "Mama said to never be without it and I haven't been."

Nodding approval, Comlan further explained.

"The brooch is a powerful amulet able to protect its wearer against harm from any human weapon. But beware. It has no power against the forces of nature—storm, sea, fire. . . ."

Grateful that her father sensed a daughter's need for uninterrupted moments to ponder the disconcerting flood of nearly unbelievable facts, Lissan sat in silence. She absently combed her fingers through cool, green blades of grass while slowly absorbing the truth of this unexpected bond with mystical beings that she'd so longed for as a child.

"The amulet has another power," Comlan said at last. "One you've exercised without realizing what you'd done."

Startled, Lissan's curious gaze lifted to meet a brilliant grin while with a deprecating motion toward himself, Comlan said, "By earnest plea the amulet's wearer can summon me."

Lissan's mouth formed a soft O of discovery. This explained how and by what magic the wish twice granted had actually been performed.

Though she seemed satisfied, Comlan had more to say on a matter pertinent no matter where Lissan might be—here or in the world of her birth. "As is to be expected from a race disdaining things either predictable or simple, this gift also comes with a unique limitation. Its call can only be heard when the wearer is in great peril." He gazed steadily into her eyes, seeking assurance that she fully understood.

"Why only then?" Predictable? Simple? Nothing her father had said could be disdained as that. Still, Lissan fervently wished for an ability to instantly comprehend all that he was willing to share.

Slowly shaking a head as golden as hers, Comlan gave another even more ambiguous answer. "There are rules governing contact between the human world and Fairy Realm that even I dare not break."

"So, I must be in danger to call you?" Lissan tried but failed to block the unmistakable note of panic in her voice. "But I wasn't in peril tonight. . . ."

"And tonight I didn't come in answer to your call," Comlan promptly answered. "Rather I came to keep my promise."

Lissan suddenly remembered that her father had said he would return to her but—

Comlan steadily held a gaze uncannily the mirror of his own while adding, "And seek a promise in return."

"Whatever you ask I will always give, Father," Lissan earnestly responded.

"Your claimed desire to retrace the path home is welcome assurance that you won't find the boon I seek too difficult to grant—a promise that you'll allow me to restore you to our family in London."

Lissan could have sworn she actually felt her heart dropping (at the pace of a particularly slow snail) all the way to her toes. On one hand she *did* want to go home, back to soft clothes, delicious foods cooked by someone who knew how, and a loving family. She did, but . . . if she truly were the White Witch of legend—and even her father had said she might well be—how could she take the coward's way by returning to the comforts of London while deserting Hildie and Liam . . . and Rory?

Knowing his daughter well, Comlan recognized the fiery spirit easily roused to defense of those who'd won her concern, he suspected the reason for her hesitation.

"Father," Lissan quietly began, gaze a silent plea. "Must I give you that promise in this very instant?"

"An immediate promise I will not demand—" Though he feared it might prove a sorry mistake, love for his daughter led Comlan to make the concession. "Yet, I strongly urge you prepare for the return to your own time and if not tonight, then soon."

"But—" Lissan was struck hard by the unpleasant prospect of abandoning not only Rory but other new friends to meet danger without the White Witch's promised aid. "Can I not linger long enough to discover whether or not I am meant to play a role in Connaught's history?"

Comlan's golden brows crashed together in a deep frown. Here, simply stated, was the precise reason that she must *not* stay. This much he dare not allow. His face went utterly emotionless. Worse still, her question wasn't clear enough to justify him in explaining how dire consequences were too easily evoked when someone strayed outside their own span in history and did something, even inadvertently, to alter time.

Having begun to think of this world and its people as hers, a somber Lissan softly asked, "Have I no choice in what era I live out my life?"

Worse and ever worse ... Comlan slowly shook his head. He had so often indulged this golden child, encouraged her independent reasoning, that now it was impossible to harshly demand she yield without question to his decision.

"Then you *don't* wish to return to your own?"

Drawing a deep breath, Lissan answered, "Yes ... no ... at least not yet."

"Odd—" Comlan murmured, gazing blindly into the distance while a wry smile drove away his stern expression. "I don't recall my spirited daughter ever being so indecisive on any matter."

Lissan was calmed by this fresh example of her father's mercurial nature; heartened by the never-wavering warmth of his affection.

"Summon me once you've chosen. ..." The deep

tone of Comlan's voice was enough to wordlessly press his wish for haste with the decision.

"How?" Lissan asked with a repressed grin. "How when I must be in peril to summon you with Mother's amulet?"

"There is another way," Comlan said. "All you need do is come and step into this fairy ring. When you call from here, I will always hear and answer."

So, Lissan inwardly marveled, her instinct had been accurate. "Then the plan to find my way here early this morning might not have been totally in vain despite being an inappropriate site to seek answers?" A quiet laugh slipped from her lips. "I meant to and would have, if only I'd known which hill to climb."

Comlan's mocking laughter filled the dark night. "You need only scale the hill directly behind the cottage where you sleep." He paused long enough to send her a skeptical glance. "How can you worry on that score after having made the same journey so often since childhood?"

Refusing to ask the obvious question already answered, Lissan accepted the fact that Tuatha Cottage faced the same direction as Aunt Daffy's Cottage from a past now become the future.

Without waiting for Lissan to speak, Comlan used a further inducement to gently reemphasize the most important issue. "No doubt your siblings are worried about the sister who promised to return but has mysteriously gone missing in the Irish hills."

Pangs of guilt for being the cause of her London family's distress immediately struck Lissan. And yet, though only this morning determined to find the way home as soon as possible, Lissan's confidence in the rightness of that path had been weakened by her father's suggestion that she might actually be the ambiguous one foretold. If it were true . . .

The fine sense of logic her brother had encouraged
and honed scoffed at the surely preposterous suggestion. And yet, after all the incredible things she'd
seen and been a part of in recent days, how could
she dismiss it out of hand? She couldn't.

"Come to this site and call out to me once you
know which route through time you wish to travel."
Though desiring an immediate choice, by the confusion clouding green eyes Comlan recognized his
daughter's need for more time to ponder. . . . "In the
meantime, though I know there's a healthy young
guard at the cottage to lend human strength in your
defense, I also will post someone from my realm to
watch over you."

Lissan was uneasy with the prospect of trying to
explain another stranger's sudden arrival, more difficult still, an otherworldly presence likely sharing
her father's exceptional looks and possibly glowing,
too. But before she could express her concern, the
sire so much more than she'd ever suspected
abruptly swept her into his arms. In the blink of an
eye, she found herself again sitting on her sleeping
pallet in Tuatha Cottage—alone.

The crash of a door rudely shoved open to smash
against the wall behind jerked Lissan from night
slumbers brief and far from restful. Sitting bolt upright while awkwardly brushing bright tendrils of
sleep-tangled hair from her eyes, she pointedly
glared at an uninvited caller.

"After other responsibilities prevented me from
being present for last eve's shared meal at Ailm
Keep—" Morag closed the door and strode boldly
forward until she could look down on the seated
stranger. "I thought it my duty to come and formally
greet the guest who—one way or another—managed to win the loan of Tuatha Cottage. And, of

course, to be assured that you have all you'll need
during your visit."

Lissan felt at a disadvantage for being positioned
so far below and having to gaze upward to the
speaker like, as no doubt the other woman wished,
a lesser creature to its master. This wordless belittle-
ment might be pardoned as an unintentional set of
circumstances but the same excuse couldn't be applied to Morag's utterly tactless emphasis on Lissan's status as a guest, a *temporary* and none too
welcome guest.

"I thank you for your solicitude and for sparing
the time and effort required to journey here although, I fear, hardly necessary as it was Lord Rory
who introduced us last night before he delivered me
safely home." Long training in social niceties en-
sured Lissan's tone and words remained the epitome
of courtesy despite the warning sparks glittering in
green eyes.

Morag, never short of confidence, ignored the
danger signals. "I appreciate your understanding."
This curt announcement contained no hint of honest
gratitude. "But I have an additional purpose for
coming."

Not the least bit surprised, Lissan responded with
a tight smile and brief nod.

"I deem it my duty to caution you, a stranger in
our midst, about dangerous matters of which you
must beware." Morag's iron-gray eyes coldly scrutinized her target for sign of the desired response.
But when no apprehension showed, she continued
in a voice lowered to an ominous whisper as if there
might be others near enough to hear. "I have heard
it said that you are the White Witch of legend but I
think you should know that I too have seen the future and the part you will play."

Morag had seen the future? Lissan fought to maintain an emotionless façade but couldn't stifle the light of skepticism brightening her green eyes.

"Oh, aye." Morag took exception to Lissan's immediate disbelief. " 'Struth." Chin lifted and gray eyes gone as cold and hard as granite, she asserted, "Though you try to protect Connaught, its people, and its lord—in the end you will fail."

Lissan slowly shook her head while in silence wondering how it could be that Morag's statement resounded more of wishful thinking than fact. Surely this woman so determined to be accepted as the Lady of Ailm Keep couldn't, wouldn't welcome the prospect of Connaught's fall?

"I trust you don't believe the Seeress Elesa of ancient times to be either the first or last person gifted with the ability to peer through the mists of time and see into the future?" Morag sneered her contempt for that possibility. "Even Elesa hadn't sufficient power to see the visions I've beheld or learn what I know . . . that your endeavors will fall prey to the overwhelming strength of another."

Though again telling herself that by now she should've grown accustomed to experiencing wildly divergent responses all in the same instant, Lissan was forced to admit herself badly shaken by those Morag's strange assault aroused. On one hand Lissan was disconcerted by hearing a *living* seeress predict that she was destined to play a role in the resolution of looming dangers—worse, an unsuccessful part. On the other hand she was relieved to learn that with her efforts she would strive to help not harm Connaught.

On open ground beyond the cottage door, Liam toiled to chop large chunks of firewood into more manageable pieces. As he tossed each length of split wood atop the growing pile, he cast another apprehensive glance toward a closed portal. Two women were inside—alone. With a final mighty blow he sank his axe into the stump atop which he'd balanced targeted log rounds.

Giving up his worthy chore as the lost battle for distraction that it was, Liam turned fully to glare at the deceptively secure view of ivy-covered walls. A personal distrust, even dread, of Morag left him uneasy with the prospect of that unpleasant woman close enough to goad gentle Lissan as nastily as she habitually preyed upon innocent Hildie.

"What woe plagues you?" a melodious voice softly inquired from behind. "Is there aught I might do to help?"

Liam spun around. Within arm's reach stood a vision of such ethereal loveliness that she caught his breath, nearly strangling a shocked question: "Who are you?"

"I am called Maedra." Her immediate answer was as succinct as his question. "What troubles you so? And if there's danger elsewhere, why do you linger here?"

Brushing fingertips over closed eyes, Liam wondered if his action would erase the image of this lithe beauty who seemed to glow with the white aura of moonlight. It didn't. Then, even though still half certain he was seeing things that were not there, Liam responded, "I wait to learn if my mistress remains unbruised by the wretched hag who arrived uninvited."

"An old hag?" the vision's dulcet voice inquired. "If your mistress is in danger, why didn't you prevent the hag from entering the cottage?"

"Morag is not old." Liam smiled sheepishly. "But she's a hag nonetheless . . . one who stands in a position of command over me."

Tilting a sweet face framed by golden ringlets,

Maedra spoke again. "Tell me why you fear your mistress is in danger?"

"I have spent several years in the hag's company and have yet to meet anyone—whether man or woman—able to escape her presence unscathed by sharp tongue or cruel schemes."

Maedra met Liam's gaze directly and nodded.

To Liam's shock, at the first creak of an opening door, his lovely companion disappeared—vanished right before his eyes. Weak sunlight of early morn picked out brighter streaks in light brown hair as Liam slowly shook his head. Plainly, he'd gone witless.

"Liam, why are you idling there?" A deeply scowling Morag demanded. "And who were you talking to?"

Liam stood mute and unflinching under the dark woman's piercing glare. Though he would willingly admit to being a simple man of humble origins, a fool he was not. No one could drive him into attempting an explanation for his apparent conversation with thin air, the critical Morag least of all.

CHAPTER 7

"Take the witch to the bridge and force her to cross over into Munster," Donal irritably demanded of his brother. Then as he, unlike Rory, was rarely quiet or content to let matters rest on succinct statements, added further reproach. "Don't you see how dangerous, how foolish it is for you to let the woman linger here . . . not merely tarry in this kingdom but coddle her within *our* borders?"

Rory's face remained impassive. Variations of this same argument he had heard from near the moment they'd set out before dawn until now when the sun was close to reaching its zenith. Every phrase had the feel, the stench of Morag, leaving Rory no doubt but that his too-easily-led brother had learned them from a constantly harping wife.

"Don't you see," Donal persisted, "that if your guest is in league with Mael and his king, you've not only welcomed their spy but granted her the perfect position from which to learn all that they wish to know. More than that, 'tis you who have rewarded their hireling by providing lodgings and foodstuffs for which others have toiled."

"Ah—" Rory spoke at last. "But Mael and his king are unlikely to learn anything from Lissan that isn't known to anyone crossing the border as easily as men from Munster have done too often in recent weeks." Rory's deep blue eyes met others of the same hue although the latter fell beneath his steady scrutiny.

"What *you* apparently don't recognize, Donal—" Rory softly reasoned, striving to bolster his seriously strained patience. "Is that greater danger might well rise from sending a possible English spy into Mael's welcoming hands. Continuing battles with Munster are challenge enough, and I see no useful purpose for risking the addition of others. Pray accept that my choices are an attempt to thwart the likelihood of a much more difficult struggle against the combined forces of Munster and the English king."

Struck nearly speechless, as he seldom was, Donal's mouth dropped open. "You think. . . . An English spy?" He sputtered over this totally unanticipated prospect. "Oh. . . ."

"Donal, journey on ahead and check with the miller," Rory directed, waving to the southeast. "If intruders have been stealing into Connaught from that stretch of the border, he would be the first to see evidence of their passing."

Although for safety's sake they should continue the patrol together, Rory was weary of Donal's endless protests and criticism. Unwilling to admit it might be more, he told himself it was for the sake of escaping before his brother's constant flow of words resumed that he'd spare time to check on the custody of the lovely witch himself.

"I'll meet you later at the bridge," Rory brusquely announced.

"But . . . Rory, you can't. . . ." Donal's objections were ignored and soon drowned out by the sound of pounding hooves as Rory urged his stallion into a gallop going the opposite direction.

Liam had nearly finished transferring split fire-wood from his disorderly pile into a tidy stack when the sound of a rapid approach halted his toil. Snatching his stave from where it leaned against the cottage wall, he whirled prepared to face the one arriving.

"Hold, Liam," Rory called out as his mount broke through the forest's green barrier. "You've no just reason to fend off your lord."

Despite the sheepish color warming his cheeks, Liam welcomed his master's gentle teasing as proof of the honorable regard in which he was held.

"Is your mistress in the cottage?" Rory took care to maintain a flat and unrevealing tone in asking this vital question.

Liam nodded. "Leastways she was there when Lady Morag went in, and I haven't seen her step out since the woman left."

Morag? Here? Rory scowled. Briskly knocking on the door, he entered without politely pausing for her response.

Sitting at an empty table, feeling utterly useless since the departure of her morning's unwelcome guest, Lissan was not prepared for the arrival of another visitor—particularly not this disturbing and unaccountably angry man.

Surprised by the trepidation in emerald eyes, Rory narrowed his own. He was irritated with himself for instinctively sympathizing with a vulnerability too likely feigned. That thought was quickly followed by others suggesting the opposite. Morag had just been here. Morag with her regrettable talent for finding and striking anyone's most vulnerable point.

"Even had Liam not told me, I would know from your expression that my sister-in-law visited you." Rory refused for the moment to acknowledge his uneasiness with these two vastly different yet equally complex women. But it was his frustration with them both that added a further thread of sincerity to what he next said. "You have my sympathy."

Her handsome visitor's consoling words and wry grin drew from Lissan a rueful grimace that gentled into a slight smile.

During the moments that followed, the warmth of Rory's face faded, leaving behind a solemn expression of entreaty. "I left my brother to continue the patrol we daily ride together for the sake of seeking answers to questions he posed but which I should have asked you much earlier."

Lissan straightened. This sounded ominous, particularly coming so soon after the professed sympathy of his greeting. She folded dainty hands together on the tabletop to prevent them from betraying her embarrassing discomfort with nervous movements. Then, silently waiting for Rory to speak, she could only hope the pounding of her heart wouldn't drown out his words.

"You said that your home was in London." Rory straddled the bench on the opposite side of the table from Lissan. "How did you get here? Did you leave from one of the Cinque ports on England's southern coast or did you cross the Irish Sea from Wales?"

Lissan gazed blindly through the unshuttered window beyond Rory's shoulder and slowly shook her head. To respond would only lead to more questions that couldn't be answered.

"It must have been one or the other. . . ." A sinking sensation of fading hope further aggravated Rory's strained impatience. "Unless you came from some Northumbrian port?"

When his last suggestion brought no response at all, Rory's jaw clenched. Lissan's determination to reveal nothing seemed proof that she must in reality

be an infiltrator, a spy for the English king. The
bench rocked as he abruptly rose.

Lissan couldn't help but watch as the intimidating
man repeatedly stomped the short distance between
table and firepit while edges of the black cloak still
draped about broad shoulders rippled in the breeze
his haste created. Though it was her silence that fu-
eled his anger, Lissan was certain the only truth, the
impossible truth, that she could share would infu-
riate him a great deal more.

Rory's fiery temper eventually cooled and he began to wonder if perhaps he'd started with the
wrong question. Halting within arm's reach of the
stubborn damsel, he gazed down to study the
golden mane tamed for the first time into a glorious
array of ringlets atop her head. It was a strange,
beautiful style, yet he perversely wanted to free
glowing curls to cascade in wild abandonment down
the graceful arch of her back. That irrational urge
brought a curl of self-contempt to his lips.

"Why have you come to Connaught? Tell me the
answer to that question and I won't pressure you for
more," Rory brusquely demanded, further vexed
with himself for issuing this offer to compromise
with an almost certain adversary.

Despite a valiant fight to look considerably more
confident than she felt, Lissan gazed helplessly up
into intense dark eyes. This powerful warrior honestly did need answers in order to guarantee that his
planned defenses for the border would be sufficient
to stand firm in the crucial battle predicted. Whole-
heartedly wishing to support his cause yet unable to
provide believable responses, she dared not answer.
Lissan felt as if she'd been unjustly trapped in a
maze with no safe path to its exit.

Rory recognized conflicting emotions in the courage of a proudly uptilted chin and the desperation

glowing from the green depths of her amazing eyes. Finding himself host to an unexpected desire to comfort the mysterious damsel, Rory sank down to share the same bench with Lissan.

While gentle fingers brushed loose tendrils back from her cheeks and temples, Lissan sank headlong into mesmerizing, night-blue eyes. She remembered too well the return from Ailm Keep and their embrace—searing, exciting, and an enticement to such intimate pleasures as she had once assured her sisters could never tempt her.

"Just tell me why you've come." Harsh words became a gentle plea as they whispered from lips Rory held a breath from her ear.

Lissan nearly cried out with the frustration of her impossible position. Surviving this tender interrogation must be the penance required of her for wicked pleasures stolen but a few hours past. Head falling gracefully forward to rest on hands still joined on tabletop, she softly moaned, "You wouldn't believe me."

"Why wouldn't I believe you?" Rory ran one forefinger down Lissan's petal-smooth cheek and under her chin before attempting to lift her face toward his. "Why wouldn't I, if 'tis the truth you tell? Or is it that you fear to trust me?"

Lissan sat upright to again meet Rory's gaze directly. She must immediately rid this man of any notion that she mistrusted him, had to for the sake of protecting the faint spark of hope that he might one day come to trust her.

"I would gladly give answers to all you've asked but, honestly, you'd find the truth unbelievable."

"Neither of us will ever know whether or not that's so—" Dark eyes held others of emerald. "Unless you share those answers with me."

Lissan had to admit that Rory's argument was eminently logical. And, having long taken pride in a talent for sound reasoning, she found herself unable to refute it. Drawing a deep breath and clenching her fingers more tightly together, she surrendered by launching into a precise account of the actions that had landed her here. Her firm statement of facts began with the journey up a hillside behind her parents and ended on the broadsword's blow.

"Nineteen hundred?" Black hair brushed broad shoulders as Rory slowly shook his head. Unbelievable? 'Struth, it was that . . . but even its implausibility couldn't smother the doubtless foolish yet persistent desire to trust her, a desire that curled his lips with a slight, self-derisive smile.

"You say your parents became younger and younger before falling *into* the fairy ring while you threw yourself *out* of it . . . and into the middle of our battle?" There was a strange logic in this but not enough for Rory to fully accept its veracity. Particularly not when the tale told by this damsel too beautiful to be trustworthy required lending credence to the superstitious fables of a pagan past.

"I don't blame you for being skeptical." Lissan inwardly chided herself not to be disappointed when he responded as she'd known he would. "I *lived* both it and the disconcerting array of odd experiences that followed. And yet with my training to use cool reasoning and trust only scientific fact, I find it almost impossible to believe any of it myself."

The mention of the unfamiliar term "scientific" meant nothing to Rory and passed unnoticed while he focused on the anxiety putting a troubled furrow between Lissan's delicate brows. There it was again, his jaw clenched, that urge to comfort, to shield her from distress of any making. The strength of willpower exercised to restrain that instinct sharpened

the edge of his voice as he asked, "But how? By what
power did you part the veil of time?"

"My father says—"

"Your father?" Rory incredulously seized on what
must be the inconsistency proving her tale to be a
lie. Anxious to suppress an ache of disappointment,
he assured himself of its insignificance even while
paradoxically claiming the pain as proof of the folly
in trusting this or any woman. "You've talked with
the father who fell into the ring and disappeared
since you fell out of it to land here?"

"Yes," Lissan instantly responded, heart thumping under the realization of just what her seeming
contradiction implied. "My father is Comlan, King
of the Tuatha de Danann. It was he who, with his
army, rescued me from captors yestermorn."

Rory took in the heart-wrenching vulnerability of
Lissan's face and gazed into the apparent honesty of
her crystal-clear eyes. Either the damsel spinning
this extravagant, convoluted tale was lost in a world
of delusions or she was an infiltrator with an incredible skill for donning a false identity.

"Then you are fairy, too?" Rory was frustrated
when words he'd intended as a flat statement of fact
came out as scorn.

"No . . . not quite." Seeing his once almost tender
expression chill into an emotionless mask, Lissan
knew how completely she'd lost but, having embarked on this path of truth revealed, answered anyway. "My mother was human, which means I am
merely half fairy."

Jerking back as suddenly as if in an instant she'd
turned into a threatening pillar of fire, Rory rose to
his feet. Nearly, too nearly, had Lissan come to
catching him in her golden snare of beguilements.
Though certain now that she couldn't be trusted,
Rory was dismayed to find the instinct to do so still

strong . . . which meant he couldn't trust himself. It was a most unpleasant first in his experience. He abruptly turned and strode from the cottage without glancing back.

Tuatha Cottage's single window was shuttered against the cold of a spring evening. Inside, wrapped in a coarse blanket and perched on a small stool at the fire ring's outer edge, Lissan leaned forward and extended her hands to the flames. She sought their cheery heat to lessen the discomfort of both the brisk temperature and the inner chill lingering after Rory's rejection of the explanation difficult to give.

"I've been sent to bear you company until your decision is made."

Lissan glanced over her shoulder while wryly congratulating herself on having finally gone beyond being startled by the unexpected. Less than a pace from Lissan's back stood a young woman of approximately her own age with the same moonglow aura as the King of the Tuatha de Danann and as golden, as stunningly attractive, though with azure not emerald eyes.

"I am so glad it's you." Lissan forced an unnatural lethargy to dissipate and rose to her feet with a grateful smile curling tender lips and brightening green crystal gaze.

It was the newcomer who was startled. How could a being never met before be pleased to see her?

"When my father said he'd send someone to watch over me, I thought he meant one of the enchanted warriors who helped rescue me yesterday." Lissan clarified words plainly misunderstood. "And I didn't know how I could explain such a guardian to my numerous unanticipated visitors."

"Don't worry." The newcomer was quick to calm the other's concern. "I am Maedra and no one save you will see me—unless you ask that I appear."

"Oh, no." Lissan lifted her hands, palms out, as if to fend off the mere possibility. "I'm having far too difficult a time explaining my own presence."

Maedra gave a sympathetic grin, motioning for Lissan to resume her seat while she pulled a second stool over to sit nearby. Though from vastly different worlds, the two females soon found themselves wrapped in the pleasant haze of an amazing harmony.

"What do you do in your world?" Lissan inquired some time later, curious and thinking this an uncomplicated topic to pursue.

"Do?" Maedra blinked in confusion. From the viewpoint of a fairy's vast life span, the potential answers were too plentiful to be easily narrowed into only a few words.

Nodding, Lissan elaborated, surprised by the need. "What do you do to occupy your time?"

Maedra hesitated no longer. "Whatever task King Comlan sets for me to accomplish."

"No—" Lissan laughed. "That's what you do to please someone else." With an amused half-smile, she explained more precisely what she sought. "I'm curious to learn what you do for your own enjoyment."

"Hmm." Maedra momentarily pondered the quirk of mortals that divided and ranked actions this way. The next instant her brilliant grin flashed. "In the king's great hall grand banquets are held, and while we feast each in turn entertains the others."

"Entertains?" When it seemed Maedra would end her description there, Lissan hastily urged her to continue. "What kind of performances?"

Maedra shrugged as if the answer were of too little interest for any waste of breath—but the dimple peeking in one cheek betrayed her indifferent manner as a mere façade. It was gone in an instant while cheerful words tripped from her tongue. "Some sing, others play pipes, harps, lutes, or any such instruments as come to hand. Then too we've fine bards who create all manner of lyrical verses along with skilled tale-spinners to share amazing stories and recount ancient legends."

When Maedra paused again, it required only a stern look from Lissan to win more.

"Then we dance and dance and dance." The sparkle in bright blue eyes made it clear that this was the source of Maedra's greatest pleasure although her enthusiasm dimmed very little when she added, "Sometimes we take our horses and set forth on cavalcade; sometimes we hunt for the ever-elusive gold-horned unicorn."

Lissan's hand instinctively lifted to cover the area of her homespun dress beneath which a brooch was pinned. During childhood she'd pestered her mother to repeat two tales for her again and again. Her favorite was the story of her namesake, the magical creature who in shedding mystical powers to live a human life had formed the fairy ring. But she'd been nearly as fond of hearing about the legendary unicorn constantly pursued but impossible to catch.

While conversation settled into the easy flow of friendship, Lissan gradually became aware that the small cottage's chill had been replaced by a comfortable warmth. And she had no doubt but that Maedra's presence was the source of this gift.

While Maedra described several particularly tasty dishes served at a recent feast, Lissan couldn't prevent her thoughts from wandering back to the meal she'd shared at Ailm Keep the previous night. That, in turn, raised a further issue and inspired another question.

"Are you wed . . . or perhaps betrothed to some-one in your world?"

Bemused by this human's fairylike ease in making abrupt subject changes, Maedra laughed but then scoffed at herself. Why shouldn't Lissan, King Com-lan's daughter and half-fairy, be comfortable with this trait?

Lingering amusement for her own foolishness kept the gleam in Maedra's azure gaze bright as she promptly answered, "Haven't yet seen a male amongst the Tuatha de Danann with whom I'd be willing to share such a pledge."

"You are real!" The gasped. words came from Liam. His knock at the door had gone unanswered, and that lack of response had left him fearing that his immediate, unannounced aid might be needed to thwart further evildoings. Toward that worthy goal he had stealthily entered.

The attention of both women shifted to the young man awkwardly standing in the open portal and blushing self-consciously over an intrusion rudely summoning their attention.

"Oops!" Maedra grinned at Liam before glancing penitently toward Lissan. "Your father will not be pleased with me," she confessed. "I was instructed not to be seen by any human save you."

"Human?" Liam repeated. What an odd statement . . . but then what else from such a wondrous crea-ture?

It was obvious to Lissan that Maedra and Liam had met earlier, though how and when she couldn't even guess. Her father's reaction to this forbidden action was difficult to predict. But she did fear that one thing could be as clearly foreseen as the seeress Elesa's prophecy: The threads of a life well ordered in London would here become ever more tangled until their snarled knot snapped under the strain.

*   *   *

"What do you mean you don't know where Rory is?" Morag demanded of her husband, planting clenched fists on hips and glaring at him across the bedchamber they shared on the keep's highest level. "You and your brother ride patrol together every day. So, how is it that now while everyone waits for the evening meal in the hall below, you don't know where he is?"

"We argued about the White Witch," Donal belligerently confessed. Morag always won, but it was his duty to fight. "I told him he was a fool to keep her here in Connaught. And, just as you suggested last eve, I told him 'twould be best if he sent her across the bridge and into Mael's less scrupulous hands."

"And did Rory agree?" Dark pleasure curdled her unnaturally sweet tone. "Is he delayed by the completion of that admirable task?"

"I doubt it." Donal deflated his wife's hope. "He says 'tis too likely she's a spy for King Henry of England and that sending her to Mael would only increase the danger here in Connaught."

By turning her back on Donal to prevent him from seeing her venomous grin, Morag hid her satisfaction over this unexpected boon. Somehow it had never occurred to her that Rory might host such a fear . . . such a *useful* fear. . . .

CHAPTER 8

Lissan peered through an open shutter into the first glow of dawn on an eastern horizon edged by the dense forest's dark silhouette. Maedra, Liam, and she had relaxed around the central firepit, talking until the darkest hours of the previous night had passed. Yet even after her companions retired, she'd still been left with sufficient solitary time to again review recent events and examine possible actions to be taken from every conceivable angle.

At last a decision of sorts had been reached. One that was neither a definitive choice nor arrived at easily but, Lissan hoped, one that would prove judicious. Though only a few days had passed since she'd tumbled into this era, so much had happened that it felt a great deal longer. In *many* ways this brief span measured in mere hours seemed infinitely more important than all the years that had gone before.

In the London of 1900 she'd had no real purpose other than to fulfill her family's wishes by choosing a respectable groom and settling into staid married life. Here in 1115 Lissan had an opportunity to possibly be of some worthwhile use. And when new friends, no matter how recently met, might have need of her it made no difference whether the aid given was attributed to the White Witch or merely to a stranger named Lissan. She couldn't simply abandon them by allowing her father to "whisk" her back to safety in the future of her birth.

More importantly, Lissan inwardly confessed, she couldn't desert Rory to meet a harsh fate that she might be able to soften. Shadows filled emerald eyes as the thought of never again seeing the fascinating man raised depressingly vivid images of a future gloomy without him in it. But it was near as difficult to contemplate denying a loving father the only boon he had ever asked of her. Dare she go on with her plan? Go out to seek aid on a first step toward making sense of incomprehensible challenges?

"Do you need my help in some way?" As had a similar query the evening before, this quiet question came from behind.

"No, not at all." Lissan subdued a troubled frown and turned to Maedra with a smile. "I've merely been making plans for a climb to the fairy ring."

"Why?" Apprehension darkened Maedra's expression.

To calm the other's distress, Lissan tried to enfuse her explanation with reassurance. "My father said that if I called him from there, he would come."

"Have I done something to offend?" Maedra's anxiety had increased not abated. "Or have I omitted some task I ought to have performed?" Although Lissan had explained the whole of her incredible experience to a thunderstruck Liam the previous night, Maedra continued to worry that the mistress was upset with her for appearing to the young guardsman.

"Oh, no, no," Lissan promptly answered. "Between your efforts and Liam's I'm as well protected and looked after as any human could possibly be."

The faint aura of white light surrounding Maedra glowed brighter for the brilliance of her relieved smile.

The fairy maiden's response heartened Lissan to embark on her planned climb to the fairy ring. Believing it unnecessary to further justify her actions, she returned a new friend's smile with another of equal warmth before moving to the door. Slipping from the cottage and around to its back, she began to ascend the hill rising there.

Compared to the broad path of the many such jaunts in Lissan's childhood, the same route now was considerably more difficult to navigate. Thick vegetation crowded narrow distances between trees in the wildwood while there were abundant stumble-traps laid by fallen branches buried beneath lush grasses, ferns, and leaves shed the past autumn.

When at last a weary Lissan stepped through the green wall of foliage that girded the hilltop glade, she glanced up toward the sky. She'd started out early and walked steadily despite a toilsome path but the sun was already near its zenith. The journey had been more time-consuming than expected, which made it more important for her to quickly accomplish what she'd come to do and start back down. Too long a delay would mean she couldn't reach the cottage before dusk. And that failure would put her at risk of a nighttime confrontation with the wild beasts—human and animal—Rory had warned her inhabited the woods of Connaught.

Legend held that nothing could truly harm them, yet Lissan took care in stepping over the fairy ring's fragrant blossoms to settle beneath the oak's spreading branches. Abruptly faced with the immediate task of summoning her father, she recognized her error in not earlier planning every detail. Although he had promised to come if she called him from here, that action seemed too simple to succeed. Thus, in spite of her father's statement that he would hear an appeal made on the amulet only if the wearer were in dire peril, Lissan laid crossed palms over her brooch and murmured an earnest wish.

"Come, Father, please come." With eyes tightly closed Lissan repeated these words over and over again like a litany, hoping her father would honor his vow to appear once she took the simple action of entering this fairy ring.

Sensing the plea had been answered even before her shoulder was touched or name softly called, Lissan glanced up to find her father sitting beside her.

"Lissan. . . ." Comlan solemnly addressed the daughter who had summoned him. "Have you made a decision? Are you ready to return to the world of your birth?"

"I don't wish my family to worry for me, but. . . ." Anxious to win aid he'd likely be loath to give, Lissan absently plucked at the skirt of her homespun gown. She'd known her father would justly expect an answer to this query and yet was not prepared to give a decisive response. "If there's even a tiny spark of hope that I might be of some aid to Rory's cause—"

Lissan broke off, appalled by what her use of a given name and that name alone revealed—not only to her father but more undeniably to herself.

"Then you've decided to remain in this past time?" Comlan's response was the epitome of a fairy nature's basic ambiguity: affection in the teasing glitter of emerald eyes but grim downward curl to one side of his smile.

"L-l-leastways for a while. . . ." Lissan sputtered, inwardly chiding herself for this new and unwelcome lack of certainty about any part of her life and this while trying to justify her actions to him. "Before I make my choice, there is something I must know. . . ."

Comlan's face went utterly emotionless while he waited for his daughter to continue with a rationale he felt certain he didn't want to hear.

"Though I've only recently met Hildie and Liam and Rory, I must know if by lingering I might be able to help them defeat the same wretches of Munster from whose captivity you rescued me."

"If you've yet to choose—" Comlan tamed his own impatience to calm his daughter's nervous fingers by gently taking them into his own. "Why have you come here seeking me now?"

Lissan drew a deep breath and then with a winsome smile began unfolding the heart of her plea. "I hope you'll grant a small boon that may speed me toward the decision."

Dark gold brows arched in silent demand for the specific details of her vague request.

"The last time we spoke you reminded me that I know numerous facts which will not be learned for many generations beyond this year." Lissan steadily met his unblinking gaze while stating both her request and the logic behind it as persuasively as possible. "My choice would be reached with more ease and haste if only I had the trunk resting at the end of my bed in London. It holds not merely history tomes telling of events soon to occur here but other books as well, including scientific volumes which contain the kind of precise data that may prove invaluable if I am fated to be the White Witch."

"And you want me to fetch that trunk with all its contents for you?" The even tenor of Comlan's voice betrayed no emotion.

Lissan nibbled her lower lip. The abrupt and utter impassivity of his face was discouraging, but without hesitation she firmly nodded, remnants of hope lighting green-fire sparks in her eyes.

"Beware, daughter," Comlan solemnly warned. "Though none here could read the words in your books, it's that very fact which when added to photographs and even drawings of things unfamiliar would assuredly be viewed by the local populace as proof that you truly are a witch."

"But they already think I'm that," Lissan promptly reasoned. "Besides, my trunk has a lock. And I'd share neither the key nor the books with anyone else."

Before further arguments could be made, Lissan froze at the sound of approaching horses. Rory and his brother broke into the glade. Lissan was startled and, but for the restraining finger laid across her lips, would've launched into an excuse to justify her presence in the fairy ring with an amazingly handsome and inexplicably youthful stranger in Connaught.

Comlan met his daughter's quizzical glance and slowly shook his bright head in a silent command to patiently wait.

As two massive stallions and their riders passed almost within arm's reach of the fairy ring's occupants, neither warriors nor steeds showed any sign of having noticed them. Not until after the thudding of hooves faded into the forest's quiet shadows did Comlan share another magical truth.

"The rising fragrance of these lovely flowers encircling us provides an impenetrable veil of invisibility to any creature resting inside—fairy, human, or animal."

Lissan could only nod. Though the two brothers' lack of response made it clear that they'd seen neither she nor her father, Lissan was grateful for the explanation no matter how scientifically implausible.

"It does not, however"—while likely unnecessary, Comlan persisted in sharing another important fact—"muffle sounds made."

Again Lissan nodded her understanding but this time with a bright grin.

"Now, so far as your trunk and its key are concerned. . . ." Comlan shook his head. "It's too dangerous and not for you alone."

Pushing to the back of her mind images of Rory riding past oblivious to her, Lissan cast her father a quizzical look and focused on picking up the threads of their previous conversation.

"I have already warned you that there are serious laws governing contact between my Faerie Realm and the human world. They are rules that cannot, must not, be broken."

Lissan nodded although she didn't see what this could possibly have to do with the books she had requested he bring to her.

"Any fairy interference in mortal concerns has the dangerous potential for altering the course of human history." Comlan held his daughter's attention. Having watched many a courageous man quail beneath his intense scrutiny, he was proud of Lissan's ability to meet it unflinching.

"Pray pay heed, daughter. Listen to the wisdom behind an ancient admonition which warns that such indefensible changes are likely to bring equally catastrophic consequences down upon both the Tuatha de Danann and the human race."

Catching a sobering glimpse of the perils her father was striving to make plain, Lissan listened carefully as he continued.

"I realize now that the first foolish misstep toward so grievous an offense was mine. I should never have suggested your knowledge from the future as a cure for the ills of this past."

Clearly recognizing danger, Lissan's heart sank along with the foundering ship of hope that she'd discovered a way to help new friends. She admitted the wrong in teaching friends from this era scientific secrets that weren't meant to be discovered for centuries. It was an action, she morosely acknowledged, almost certain to wreak a grievous, major impact on the intended path of human history. Yet even as she accepted this bleak prospect, her father quietly spoke again, provoking a deeper insight.

"However," Comlan reluctantly conceded, "if you *are* the White Witch, who is to say that precisely this kind of inexplicable magic isn't to be wielded for the sake of securing the goal desired?"

Lissan's grin nearly outshone the sun. "Then so long as I don't reveal how to *create* the magic, but rather simple methods to use whatever mystical instruments the White Witch provides. . . ."

The approval in a flashing smile intensified as Comlan slowly nodded. He was again pleased by his offspring's sharp wits. In this instance Lissan's mental acuity enabled her to quickly comprehend details which one of his ambiguous breed found difficult to explicitly state.

"When you wake on the morrow, your trunk will rest nearby."

"Wait." Fearing her father meant to leave as quickly as he'd come, Lissan reached out to clasp his arm. "Tell me, then, am I truly the White Witch?"

Required by ancient laws to answer any question posed by a human, Comlan reluctantly said, "The Seeress Elesa predicted that the mythical White Witch would fall out of a clear blue sky—as you did."

Tilting a golden head, Lissan sent her father a probing sidelong glance. "Surely it is unlikely for so peculiar an event to happen a second time or to someone else at so propitious a moment in time?

"How could your quote from the ancient seeress be either disbelieved or ignored?" Though her companion remained impassive, Lissan continued. "And yet though my loyalties lay solely with my current homeland, there's another now residing in Ailm Keep who swears she foresees a future in which I am destined to destroy rather than aid Connaught."

"Another seeress?" Comlan looked skeptical. "I've heard of no other, which makes the claim unlikely to be true."

"But surely you see that I must be certain—" Lissan sought to convince him of a rightness in the request that had brought her here. "Certain that the White Witch is fated to *help* not harm Connaught and toward that end must have my books from London?"

"I fear that—your history books notwithstanding—yours is a question only the White Witch can answer." Comlan slowly shook his bright hair while with gentle fingers trying to wipe away the slight frown of frustration between Lissan's brows.

Lissan wished she could be confident of being the legendary figure. But lacking that assurance, she purposely blurred the focus of their topic with another curious question.

"Was the Seeress Elesa herself a fairy or a witch?"

"Neither." Amused by his daughter's simple query, Comlan smiled wryly once more. "She was a Druid-trained prophetess.

"Now that I've responded to your questions, answer one for me?" Comlan paused, waiting for a suddenly wary Lissan to nod before continuing. "Earlier you mentioned three humans. And though I know of Lord Rory, tell me about Liam and Hildie."

"Liam is the human guard Lord Rory set to watch

over me. Hildie is Rory's young daughter. She is a winsome little thing whose mother told her before dying that they were directly descended from the magical Princess Lissan responsible for the fairy ring on the hill behind their home—Tuatha Cottage."

Comlan's expression settled into one of pensive thought. His sister had borne mortal children. It was only reasonable that they, in turn, would've borne their own—on and on and on. It was possible that this Hildie truly was his niece though divided by many human generations.

"I had better start my journey down to the cottage before twilight comes." Although her father had become unaccountably withdrawn, Lissan hated to leave his company behind. Still she dared not allow herself to forget the perils of a night forest best avoided and reluctantly stood up.

"I'll whisk you to the edge of the cottage garden," Comlan reassured Lissan, equally unwilling to see her fall prey to night dangers—more dangers than she knew. "But first I think it best to remind you of yet another important fact. Your mother's amulet protects you from the weapons of mankind but *not* from natural forces." Rising to his feet, he gazed solemnly down into her eyes and added, "Only a true fairy can meet such challenges as fire, storm, and flood to emerge from their threat unharmed."

Before Lissan could finish nodding, she found herself alone a few steps from where lay the cottage's garden, once neglected but now diligently tended by Liam's generous attentions.

Morag risked a quick glance up toward the moon only half hidden by drifting clouds. Then tugging the hood of a black cloak lower to cast her face deeper into shadow, she urged her mare to move more hastily along a hidden pathway known to few.

On this dark journey she was joined only by small animals dimly heard scuttling through forest undergrowth and night birds swooping down to capture prey in near silence.

Fortunate, Morag gloated. Yes, fortunate to have the fine subterfuge provided by her façade of onerous duties rightly taken on by a keep's chatelaine. It was a position for which she was well qualified, one in which her study of herbs was an asset. She knew which plants healed and which possessed useful applications for other purposes equally important to her goals.

Morag's pleasure in this fact was tested only by the sour prospect of what lay ahead. Between a naturally foul disposition and an overfondness for both wine and ale, Mael was almost certain to be awaiting her arrival with an impatience bordering on madness—not a propitious way to embark on the quest for his support of her scheme, an unavoidable one.

As the hooves of Morag's mount left the muffling thickness of forest path and began loudly pounding across the drawbridge leading to the only entrance into Mael's wooden keep, doors barred from within swung wide. Once safely inside palisade walls with gate closed behind, she descended from the horse's back aided by a man deputized to meet and lead her to his lord.

Though Paddy spoke not a word, the trepidation in his eyes made it abundantly clear that he feared his master's sorceress—a woman whose mere presence represented a betrayal of her own and was to him proof of her untrustworthiness. How could Lord Mael have failed to recognize the same truth?

Anxious to be quit of his charge, Paddy hustled to open the keep's door and waved into the great hall a woman still moving at her own measured pace.

"Surely," a fuming host snarled once Morag came into view, "in order to justify a more timely arrival you could've seen to it that the people of Connaught were visited by some small plague?"

"Calm yourself, Mael." Venom burned openly in Morag's gaze and yet she smiled with cloying sweetness at the man who, despite the late hour, was still seated behind the remnants of a generous meal. She languidly pushed back her hood, refusing to let this self-important creature rule her, particularly when to do elsewise would weaken her credibility as one possessing unearthly powers.

"I'm here now and bring welcome news of a fresh and unsuspected weapon to wield in neutralizing our quarry's threat."

Mael's colorless eyes narrowed suspiciously, but he waited in silence for the sorceress's explanation of her bold claim.

"Rory O'Connor's qualms go beyond mere concern for the White Witch's purpose." Morag paused, finding peculiar pleasure in prolonging this revelation—an action certain to intensify Mael's irritation.

"What?" Mael snarled, further agitated by this woman's blatant attempt to provoke his anger. "Of what possible interest and less use could O'Connor's troubles be to me?"

"A great deal, I should think," Morag responded and paused again. But when Mael's fists clenched and he shifted in his seat as if to rise, she relented and with a merry smile announced, "He fears that the pretty foreigner he finds so alluring is in truth an English spy sent by the sly King Henry."

"An English spy? Hmm. . . ." Mael pressed his mouth against the inner edge of hands pressed together, palm flat. It was an intriguing notion and posed vague possibilities, but—

"We haven't the time to waste on elaborate plots."

He made this statement with the harshness of indis-
putable fact. "Days and weeks have already been
lost. It's *now* that action must be taken for hope to
clear the way and see a successful invasion concluded before the cold returns."

"An elaborate plot is unnecessary," Morag
snapped, gliding forward to face her host from directly below his position on the dais. "All you need
do is arrange for some man unknown to O'Connor
to be caught carrying an incriminating message addressed to the guest in Tuatha Cottage and closed
by King Henry's seal."

"Hah!" Mael hooted sarcastically while rising,
stepping down to a rush-strewn dirt floor and moving to stand within arm's reach of the woman he
wished to intimidate. "I haven't the English king's
seal, have you?"

Morag slipped the fingers of one hand beneath
where a sleeve ended just above the other. Then like
a traveling conjuror with a flourish she extended her
fist and opened it to reveal a shiny object lying in
the center of her palm.

A dubious Mael picked the lopsided oval up between thumb and forefinger. He peered closely at
the crude image pressed into the metal for an instant
before closing meaty fingers over the prize.

" 'Tis only a coin."

"Yes," Morag instantly agreed, "a coin that bears
the king's image and the opening year of his reign.
What more could one expect of a king's seal?"

Mael shook his head and vivid red hair reflected
the dancing flames of a roaring blaze in the room's
central firepit. "I think O'Connor is unlikely to be so
easily misled."

"Why?" Morag demanded. "Is he more apt than
you or I to have seen the seal of a foreign king?"

"Nay." Mael growled his disgust. "But if you possess such a coin, then likely Rory has seen another much the same."

"A coin? Oh, indeed." Morag smirked. "Since I took the one you hold from the strongbox at Ailm Keep, I'm certain he has. However—" She shrugged in a fine demonstration of unconcern. "On the intercepted letter he'll view a seal's reverse image, an image distorted by hot wax."

Lightly pounding a coin-containing fist into the palm of his other hand, Mael strode completely around the hearth several times before coming to a halt directly in front of Morag.

"Before midday on the morrow, I'll send for my scribe and set him to the task of composing an appropriately cryptic message from king to an agent concealed by a façade of innocence. Then while the scribe labors I will go out to bargain with someone perfect to pose as a royal messenger destined to be captured."

"Who?" Morag coldly inquired. She wanted to be consulted on every detail of this scheme she'd devised but felt control rapidly slipping from her hands.

"Stephen," Mael answered with an unpleasant smile, reveling in a rare opportunity to seize command from this domineering woman. "He's a slave from England who will do whatever I ask in exchange for his freedom."

Furious with Mael and frustrated at having no better plan to propose, Morag chose to say nothing at all while pulling up her hood in preparation for a hasty return to Ailm Keep before dawn.

"Wait." Mael placed a restraining hand on her shoulder. "I accepted your suggestion but have not forsaken my own plans."

Morag scowled. She didn't like to think what ruinous complications this red-haired madman might yet wreak upon the smooth execution of her scheme.

"While we'll both wait to see what results your fine, bloodless ploy brings, I will hesitate no longer to put my own strategies in motion." This pompous announcement was calculated to further irritate the ambitious woman with whom he shared an uneasy alliance. "My methods require neither the supernatural spells nor worthless talismans you've previously proposed. No, for me honest battle will suffice—and bloodshed there will be."

When the man wildly shook two clenched fists in the air, Morag cringed a step back. It was an instinctive yet traitorous reaction that grated over her already chafed temper.

"No need to play the squeamish faintheart when blood you wish to spill will join the flow." Mael sneered, relishing this chance to mock Morag's hypocrisy. "And furthermore, you owe me for delaying your departure long enough to share a few words of caution: If you wish Donal—the key for achieving all your goals—to remain healthy, best you ensure that he falls ill before the morrow's dawning."

CHAPTER 9

Hildie sat snugly tucked into the fork where a stout timber angled out to further brace a first in the parade of oaken joists fitted into notches on opposite stone walls. These parallel beams in turn provided framework for what served as the ceiling of this level and floor for the one above. Viewing her actions a game, Hildie remained as motionless as ever had Shadow, the grey stable cat, while patiently watching for any rodent foolish enough to intrude on her domain. The analogy was apt as from amid this gloom high above the great hall it was Hildie's habit to watch unseen while people gathered for each day's first meal.

Every night Hildie slept in a loft above the great hall and opposite from the dais. It had originally been built to accommodate musicians playing for diners below. With a child's inquisitiveness, she had soon discovered how easy it was to climb into the network of rafters and braces. There was no doubt but that if this practice were known, it would be instantly forbidden for being both dangerous and nosy—a prospect which merely increased the rafters' lure for an adventurous Hildie.

This morning, before servants arrived to begin

their domestic chores, Hildie saw something of considerably more interest than usual. Morag, who
rarely appeared before midday, had already been
busy when Hildie took up her perch.

Hildie's favorite position was catercorner from the
alcove where the woman posing as chatelaine kept
an array of bottles, bowls, and baskets filled with
items used in medicinal potions. By curtains left
open it was clear Morag wrongly thought herself
alone while, in truth, the child was afforded a fine
view into the small room built within the stone
wall's width.

Interest piqued from the outset, Hildie closely
watched as Morag reached for the valuable glass jar
even she knew contained seeds from which a potent
sleeping tisane was brewed. The woman placed an
apparently precise number into an undersized cal-
dron. Next she added water from the ewer waiting
on one end of the table. Lifting the pot holding her
potion by the thin chain attached to opposite sides,
Morag turned the brief distance required to hang it
from a hook protruding out from the wall. She then
left it suspended there above a torch's steadily glowing flame.

Had recipe preparations stopped then, Hildie
would've been curious yet unconcerned. But midnight-blue eyes widened when Morag singled out
the smallest key amongst the ring of many marking
her as lady of the keep. Hildie stifled a gasp when
the woman used it to unlock a small chest of brass-
bound leather. The girl knew that in the time since
her own arrival at Ailm Keep, and likely long before,
there had been wild conjectures amongst its inhabitants about what dark secrets this never-opened
chest might conceal.

Holding so tightly to the coarse surface of a sturdy
oak beam that it would leave its imprint in tender

flesh, Hildie leaned forward to peer more intently into the alcove. While she watched, Morag withdrew from the box a tightly folded square of parchment. This the woman carefully opened. Then from its creamy surface she lifted something so tiny that a frustrated Hildie couldn't identify the item before it was dropped into the pot where a greenish liquid had begun to boil.

Hildie sensed worse was to follow when Morag filled Donal's favorite mug with the steaming brew, after which she moved quickly toward the arched opening to the spiral stairway constructed within the thickness of the keep's stone wall.

Was the sleeping potion for Morag herself? Was an inability to find rest the reason the dark woman was still fully dressed? Hildie grimaced. Although Morag was garbed for a journey with black cloak fastened at the throat by her magnificent scarlet brooch, Hildie could hear footsteps climbing up steps toward the bedchamber, not down to an outgoing door.

Hildie had yet to free herself from a bewilderment of unanswered questions when her thoughts were interrupted by the sound of her father arriving to join others gathering for the morning meal in the chamber below. On the verge of making her own way down, Hildie's attention was caught by the keep's lord as he summoned his elite guard of most skilled warriors to join him at a trestle table lower than his usual position on the dais.

With great care Hildie began quietly scooting down one long, wide beam toward a point directly above the group speaking too softly to otherwise be heard—but not in time. Just as she reached the desired position, her father rose to his feet, which was a clear signal for others to make haste with their preparations for departure.

Hildie caught only a single disappointing morsel
of information and that when a particularly toady
guardsman questioned an unusual absence she
ought to have noticed but hadn't.

"My lord, is your brother not to accompany us?"

Firmly planted on the beam above, Hildie cringed
at the sound of this too smooth voice yet listened
closely for her father's answer.

"Donal's wife informed me that he has fallen ill."
Rory no longer held his voice to hushed tones. "And
though she is certain her husband will fully recover,
he won't be joining us on patrol today."

Ailm Keep soon emptied of fighting men, but Hildie lingered amid the welcome shadows of her private perch to consider the significance of what she'd
learned. Not that it required more than a moment's
thought to realize Morag's potion was responsible
for Donal's illness. The question to be resolved was
why?

After assigning guardsmen in pairs to ride specific
stretches of the border between Connaught and
Munster, Rory was left to patrol alone. He instructed
his men to check the well-being of each hamlet and
every farm while accepting for himself the most sensitive and likely most hazardous duty.

Rory would personally inspect the bridge below
Tuatha Cottage to assure himself of its security.
Though closely watched over by rotating guards and
spanning some of the roughest terrain on his lands,
if this bridge were captured it would provide the
most direct route for invaders from Munster.

Plans made, Rory rode from Ailm Keep and down
the narrow forest path that would eventually lead to
a cottage hosting the incredible colleen who too easily slipped unbidden into his thoughts and haunted
his dreams. The never-fading image of her emerald

eyes, her winsome smile, tantalized him with the
same indefinable sweetness as the fragrance of flowers that forever bloomed in the fairy ring.

Fairy ring . . . The term jolted Rory back to harsh
reality. That Lissan claimed to be even part fairy was
surely proof of how little she thought of his intelli-
gence. How could she have believed him so gullible,
so . . . Rory scowled. Hadn't she warned him that he
wouldn't believe? And yet, he chided himself, surely
her reticence, so persuasively enacted, must further
convince him of her untrustworthiness. It must be
so—but why then did he feel so guilty, as if he had
been unjust?

Rory coldly glared down the path dividing leafy
undergrowth into walls of thick foliage on either
side. Close-grown trees towered overhead while in-
tertwined branches so thoroughly intensified this
route's gloom that Rory irritably shrugged broad
shoulders in an attempt to shake off a vague and
most uncomfortable sense of foreboding.

It was hardly the first time Rory had covered this
ground alone. He feared neither the wild beasts na-
tive to this forest nor the craven outcasts skulking
through its shadows to steal what honest labor
hadn't earned—neither were likely to attack during
daylight hours. Moreover, still far from the border,
he very much doubted invaders from Munster
would dare an incursion this deep into Connaught.

Despite confidence in his ability to deal with even
hidden dangers, Rory's unease did not lessen. It was
a wariness proven justified when his attention was
caught by a rustling in the branches overhead. He
glanced up in time for one quick glimpse of the
huge, dagger-wielding man dropping from above.

Knocked from the saddle of his bolting horse,
Rory crashed down on rutted and rocky ground,
landing in a painful tangle of awkwardly twisted

limbs. He fought both the agony of his injuries and
the incredible weight of his assailant which forced
breath from his lungs.

Rory wrapped powerful hands around the wrist
of a man striving to pierce his throat with the blade
already responsible for inflicting too many jabs and
cuts. Struggling mightily, he finally succeeded in
wresting the dagger free. It traced a glittering arc
through the air when, to be rid of at least this danger, Rory tossed it far into dense undergrowth.

Growling his fury at being disarmed, the assailant
resumed his violent attack with even greater fervor
and gauntleted hands.

Rory was unable to reach either the sword caught
under a badly twisted leg or pull his own dagger
from a sheath trapped between his body and that of
the man now trying to strangle him. Desperately
searching fingers at last found a sizable stone. With
this improvised weapon, he struck the back of his
foe's head repeatedly until the man sagged lifelessly.

Although Rory had won this fight, he was horrified to discover that the task of merely rolling his
opponent's limp form aside required more strength
and endurance for pain than remained at his command. Senses swimming, Rory felt his hold on consciousness slipping and sank into darkness.

Finding the stable of Ailm Keep deserted, save for a
grey cat, Hildie was left with the challenge of read-
ying her own mare for the ride. She succeeded after
a lengthy struggle with the heavy saddle and its re-
calcitrant straps.

Hildie knew that Donal daily shared a patrol route
with her father. So, now that Donal was ill thanks
to Morag's fearful concoction, her father had no
partner to lend help were he threatened with danger.
Exercising the sharp wits she liked to think inherited

from him, Hildie quickly realized that Morag wouldn't have gone to so much trouble without there being a purpose for it. Likely a dastardly purpose.

Reluctant to consider precisely what this meant, Hildie chose to waste no further time in idle wondering. She would take action instead! And yet to perform this task well, for safety's sake, she also would need a partner. Beyond the father often uncomfortable with her, yet undeniably worthy of the faith she put in him, the only two people the girl dared trust currently resided in Tuatha Cottage. Thus, to that location she must and indeed meant to go.

Urging her mare to canter and even gallop where the path permitted, Hildie soon entered a particularly shadowy area. There amidst its gloom she encountered the disturbing sight she had fervently hoped would never appear.

Ignoring the prone and motionless figure of a second man, Hildie concentrated on the dark shape of her father's crumpled form. Bringing the mare to an abrupt halt, she slid from the saddle and tossed her reins over a bush with little care. She rushed forward and dropped to her knees at his side, terrified that she'd arrived too late. But then as small fingers gently probed the source of blood slowly oozing from his temple, the lord of Ailm Keep groaned.

Hildie's instinctive yelp of relief was quickly stifled by an ominous certainty that he would truly be lost to her unless she secured help for him—and very soon. She jumped to her feet and jerked carelessly thrown reins from their entanglement in the thick foliage of her poorly chosen tethering site. To mount her mare without the aid of another human or even the stump at Ailm Keep that she'd earlier

climbed atop for this purpose was a nerve-
wrackingly long process.

Once ahorse Hildie spurred the animal into a flat-
out gallop, racing down the narrow path. An overwhelming need for haste was the driving force
which left her heedless to the sting of branches
whipping at her and thankful that only a blessedly
brief distance separated her wounded father from
Tuatha Cottage.

Inside that structure at track's end, two females
sat on either side of a trestle table after having vir-
tuously earned their respite.

For Lissan the pastels of dawn had been brightened by the small joy of a boon granted. Her father
had kept his promise. A chest filled with precious
books waited at the end of her pallet. Yet, knowing
the likelihood that others would soon appear, with
wise caution she had restrained the urge to immediately immerse herself in its contents. Rather, comforted by the prospect of delving inside once the
solitude of night returned, she'd wasted no moment
to make certain it was safely locked. Next the key
was hidden in the toe of a white walking shoe not
worn since Hildie had brought her a sturdier pair of
boots.

Heartened by a pleasant beginning to the day, Lissan had soon turned her attention to diligently re-
peating actions she'd once seen Liam perform when
prodding flames into a tolerable state to be cooked
over. The glopping of lard onto a flat metal surface
quick to heat was distasteful and anything but appetizing. And yet, even though prepared by a novice
chef, once fried the cuts of venison retrieved from
the cellar were surprisingly tasty.

That meat, supplemented by hunks of cheese and
the apples of which Hildie had been so proud, con-
stituted a satisfying meal for two females and the

young guardsman they'd called inside to join them. It was after this that Lissan truly learned the work of a meal so quickly consumed was not finished until the additional toil of clearing away was completed.

From the outset Maedra lent help to her charge, despite an unconcealed amusement over these difficult and time-consuming rituals required of humans. Then while Liam returned to his gardening, she joined Lissan to idly chat and relax in the satisfaction of a shared task well done.

Shrill screams rudely shattered their peaceful harmony. . . .

Lissan dashed from the cottage only to find Maedra already hovering behind an agitated, sobbing Hildie while Liam knelt in front of the trembling child firmly clasping slender shoulders with comfort and support.

"Hildie . . . poppet. . . ." Lissan began while approaching the tender tableaux from one side. Under the circumstances her unthinking use of Rory's pet name for the girl could have deepened distress but happily it instead had the opposite effect in sharpening the focus of a determined plea.

"He's hurt something awful," Hildie clearly announced while her solemn eyes directly met Lissan's worried gaze. "And if we don't help him soon, he will almost surely die."

The listeners wasted no time to ask what they already suspected or knew—who. However, as if the communal chant of some religious order, in unison all three posed a single-word query: "Where?"

"Up the path to Ailm Keep not too very far from here," Hildie stated calmly although shaking still. "Come, I'll show you." She turned to the mare yet wheezing with an exhaustion caused by the speed demanded during the last part of their journey here.

"No, Hildie." Lissan laid a restraining hand on the girl's shoulder while at the same time heartened by the possibility that a wounded Rory lay near the magical fairy ring.

An instant later Lissan became aware of the dark glare half disappointment and half disgust that Hildie trained on her and lost no moment to correct a misunderstood intent. "Your horse is too weary for a safe return but I'm quite certain our friend Liam will permit the use of his for this important journey."

Hildie flashed Lissan a relieved grin before shifting her attention toward the again standing Liam with a wordless plea for this boon she knew he'd find difficult to deny her.

"But if the pair of you take my steed, how am I to go to my lord's aid?" To Liam as a man of honor, faithful to his lord, and—most significantly—the only warrior amongst them, this logical question was of overriding importance.

"And yet, Liam," Lissan reasoned calmly, despite the anxious Hildie's impatience to be on their way— an anxiety and impatience which beneath a serene façade she shared. "As Lord Rory has been assaulted, is it not logical to assume invaders are near?"

Liam warily nodded, suspecting his mistress— whether half fairy as she claimed or no—more than capable of making even the rightness of a straight and true path seem utterly wrong.

"Then who," Lissan sweetly inquired, "if we all desert the cottage, will protect it?"

"I've sworn my allegiance to Lord Rory." Liam fought to stoutly maintain his position. " 'Tis him I must protect."

"Ah, but it is by his order that you are charged to guard Tuatha Cottage," Lissan reminded with the confidence of a blow well struck. "And surely your duty to obey his command comes first?"

Flustered, as he'd feared, by her arguments, Liam obstinately stated, "Then if I stay, you must remain here, too."

Desperately striving to control her own deep fears for Rory's survival, Lissan firmly shook her head. "One of us *must* go out to help your injured lord else he'll die."

And, Lissan forcefully told herself, she must win this verbal battle. She must in order to clear the way for seeking an assistance without doubt more effective than even that provided by the medical texts contained in a trunk which had mystically appeared in the cottage that morning.

Face gone a pasty white, Liam fell a step back under the distressing image of his master, O'Connor, in mortal peril.

"Don't fret so, Liam." Maedra joined the debate at last. "While you remain here to guard the cottage for your lord I will protect Lissan as she goes forth to treat his wounds."

Though no better pleased by the thought of both females, nay, three subjected to the danger of lurking foes, Liam sent Maedra a gentle smile of gratitude for her offer.

The tender moment was shattered by a single word from Lissan. "No."

"No?" Maedra echoed in disbelief.

"Your talents are needed here." Lissan stared steadily into bright azure eyes, willing her fairy protectress to comprehend the importance of preventing an earnest Liam from complicating simple plans, albeit with the best of misguided intentions.

Within moments Maedra yielded to an emerald gaze as potent as her king's. Truth be known, she was at least as anxious as the mistress to ensure that

Liam remain wrapped safe inside the boundaries of
a protective spell earlier cast over Tuatha Cottage.
But still she couldn't quell niggling doubts about the
wisdom of freeing Lissan to pursue an unknown
strategy of uncertain value.

While a wordless exchange passed between the
two women Liam's tension increased, a silence he
ended with a flat assertion. "Lissan, you cannot take
only a child and go *alone* to rescue a man so recently
attacked by foes all too likely skulking nearby."

Lissan, ably backed by Maedra, immediately advanced a compelling argument for precisely how she
could and must do that very thing. That her logic
was incredibly convoluted and in the end meaningless Lissan knew full well but fervently hoped the
befuddling desperation of this dangerous moment
would prevent Liam from recognizing it, too.

"Maedra—" Lissan added, aware that her protectress's support had begun to waver and anxious to
bolster it with a less than subtle hint of her strategy.
"If Rory isn't too far down the path, he must be very
near the fairy ring."

Catching a glimpse of what Lissan intended, Maedra nodded while a merry sparkle brightened blue
eyes. If this new friend and her young companion
could help the wounded man into that circle, all
would be well. Despite Liam's fierce scowl, she hastened to help the pair mount a warrior's stallion and
begin retracing Hildie's path of arrival.

A nauseating dizziness and fiercely pounding head
greeted Rory's return to consciousness. Lying in near
the same position into which he'd toppled after being violently knocked from his horse, memory of the
ensuing struggle flooded back.

Rory suddenly realized that a prone body lay
within arm's reach. Despite waves of sickening pain,

he reached out to check for signs of life ... his assailant's threat had been permanently neutralized.

But that welcome fact brought renewed awareness of other continuing menaces. It was unlikely that this man had slipped into Connaught alone. Worse still, it was even less likely that he had been the only man dispatched from Munster with an order to see the impediment of Rory O'Connor eliminated.

Trained by hard experience, Rory knew the importance of moving away as quickly as possible before associates of his slain opponent came looking. Toward that end, he took a quick inventory of physical damages. The blow his head had sustained in the fall seemed the most ominous but his dagger-wielding foe could be blamed for a myriad of stinging wounds and aching bruises. However, under these circumstances his awkward plummet to the earth was responsible for the most disabling and regrettable injury—his left leg was broken. And by the agony incurred under the slightest movement he suspected the limb fractured in more than one place.

Fierce determination blanked the expression of pain from Rory's handsome face. No matter what must be endured, the realities of the moment demanded action. His destrier had apparently been spooked into wild flight. He exercised great effort of will to sit up and begin scooting backward into the thick undergrowth edging the path. Although a hiding place of dubious value, it was the best his current situation had to offer and one he was grateful for when moments later the thudding hooves of an approaching horse was heard.

"There's the assailant," Hildie announced, excitement increasing the volume of her voice. "See, all I told you is true."

Lissan motioned for her companion to speak more softly. Lessening the abruptness of her directive with a gentle smile, she was subjected to a pang of guilt. She had been so preoccupied by her own concern for the wounded lord that she'd failed to sense Hildie's growing uneasiness over time elapsed and distance traveled without reaching their destination.

Even that guilt couldn't stifle the all-important question escaping Lissan's worry-tightened throat. "Where's your father?"

"I'm here in the bushes ahead and on your left."

Peering into shadows where directed by the deep velvet voice that never failed to make her heart pound harder, Lissan caught a glimpse of one foot not completely hidden—and the trail of blood leading to it.

"Father, are you all right?" Hildie slid free of the stallion with the amazing agility of childhood. Rushing forward, she broke through bushes to kneel at their goal's side.

"I'm alive, poppet," Rory responded with a wry smile. "And the wounds will heal."

Stepping into the nest created by his movements in the midst of a thicket, Lissan gasped. Not only was Rory's clothing ominously stained with dark patches brown where dry and deep crimson where wet, but one leg was bent in an impossible angle. His face was discolored with bruises and a huge lump had sprouted just above the right temple from which blood oozed down to cake black hair. This sight was infinitely more brutal than any a well-bred Victorian miss would ever be expected or even allowed to view.

By gazing into Lissan's revealing expression, Rory saw a reflection of how serious his wounds must truly be. That she didn't turn away repelled but rather sank down next to him and with gentle fingertips probed to judge the extent of his injuries for herself showed this incredible beauty to be the kind of strong yet compassionate woman he had thought didn't truly 'exist. This was a discovery with more serious repercussions than he was willing to acknowledge.

"Can you stand?" Lissan brusquely asked, pulling back to sit on her heels. One glance over her shoulder had already betrayed an unpleasant fact. Liam's stallion, left untethered by two worried females in great haste, had already disappeared on a return to his master.

Startled, as he would have sworn he could never be, Rory's penetrating eyes narrowed on the questioner. Hadn't Lissan just confirmed his badly broken leg? Did she lack the knowledge to recognize even so blatant an injury?

"If you can stand on one foot and hop while Hildie and I steady you on either side," Lissan continued, purposely ignoring his blatant skepticism, "despite the steed that left without us, we'll have hope for reaching a location of safety which lies very near."

Safety? Near? Rory scowled. These were his lands and he knew of no such place so how could she?

"Please, Father," Hildie begged, lifting one of his battle-bruised hands. "Please try."

It was difficult and painful in the extreme but with two supporters to urge him on, Rory accomplished the feat of balancing on one foot. That, however, was only the first in an excruciating test of his willpower and endurance.

Eyes refusing to focus, Rory had little notion where they were or in what direction they were heading, except upward, always upward. Renewed waves of dizziness threatened to overwhelm and take him down despite the determined attentions of the two nearly carrying him.

Having accepted by far the majority of their load

to spare Hildie, Lissan was exhausted by the time
they reached the hill's crest. Yes, exhausted but also
more relieved than she dared admit even to herself.
She *had* chosen the right hill to climb, the magical
ring of flowers blooming here proved it.

Lissan stumbled forward, nearly buckling under
the weight of a barely conscious burden. She and her
young cohort more dragged than helped Rory beyond the bright border. Once inside the circle, Lissan
gratefully sank to her knees and allowed the man to
gently slip onto a green cushion of lush grasses . . .
overcome again by an unnatural sleep.

While Rory was lost in peaceful oblivion, the pair
who'd struggled to see him reach this spot were all
too aware of the noisy approach of others.

"We've been tricked," a fuming red-haired warrior snarled as he burst from forest shadows and
with menacing blade at the ready marched several
paces into the clearing. "Tricked like fools!"

Lissan realized this speaker was the same man
who once had slashed a broadsword completely
through her. Even as this fact sank in, she recognized a greater danger in Hildie's opening mouth
and immediately placed fingertips over parted lips
to seal betraying sounds inside.

"But the blood trail ends here," a second queru-
lous voice impatiently argued. "So the O'Connor
must have come here, right here at the edge of this
wretched ring of flowers where last we battled."

Holding her breath and praying the man standing
within easy arm's reach wouldn't hear her pounding
heart, Lissan stared up at him—a face only vaguely
familiar but a voice she'd never forget, the voice of
one of her erstwhile captors.

" 'Struth, Fergil." This ill-humored response from
the first man who must be Mael jerked Lissan's attention back. His face flushed with ever deeper color

while he peppered his cohort with a barrage of scornful questions. "But what do you make of that fact? Do you believe it some mystical omen? Dream that our prey has magically become invisible? Worse, do you honestly think it an adequate excuse for the undeniable fact that we have lost him?"

Lissan's one-time captor cringed. Without risking answers, Fergil slunk away two paces behind the leader who was stomping his own path down from the summit.

Not until after the last faint sound of their passing faded into the distance did Lissan respond to the wordless wonder in Hildie's gaze.

"This fairy ring has mystical powers." Lissan gracefully motioned toward the spot where they'd entered into the circle of blossoms. The delicate flowers crushed by the crossing of two nearly dragging a third were now miraculously restored. "Once resting safe within its boundaries neither human nor animal can be seen by anyone on the outside looking in."

Hildie slowly nodded, dark eyes wide with awe. Though her own mother had shared tales of such things, she'd been afraid to believe—until now.

Lissan was pleased that the girl accepted her words without question and glad that she needn't attempt to explain the same to Rory, who had lost the open faith of a child and wouldn't believe.

"Daughter, why have you come?" Comlan's stern question contained a hundred layers of emotion ranging from slight disapproval to restrained fury. "Why have you brought two humans to intrude on the secrets of *my* realm?"

Having rarely been the focus of her father's censure, Lissan shivered but the crucial purpose behind her actions held her steady.

"Hildie, the child I told you about, came to me

with news that her father had been ambushed and badly wounded. She requested my help in rescuing and treating his injuries." Lissan motioned toward the unconscious man. "As you see, Lord Rory is in desperate need of aid—more than is in my power to provide."

The arching of dark gold brows was Comlan's only response.

"Can you heal him?" Lissan persisted, refusing to glance toward a youngster first awed by the fairy ring's powers and now doubtless stunned by the sudden arrival of a figure who glowed as if by moonlight.

Comlan shrugged. "Humans are fragile but easily mended. The repair of shattered bones needs but a simple deed while sore muscles and bruises will re-quire the administering of elixirs and the application of potions near hourly from now until this time on the morrow. Will you see to these tasks?"

Lissan nodded an immediate acceptance. And, re-membering her father's claim that the logic prized by humans was anathema to the Tuatha de Danann, she recognized the perverse rationale in this strange order of healing—most serious wounds first cured while lesser injuries required lingering treatments.

CHAPTER 10

Though the day was near half done Liam stood morosely currying his stallion amid the gloom beneath eaves extended to the ground as shelter for animals. With every stroke over his horse's hide, he reviewed again and yet again the wrongs done him since the previous day. It was inexcusable for the warrior he was to have been denied a role in the quest to save his lord. But it was even more an insult to his honor that access to the cottage had been refused him even today although he was certain the rescued man lay inside.

When something blocked the flow of sunshine, Liam glanced toward the lean-to's open end. Golden light from behind outlined Maedra's form and joined her natural moonglow aura to surround her in a nimbus of unearthly beauty.

Liam gaped in open wonder. Although to please both women he had outwardly accepted his mistress's explanation of a fairy heritage shared in part with Maedra, he hadn't truly believed. Indeed, he had nearly convinced himself that it was only the two women's incredible beauty that led his romantic soul to see magic where there was none. But now his doubts evaporated like rain puddles subjected to a noonday sun.

Maedra moved a step toward the gentle human so different from males in her sphere and forlornly announced, "My king says that I must leave your world."

"But why?" The words sighed from Liam on a dismal wail. Though he couldn't explain it, the prospect of never seeing Maedra again was painful. His only consolation lay in the fact that this ethereal beauty seemed as dispirited by the ordered act as he.

Constrained by rules governing fairy interaction with humans, Maedra must respond to a question asked even though fairly certain the answer bespoke a principle as true in Liam's world as hers.

"In the realm where I live we do not question our king's orders, no matter what they be."

Liam frowned but was forced to accept her explanation when he couldn't imagine the questioning of Lord Rory's commands by himself or anyone else— save, perhaps, Donal or that man's cold wife. Thus barred from further debate on this point, he focused upon the first words of her statement by issuing another simple request.

"Tell me about your realm—what is it like?"

A gentle blush warmed Maedra's cheeks. She'd already fractured laws governing contact between fairy and human merely by appearing to him and had intensified that wrong by warning him of her upcoming absence. But, she comforted herself, that code required even King Comlan to answer a mortal's directly stated question.

" 'Tis a joyous place more beautiful than you could possibly comprehend." Recognizing an unintended condescension in her words, Maedra guiltily dropped her azure gaze.

"But—" Liam gently coaxed this amazing visitor apparently gone shy to tell more. "I thought we shared the *same* world."

"True . . . but untrue as well." Although sincerely regretting his inability to recognize the fairy logic in this statement, Maedra laughed. The sound contained the sweet tones of a silver bell. "And could you but see through my eyes what wondrous sights of extraordinary beauty are hidden from yours by the veil of humanity. . . ." She gave a delicate shrug.

Liam was more than a little peeved by her slight on all humanity and their reality—something she clearly deemed dreary. "Then how can you bear to waste so much as a single moment in our dismal environment?"

" 'Struth, I see things that you cannot." Maedra laughed again but greatly mitigated any insult by adding, "Besides, your world has interests to offer that mine does not."

"What?" Liam wanted to believe Maedra found something of interest to hold her near but feared her suggestion simply the preface to an additional unhappy contrast between their worlds. "How can that be?"

"While we in the Faerie Realm enjoy unlimited pleasures and delights, few are the changes and rarer still the challenges we cannot easily overcome." Maedra's forlorn smile returned, a dark contrast to the brilliant glow of golden curls framing her face and seeming to cloak her shoulders in sunshine itself. " 'Tis a strange truth for a race who treasures the unexpected."

"Nothing changes?" Liam was surprised. "No challenges?" He wasn't sure he could be satisfied with such a bargain and said so.

" 'Tis doubtless one reason why I so enjoy your company." Maedra's smile intensified while she glided forward and lightly trailed dainty fingertips across his cheek. "I never know what you'll say or do . . . nor what unexpected events, sudden demands will next require your attention—whether a daring dash into the forest to rescue our charge or the honorable fulfillment of a duty to guard the cottage."

Though deeming himself the most ordinary and predictable of men, Liam was inordinately pleased by Maedra's admission. At the same time it renewed his despair. "*Must* you go?"

Maedra nodded. "But I'll return."

Before Liam could appeal for her to tell him when, the fairy maiden disappeared.

The sun had just begun its descent from the apex of a sky now free of early morning clouds when Lissan stepped beyond cottage door and closed it quietly behind. Rory was at last sleeping peacefully and she was unwilling to see him disturbed.

The previous day her father had magically whisked his daughter, injured warrior, and a girl-child from the fairy ring into the safety of Tuatha Cottage. After that, true to his word, he had mended the shattered leg in a few brief moments. Also true to his prediction, the healing of cuts and easing of bruises was taking considerably longer while Lissan followed his instructions in applying balms and administering elixirs to see Rory's health restored.

Green crystal eyes gazed across new-tilled ground and into forest shadows while their owner wondered what had become of Maedra. Not since Lissan had ridden off with Hildie on a rescue quest had she seen her protectress. Then once back in the cottage, anxious to forestall Hildie's possibly awkward questions about Maedra, she had urged the child into a quick return to Ailm Keep. And yet Maedra, plainly sensitive to her king's order to be seen by no human beyond Lissan, remained absent.

Before Hildie departed from the cottage, Lissan had directed her to share with the keep's inhabitants nothing of what had occurred—not the assault on Rory and even less the inexplicable actions taken to care for him. Now it was time to address these same issues with the earnest guardsman left behind for the rescue and, of necessity, excluded since their return. She resolutely turned toward the lean-to on one side of an abode she'd begun to think of as her own.

When the flow of sunlight into his rustic shelter was again blocked, pulse leaping with hope, Liam turned toward the source.

"Forgive me for leaving you here yesterday," Lissan began.

Guiltily quashing disappointment that it wasn't a returning Maedra who stood in the opening, Liam gave a broad grin of welcome to his mistress.

Lissan responded with a smile of blinding sweetness. "Someday I hope you'll understand the circumstances making such an action necessary."

For that brilliant smile Liam knew he could forgive near anything. Besides, though Lissan had claimed and might well be half-fairy, it seemed ever more certain that she truly was a being even more important to the future. And were she in truth the White Witch, what earthly right had he to challenge her choices?

Acknowledging the impossibility of immediately providing any adequate explanation for recent events to this earnest young man, Lissan returned to her initial purpose in coming. "I have a charge to relate from your lord, along with a request of my own."

Liam immediately nodded and a beam of welcome sunlight stole through gloom to ripple over the lighter streaks in his wheat-colored hair.

"Go to Ailm Keep." Lissan spoke softly but with a steadiness of purpose that belied her small untruth. Though her patient had yet to rejoin the conscious world, she was certain that, were he able, Rory really would issue such instructions. "Assure its inhabitants that their lord is safe and will return to them tomorrow—but don't distress them unnecessarily by speaking of the events that brought him here."

Liam frowned. It was an expression once rare to him that had of recent days been too commonly observed. He couldn't see the sense in failing to warn the rest of Lord Rory's people about dangerous intruders and the evil they'd wreaked upon him. But for the woman who'd rescued his lord, the woman surely destined to save the whole of Connaught, he would obey this directive.

Lissan lingered in the lean-to, watching Liam saddle his stallion and ride away. All too aware how her father had said that with his prescribed treatments Rory's full recovery could be expected within a day's time, she uneasily wondered what emotions might soon fill the cottage. Would Rory be grateful, suspicious, or angered by her part in his rescue? Particularly when it was a part whose honest explanation he was no more likely to believe than he had accepted the account of events landing her in his sphere.

On dragging feet Lissan made her way back to an iron-bound door and held her breath while swinging that oak barrier wide. As the loud creak of heavy wood reluctantly moving died away, she slowly exhaled. She'd been granted a reprieve. The man who must by now be nearly recovered still lay unconscious. Yes, she been given a reprieve, temporary but appreciated.

During the past night she had briefly dozed, wrapped in a coarse blanket and leaning across the trestle table. This while with the aid of her father's elixir, Rory slept on her straw pallet unaware as she applied soothing balms. While rubbing ointment over the cuts and bruises on his face, throat, and powerful chest, she'd been so concerned for his pain and her wish for his quick healing that she hadn't permitted herself to be distracted by either admiration or personal longings.

Moving to stand beside the straw pallet, Lissan gazed downward. In her absence Rory had apparently found the fire's heat too strong. He'd thrown back the coverlet allowing flamelight to play a golden melody across the hills and planes of his strongly muscled body, leaving it clear that his injuries had truly healed. She'd never seen a nude man before, and the impressive sight caught breath somewhere in her throat.

With fresh memories of recent salve applications, Lissan could almost feel the texture of Rory's flesh beneath her fingertips. He hadn't awakened during the many treatments, allowing Lissan to convince herself he wouldn't now while gracefully sinking to her knees. She extended one hand to tentatively caress the hard, cool width of his massive chest. This time she embarked on a purposeful exploration, discovering the fascinating combination of rough satin skin and abrasive hair with steely muscles beneath.

Struggling through layers of dreams tormented by the endless caresses of an enticing, impossibly lovely yet dangerously untrustworthy colleen, Rory forced heavy lashes to lift a small distance. His eyes immediately clenched shut against a delicious apparition that could only be another of the hot night fantasies plaguing him since an exquisite beauty fell into his life.

Hesitation overcome by helpless yearning, Lissan touched more firmly, burrowing gentle fingers through crisp black curls to stroke the powerful expanse of his wide shoulders, feeling every line and curve begin to burn.

Certain now about the reality of her, through a fog of kindling desire, Rory fought for sufficient control to reject sweet temptations—surely practiced lures that proved her an experienced woman rather than the innocent she so skillfully pretended to be. That being the case, why must he deny himself all the pleasures of her company?

Enthralled, Lissan gazed at the man still lying quiet beneath her caress, at his superb masculinity. Nothing existed but the feel of his skin, heat and iron thews beneath, and the fiery sensations that blossomed with this freedom to touch where she would. A small pink tongue lightly touched lips suddenly dry.

At the sight, Rory groaned. Never breaking their visual bond, he rose up to wrap her in an embrace of shattering intimacy. Robbed of sanity by a gaze burning with the hypnotic power of a predator for its quarry, Lissan parted her softly bowed lips on a silent gasp as he rid her of a homespun gown far too large and laid her across the pallet. He stretched out at her side, urging soft flesh to melt against the hard muscle of his body.

Lissan's gasp faded into a sigh of welcome as Rory's mouth found hers. With blatant expertise he built their kiss to such a fever of hungry passion that he'd never believe an inexperienced woman able to be as responsive as the beguiling wanton in his arms. While a masculine hand gradually laid its searing path up Lissan's side, over her hip and narrow waist to the sensitive flesh beneath one of the arms clinging to his broad shoulder, heat-thickened blood slowed her pulse to a dragging and uncertain rhythm.

Rory pulled a whisper away, dark eyes glittering with silver sparks beneath half-lowered lashes as slowly, gently, he allowed an outspread hand to glide over skin the velvety texture of rose petals. Finding the first slight swell of her breast, he watched in satisfaction as wild shudders of excitement shook the enticing woman who had invaded his dreams and now his bed. No matter his disdain for the trickery in her practiced façade of virginal naïveté, she was a temptation too potent for him to easily resist.

Of a sudden Rory rolled over to align his body carefully above Lissan's yielding form. She gloried in his strength and savored their contact—hard chest pressing against soft breasts, and hip against hip, thigh to thigh. This heady intimacy was a sweet torment eliciting a faint whimper from her.

Rory responded immediately, crushing the alluring beauty even closer to his power while both giving and taking the potent kiss he craved. Lissan's once-slowed pulse blazed and sang. Subjected to silver fires in the depths of a dark gaze, she lay beneath him vulnerable and utterly, willingly defenseless.

After again pulling back a brief distance, Rory rested his weight on a forearm. He let one palm return to move more firmly against the outer edge of an aching breast and watched her twist sensuously in response to that tantalizing pleasure. Incapable of preventing the action, Lissan reached up to clasp his hand to needful flesh. He lightly pressed the warm softness and she gasped. Succumbing to an unfamiliar, smoldering need while his hand cupped the full weight of her breast, Lissan mindlessly tangled her fingers into cool black strands and urged him nearer.

Gladly complying, Rory bent to nuzzle her
breasts, cherishing her bounty until she trembled under flashes of wildfire. For long moments he sampled her delectable flavor, an addictive pleasure. But
still these caresses were not enough to appease either
of them. And at last came the mist-faint brush of his
lips across one peak, teasing her senses unmercifully
and sending her deeper into a hungry blaze.

Even then Lissan wanted more. Plunging further
into the dark flames of wicked sensations and wandering through a dense haze of desire, she arched
against Rory's mouth until his lips opened to draw
the tip into a starving need.

Again writhing against his hard form in shattering
intimacy and overwhelmed by blazing sensations,
from Lissan's tight throat escaped another sweet
moan. Rory couldn't prevent his body from moving
above hers in a rhythm as old as time. When she
instinctively met the motion, he knew the moment
had come to claim from her the price for dangerously daring him with irresistible lures.

When dark eyes shut tightly, Lissan mistook his
action for an intent to put her aside—a further demonstration of how unworthy he found her? She
wrapped her arms more tightly about his strong
neck and recklessly arched up to brush generous
curves across the width of his torso, reveling in the
sweet rasp of wiry curls across tender tips.

As Rory gazed down at the exquisite creature
driving him beyond hope for any measure of control, a deep velvet growl rose from his depths. The
sound sent a shiver of desire through Lissan just as
he lowered himself fully atop her.

Lissan pressed even closer, shaking in an agony
of need. She yearned to be nearer, wanted more, and
wrapped her arms about wide shoulders, urgently
running her palms over the hard contours of his

back and up to lock about his neck. Her nails dug
into the smooth flesh beneath as she again twisted
against him, exciting, enticing.

Rory's mouth claimed the nectar of hers as he slid
his hands down skin like hot satin to tilt her hips
into his and ease the joining feverish hunger demanded. To his shock she yielded not only the wild
passion of her kiss but a short gasp of pain. He went
motionless.

Refusing to be so belatedly rejected, Lissan moved
against Rory, driving him to begin rocking them
both higher and ever higher on the searing delight
at the blue-white extremity of flames like those burning in his eyes. The rhythm growing wilder and wilder swept Lissan up into the vortex of a firestorm.
Though fearing the impossibility of reaching its pinnacle, she strived toward the unknown goal beyond
her reach. Lissan's feverish cry blended with his
deep growl when the whirling blaze of incredible
sensations exploded, scattering a glittering shower
of sparks to ripple through every nerve in her body.

Lissan floated through the gentle smoke of blissful
lassitude and drifted into dreams. Rory watched the
tender innocent a virgin no longer thanks to his unfounded suspicions. Oh, yes, she'd provoked him to
that wrong which could never be undone, but as a
man at least a decade her senior he should've been
able to restrain himself.

Shifting his gaze toward a shuttered window
where the faint light seeping in revealed descending
dusk, Rory admitted his error in allowing himself to
use what now seemed an unwarranted indictment
to justify the wicked taking of what he'd badly
wanted.

"Lord Mael—" Morag's voice was strained by an
irritation reined in only with great difficulty. "I

swear on the Holy Cross that Rory O'Connor is alive and plans a return to the keep on the morrow—unscathed by your futile assault." She paused before adding with a sneer no more than cursorily masked, "Yes, unharmed by the attack you swore would be a bloodbath but instead cost merely the life of one of your own men."

"And how many times have you attempted the same deed only to fail?" Mael demanded, refusing to falter beneath this woman's criticism and justify himself by explaining like an errant child how O'Connor's forces had split into small parties, preventing a mass assault.

"Ah, but I haven't an army to do my bidding." Morag's gaze slipped past her red-haired protagonist to pointedly settle on Fergil, Mael's most loyal— or was it intimidated?—supporter.

"Ah, but you possess extraordinary powers. Leastways you have repeatedly claimed it to be true although I've seen little enough proof to back your grandiose assertion."

"For that insult, my lord," Morag hissed, glaring directly into his unnaturally pale eyes, "I will demonstrate the full scope of my powers *on you* once our goal has been secured."

Mael's belligerent expression did not change one whit and yet he was the first to blink.

"Come now, Mael." Saccharine tone a poor disguise for poisonous fangs, Morag purred like the slyest of predatory cats hunkering down to pounce on a helpless mouse. It was an apt analogy even though the red-haired lord was neither smaller than she nor helpless in the least. "Though O'Connor is an initial impediment to our goals, to reach him we must first remove the White Witch's threat."

"For what purpose?" With a scoffing laugh followed immediately by a faint growl of scorn, Mael let his poor opinion of this visitor's reasoning be known. "Once O'Connor is gone, even the White Witch can do nothing to preserve Connaught from Munster's might."

"You're a fool, Mael." Disdain dripped from Morag's words like corrosive acid. "A fool not to understand that she represents by far the greatest danger to your plan to subjugate Connaught."

"*My* plan? Only my plan?" Mael feigned amazement. "Pray forgive my confusion but if 'tis not the same end that you desire, then what draws you so often to my hall here in an enemy's kingdom?"

Grey eyes narrowing, Morag spat out, "What need have we for such useless games? At the outset I clearly stated my reason for aiding your goals. I will help rid you of Rory, a boon to your stratagems that also clears the way for Donal to assume a deceased brother's patrimony. Once my spouse secures that position, I will be confirmed in the one whose duties I already fill."

" 'Struth," Mael snorted. "The Lady of Ailm Keep you'd be . . . but 'tis a higher status you seek and don't add further insults by deeming me too foolish to recognize this blatant fact." He stomped several paces toward her, pale gaze sharpening into dagger points. "You think that by helping to see my king triumphant, your husband's claim to the throne of Connaught will be advanced, and your hope to be queen brought nearly within reach."

Seeing no reason to dispute facts so evident, Morag merely gave a regal nod.

"And your dreams might become reality—" Mael continued, voice dropping into an utterly unnecessary, conspiratorial undertone. "If you but tame your viper's tongue and rather than criticizing me and mine, concentrate on freeing a bright future from O'Connor's lethal cloud."

CHAPTER 11

The first glimmer of dawn had just begun to lighten an eastern horizon shrouded in clouds heavy and dark with unshed rain when two riders approached Tuatha Cottage. Its window remained shuttered, but gleams of firelight from within escaped through slight cracks between the broad slats that formed them.

Before Donal could dismount to aid his wife's descent, Morag swung down on her own. He grimaced against this further demonstration of her indifference to—no, worse—her disdain for him despite the years he'd spent in earnest attempts to please.

"Come, come, Donal." Morag spoke sharply, impatient with the man. "Your useless lingering serves no purpose when 'tis action that's required."

"Yes, Morag," Donal murmured, despising himself for this spineless response too commonly given.

Once her husband, weak for all his physical strength, towered behind her, Morag pounded loudly on the oak door. She waited with an impatient frown deepened by the sudden disturbing sounds of bustling activity and hushed whispers beyond the barrier. These noises were, Morag feared, the too revealing indication of a new alliance likely to be a far more serious hazard to her goals than any threat posed by either partner acting alone.

"Who is it?" Lissan called out from beyond the closed portal, temper grated by the harsh hammering which had unceremoniously shoved her from the new thrilling yet gentle embrace of sweet dreams inspired by fresh and fiery memories.

Morag's firm response was succinct. "Donal has come to fetch his brother for their morning patrol."

Inside the cottage Lissan fell one step back as if pushed by an unwelcome voice somehow lent a physical force. The declaration explained Donal's arrival, but in no way could it justify this distinctly unappreciated visit from Morag which waved the prospect of a truly dismal day.

Rory, already garbed in chausses and cross-garters, lifted from the tabletop a tunic earlier cleaned and carefully folded by someone else's hands. Before shrugging into its folds he gazed for an instant at the slender back of a tender beauty rudely awakened from her night spent drifting through the gentle slumber of first passion's sweet satisfaction. To open the door, he next stepped beyond the flustered Lissan while casting her a potent smile supported by a quick, conspiratorial wink.

"Grant me a moment to buckle on my scabbard and don my cape." Rory ignored the woman in the doorway and spoke directly to his brother. "Once done we can be off on our rounds."

Donal nodded, face burning against yet another in the endless round of slights aimed at his wife. But, although resented, it was knowing how truly Rory's contempt was deserved that allowed Donal to again shirk the hopeless duty of defending Morag.

Unbeknownst to Donal, the woman he'd wed had earlier been spurned by his older brother. And in the decade since the union contracted while Rory

was absent fighting on their king's behalf, Donal had
learned from bleak experiences in an uncomfortable
life with a domineering wife the wisdom behind rejection of Morag's advances.

In near all instances Morag demanded and got her
own way—except where Rory was concerned. It was
Rory's ability to not merely defy Morag's wishes but
to ignore the woman herself which had earned her
ever-increasing, undying enmity . . . and perversely
strengthened Donal's resentment of the sibling he'd
long deemed unfairly blessed on every count.

"I thought—" To cover an uncomfortable silence
the man habitually talkative burst into speech.
"Coming here would save the two of us from an
unnecessary waste of time required by your return
to the keep before immediately joining me to retrace
the same path on a journey back in this direction."

While Rory nodded and moved to do what he'd
said, Morag stepped uninvited into the cottage's
small interior. Both Lissan's tousled golden hair and
the disheveled appearance of her clothes, as if too
hastily pulled on, seemed to confirm Morag's worst
fears, further darkening a mood unpleasant at the
outset.

The self-professed seeress's bold action made it
clear to Lissan that her feminine caller intended to
remain even after the men departed. Small white
teeth firmly bit down on a full lower lip to stifle an
ungracious demand that the woman coolly settling
atop one fireside stool leave.

All too familiar with Morag, Rory refused to suffer
under any such courteous restraints. With a stern
glare for the brazen visitor carefully arranging the
folds of her gown to flow in smooth waves, he issued a curt announcement. "You needn't make
yourself comfortable. You won't be staying long."

"And why not?" Morag softly inquired, adopting

a mendacious expression of polite concern. "I've been sadly remiss in not earlier making our guest welcome and mean to remedy that lack with a lengthy visit and quiet morning of cozy conversation."

"No—" Realizing Morag was unaware that he knew about her previous call upon Lissan, Rory immediately disabused her of the proposed action. "This cottage belongs to *me* and you are not welcome to tarry here either now or on any other day."

Grey eyes narrowing to pinpoints dueled with the dangerous silver glitter in Rory's dark gaze. Morag's steady stare did not falter despite the instantly regretted compromise falling with disgusting ease from her lips.

"Very well." Resentment burned in Morag's each word. "I will linger for but a few moments after you have departed."

"See that you don't stay longer." Rory was not satisfied with a plan that would leave this treacherous woman too near Lissan after he'd departed and took action to avert such danger to the one he feared already wronged by his rare loss of control over unmanageable passions. "I will direct Liam to ensure that your visit is brief."

With neither further words nor the risk of so much as a brief glance toward the too seductive sight of a temptingly disarrayed colleen, Rory led his brother from the cottage.

Worried that this brusque departure signaled Rory's morning distaste for the previous night's easy prey, a dismal Lissan watched the ebony hair brushing his broad back until her view was blocked by a door slammed shut. More depressing still, once Rory's strong presence was removed, she felt trapped inside an unaccountably shrinking room with an unpleasant woman of questionable intentions.

"So, 'tis true that you have become Rory's latest trollop?" Dark brows disdainfully arched in a query whose answer Morag deemed all too clear.

Lissan's chin tilted proudly upward although she refused to dignify the question with a response. By what perverted logic did this condescending creature think herself owed such private information?

"But then—" Morag smugly leveled a piercing gaze on her prey. "I suppose it was to be expected after he installed you here in the same cottage where so many in his long line of female conquests have resided. And I'm sure you realize 'tis a temporary arrangement destined to last only so long as his shockingly fickle attentions are engaged."

Despite an expression carefully held blank, Lissan felt as if emotions already unsteady had been jerked into a wild ride atop a bolting horse. Did Morag speak the truth? Was this confirmation of her fear that in succumbing to the devastating lord's charms, she had devalued herself by proving a woman of easy virtue? Or, worse, had she betrayed the love for him so recently discovered? Lissan's hands went cold while wild rose tinted her cheeks and she couldn't quiet the unsteady thumping of her heart.

"Oh, it's true," Morag assured her plainly shaken listener, proud of her ability to feign a compassionate sincerity. "But don't envision respect from either Rory or the decent people of his domain. That can never be when, like Hildie's mother before, you reside not in Ailm Keep, not in Rory's own home, but rather in this simple hovel tucked safely away from prying eyes amidst the woodland's concealing shadows."

No matter the sharp pangs of shame stabbing Lissan for having willingly yielded to Rory's undeniable charms and devastating seduction, she defiantly refused to be humbled by her tormenter.

A brisk tapping on the door reminded both women of the forewarned time limits Rory had placed upon their exchange. However, before Lissan could answer Liam's knock, Morag hastened to add one more taunt.

"Remember the disastrous end to your interference here that I predicted." Morag couldn't quell the glow of pleasure in her eyes although she tamed her smile into lines of false concern.

"I earnestly counsel you to escape from Connaught now." Morag's voice dropped to ominous depths. "Go before being publicly disgraced by your illicit relationship; go before the terrifying conclusion to your days that I have foreseen descends upon you."

Fighting to restore cool reasoning even while listening intently, Lissan caught an odd undertone in her visitor's arguments. Was it desperation? Or merely the wishful thinking of a woman knocked off stride by awareness of an ill-fated love?

Seeing confusion cloud normally clear green eyes, Morag didn't bother to hide the gleeful bubble of pleasure for a near triumph while solicitously extending what could be mistaken as a generous invitation. "Come, flee with me now and I'll accompany you to a safe haven."

The door burst open under Liam's energetic shove and even the weak light of a cloudy day flowing into the room from behind him gilded Lissan's soft mass of hair as she emphatically shook her head to refuse the less than sincere offer.

"Mistress," Liam called, concerned by a new, unnatural pallor to Lissan's cheeks. "Are you ill? Have you need of help?"

Mistress? Lissan cringed but did not chide him for again using the title now undeniably, shamefully hers. Rather, she invited him inside, welcoming his unquestioning support while assuring him that she had no need of physical aid.

Directed by sunlight streaming through the abruptly opened portal, Morag's attention narrowed on an unfamiliar addition to a cottage she'd visited more than once before. A massive and oddly constructed trunk now resided at the foot of a straw-filled pallet. The witch's? How could that be when the woman had arrived with nothing? Never mind, it clearly was hers and surely contained damning items revealing her true nature.

Well satisfied with her morning's achievements and discoveries, Morag gladly slipped away while Liam and his lady purposefully ignored her as they quietly discussed a variety of unimportant matters.

In the waning light of a gloomy day, Rory sent his unusually quiet brother off alone on the return journey to Ailm Keep. Donal's strange silence had somehow seemed a mere reflection of the disturbing atmosphere filling wooded hillsides and valley meadows with an unnatural stillness.

During the hours since his rude awakening, tantalizing images of Lissan had crept endlessly into Rory's thoughts. Beyond even the fiery delights shared the previous night, he found himself longing for the gentle solace of her company, certain of its ability to revitalize flagging spirits and add the spark of joy to an otherwise bleak day.

Despite knowing it meant loosening his grip on the reins of a long-ingrained caution against feminine wiles, Rory sent Donal home without him . . . freeing him to take the path toward Tuatha Cottage.

In that cottage filled with the deep yellow light of its central hearth's fire, Lissan sat across the table from Liam while their honest laughter further warmed the room. During quiet hours shared after an evening meal, she had welcomed the discovery of Liam's wry humor. It provided at least a momentary diversion from the depressing daylong repetition in her thoughts of all that Morag had said.

When the door suddenly opened, a gust of wind whipped flames into an amazing display that caught Lissan's attention but held it for only an instant before she became aware of a dark figure filling the portal. A small gale swirled the edges of Rory's black cloak around his powerful form. Lissan jumped to her feet, caught between the excitement of his unexpected arrival and lingering fear that she'd cheapened herself in his eyes by so easily succumbing to his wiles the previous night. With the sudden movement she bumped the table, making it rock so violently that the spring water filling pottery mugs sloshed over sturdy rims.

The discovery of this winsome beauty in such close harmony with the younger man struck Rory with a distinct stab of unreasoning jealousy which he immediately denied. He'd never been jealous, never in his life. And, after living three decades and more, he cautioned himself against being caught in that snare.

Yet in the next instant even these dark thoughts evaporated as his gaze met vulnerable green eyes dominating the blush-tinted face of an exquisite colleen tangling fingers in golden tresses to lift their bright weight from a graceful neck.

Instead of the chill greeting Rory had intended, a revealing confession escaped from his lips. "I've thought about little save you all the day long . . . ached to see you again."

Unnoticed by the two who of a sudden had become completely oblivious to his existence, Liam's eyes widened. He gaped in wonder at the sight of an intimate communion to the likes of which he'd never thought his lord would yield. Carefully rising, Liam slipped quietly from the building and closed the door behind.

Responding to words spoken in a too potent but familiar voice like distant thunder, Lissan slowly shook her head, setting a luxurious, fire-gilded mane to rippling. It was happening again! She was falling easy prey to his charms—wicked charms. . . . No! Lissan heatedly scolded herself. No, she had more pride and more spirit than that! Though trapped between bench and table edge, she leaned sharply away from the dangerously attractive man advancing to stand within arm's reach of her.

"I will *not* be your trollop!" Lissan's defiant words were prompted by a desperate need to bolster defenses flagging against his too-potent allure.

Rory was offended by an accusation that belittled their intimate time together, inexplicable and most unpleasant. His face went as hard and cold as granite. He hadn't asked her to be his trollop. Moreover, that she would suggest such a thing after *willingly* gifting him with her virginity was unthinkable . . . unless. . . . His suspicions leapt to new heights.

Had Lissan's sweet surrender merely been a part of some plan to further entrap him with guilt for what he'd taken from her? Did she foolishly think to bend his will with her schemes? (That she had already made inroads toward that despicable goal made ensuring that it stop here all the more important to Rory.) Anger soon overshadowed the tender emotions he now felt certain she had deviously intended to inspire.

Refusing to be no more of a fool than she'd already made him, Rory abruptly turned on a booted heel. He strode from the cottage, mounted his stallion, and pushed the beast to such relentless speed that he soon caught up with Donal. However, despite their shared journey, no words were exchanged between two men each lost in their own bleak thoughts.

CHAPTER 12

Night had truly fallen and a delayed evening meal had begun to cool by the time inhabitants of Ailm Keep scattered before their returning lord's fierce scowl.

Rory had thought a day dreary from its start could grow no worse. He'd been wrong. Even before reaching the stairway that led up to his home's entrance, he was intercepted. The two men assigned to patrol his domain's westernmost border had happened upon a furtive stranger. They had captured the intruder as he sneaked through the forest on a course running parallel with the path leading to a single destination—Tuatha Cottage.

Now as Rory strode down the path his frown had cleared through a crowded great hall, he held clenched in one hand a still-sealed message taken from a sullen captive.

Settling into a comfortably padded chair at the center of the high table, Rory was as oblivious to his warriors' speculative gazes as to the curiosity poorly hidden in an army of servants waiting to deliver a belated meal's parade of courses. With an intense scrutiny of the seal closing folded parchment, he ground his teeth. It clearly depicted the English king.

Impatience increased by the acrid taste of desperate hopes betrayed, Rory broke the wax closure with far less regard than was his wont. He pushed his trencher aside, then spread the day's unwelcome prize over a table covered by white cloth that brushed the floor both front and back. Using open palms, he took great care to smooth out creases until a sheet filled with hastily inscribed words lay flat, message exposed.

"From whom does it come?" Donal asked, unwilling of his own to wait and even less so while sitting at the high table beside a wife intent on forcing the question. Seated just beyond Morag's position on his brother's right, Donal knew that by morning his legs would bear bruises from the merciless kicking of feet hidden by a tablecloth.

"King Henry," Rory curtly answered, reluctant to discuss the matter either now or here.

"But for whom was it meant?" Morag couldn't resist the jab, knowing the answer was certain to make Rory squirm.

Rory's lips went tight and as his only response focused the full force of a penetrating gaze on his inquisitor. He refused to be a party to his sister-in-law's machinations.... "Machinations," the term had come to mind without forethought but instantly inspired an odd suggestion that the untrustworthy Morag might have had a hand in these nasty doings. But, no. He reluctantly dismissed the silent and likely unjust accusation. After all, even this cunning woman so adept with clever deceits couldn't possibly have access to a royal seal.

Staring down at the paper stretched between two powerful hands, Rory was irritated with himself for having allowed Morag's repugnant ways to even momentarily divert his attention from this message sure to prove important. It didn't. A fact that roused deeper and more ominous suspicions. Why would King Henry either waste time or put his emissary at risk merely to restate information obvious even to casual observers long before Lissan's arrival?

"Are you ready for the first course?" Harvey, the keep's steward, hesitantly inquired.

Rory's eyes briefly widened at this reminder that, since none could eat until their lord had been served, a meal already delayed by his late return had likely gone cold. Embarrassed that his distraction was the cause of so many others going hungry, Rory nodded. An unusual pang of guilt assaulted him for the fact that their patience would now be poorly rewarded with foodstuffs served tepid at best.

While anxious servants approached with heavily laden platters, Rory refolded the strange message and tucked it inside his tunic. Leastwise for the length of this meal he would put aside difficult questions, misdoubts, and suspicions.

Rory warned himself to employ his best defenses to fend off concerns about the truth of Lissan's intriguing nature. And more importantly, he must block those persistent images of the exquisite, self-styled fairy damsel threatening a subtle invasion of his mind . . . and heart.

The first light of another day found Hildie again secure on her secret perch amid Ailm Keep's rafters. Gazing curiously down upon a rapidly filling hall, once more it was the dark Morag who captured and held her earnest attention.

Although today there were no oddly mixed elixirs, Hildie unsuccessfully strained to hear sly words spoken in an annoying undertone. Secrets? How could that be true of matters indiscriminately shared with an ever-widening group of listeners?

Their dark lord's arrival brought an immediate

end to the hushed sounds of mumbled gossip. And Hildie, wedged into the angle of one bracing beam, let her forehead drop forward to rest against sturdy oak while a puzzlement of questions filled her thoughts.

Since Morag was neither liked nor trusted by the keep's inhabitants, what might she have said of such interest that it drew a great many to listen so earnestly? It was gossip, of course. But what information could, nay, what would the proud and secretive Morag willingly reveal to a mass of common folk? Far less everyone save their lord. And why?

Coming to a decision, Hildie straightened. She would skip the morning meal. Her absence was unlikely to be noticed. Most mornings Ailm Keep's people paid little mind when she quietly came and went. In truth, only Liam ever had and he wasn't here.

Although the emotion of being lonely in a crowd had at times dropped Hildie into the dismals, now her obscurity might finally serve some good purpose. She could remain concealed in this position until the men departed for their daily rounds. After that she had no doubt the tale-telling chatter would resume and this time she would find some way to hear what was said.

In Tuatha Cottage at that same moment Lissan rose from a pallet which after nights spent enduring its lumps seemed more comfortable than it had at the first. This ability to adjust to realities neither dreamed of nor experienced during her first two decades of life amid a century far in the future reminded her of the difficult choice she must soon make.

By Rory's understandable and likely unshakable skepticism for the confession of her honest experience, Lissan saw how improbable it was that she

would ever earn his trust. And, despite her love for
the stunning Irish lord, without trust he could never
love her nor could there be a basis for any deeper
relationship between them. Lissan felt forced to acknowledge anew the depressing truth which Morag
had made abundantly clear. It was an unhappy,
shameful fact that she meant no more to Rory than
a convenient mistress, a trollop unworthy of better.

The notion of remaining in his world under such
circumstances was heartbreaking. And yet the
ghastly prospect of leaving and never again walking
the same ground he trod upon, never seeing him
again, was far more devastating.

Pushing bleak thoughts aside, Lissan reached for
the moss-green gown Liam had brought for her on
his return from the trip to Ailm Keep with news of
Rory's health. While quickly donning wool folds
considerably softer than the dowdy homespun most
often worn in recent days, she dropped her gaze to
the sturdy box from which she'd lifted the dress. It
was the trunk her father had magically retrieved
from their London home of 1900 and delivered to
her here in 1115.

The rapid succession of events begun the morning
after her request for this boon seemed to have joined
in a conspiracy of distraction. Lissan wrinkled her
nose in self-mockery. Perhaps that was a bit of an
overstatement? No! How better could the situation
be described? It had truly been a mad tangle what
with Rory's capture, his rescue, a desperate climb to
the fairy ring seeking her father's aid, and her treat-
ment of the wounded warrior—overshadowed by
the fiery magic of loveplay soon cheapened by Morag's scorn. Surely all that was explanation enough
for how and why her attention had been diverted
from this precious gift.

Retrieving the key from its hiding place in the toe

of one shoe, Lissan sank down directly in front of the brass-bound chest. She released its lock and lifted the heavy lid, arched like an angry cat's back, to lay it gently back and rest on the pallet beyond.

Books! Wonderful books. Lightly running fingertips over hand-tooled leather covers, Lissan realized how much she'd missed such mundane possessions as these works of science, history, and fiction. Pulse pounding in trepidation over what undeniable facts might be revealed, she selected a thick volume of history prepared by a much-respected historian and shifted to sit cross-legged on the pallet. Savoring the pungent odor in pages of volumes lovingly stored, she started flipping with care through pages near its beginning. . . . All too quickly what she sought was found. . . .

In bold lettering of the fourth chapter's title no room was left for misinterpretation: MUNSTER'S DEFEAT AND ENSLAVEMENT OF CONNAUGHT.

Heartsick, Lissan slowly closed the book. Then, despite vision blurred by gathering tears, berated herself for being so weak as to even momentarily surrender the cause with such ease. She brushed shameful tears from her cheeks and straightened slumped shoulders. Hadn't her father said that someone acting outside their own timespan might change the course of history?

She knew perfectly well that it was the prospect of such a deed that her father most feared her presence would bring about. But surely—so long as she didn't err in teaching people in this year what they were not meant to learn for centuries to come—lending aid which they would perceive as the White Witch's magic couldn't be wrong.

Closing her thoughts to the very dark suspicion that her father wouldn't agree with this assessment, Lissan instead concentrated on a comforting idea.

Somewhere in these pages there must be a way to help Connaught defeat Munster, a gem of incomparable value buried in her very own treasure chest!

Knowing there wasn't time to embark on the earnest search at this bright hour, Lissan gently returned the book to its place in the trunk. Though meaning to close and relock her treasures, she found her eye caught by a personal favorite. Without thought, she lifted the novel and was unintentionally caught up anew by the adventure of H. G. Wells' *Time Machine*.

It was amazing, Lissan acknowledged, how the author had used his scientific curiosity to theorize a machine for exploring the future, envisioning a world full of marvels to come. She wondered what H. G. would think of her more far-fetched but absolutely true adventure into the past.

"What's that?"

Startled, Lissan glanced up. As on that first morning in Tuatha Cottage, she found herself again the steady focus of Hildie's solemn gaze. The child skilled at slipping into and out of places stood only a few paces away.

Certain a truthful response could only further complicate already difficult matters, Lissan warmly smiled but chose not to attempt an explanation for her treasures. And, wishing to avoid betraying her uneasiness at being observed inspecting them, she closed the book and with unhurried movements returned it to a trunk soon shut and relocked.

Wise beyond her years, Hildie allowed the matter to drop unchallenged and instead exercised an amazing maturity by tactfully changing the subject.

"After trying many times without success, Morag has at last found a lure tempting enough to snare and hold the people of Ailm Keep's attention."

By the complete lack of emotion in Hildie's words,

Lissan recognized a trait surely inherited from her father. Bright hair falling forward as her head tilted to one side like a curious bird, she wondered if the girl had truly made the early journey here merely to tell her about Morag's latest schemes.

"What lure did Morag use?" Lissan quietly inquired, hoping for a more revealing answer. "Perhaps something similar would be as effective for me."

Though Hildie immediately grimaced and gave her head a sharp shake, she remained oddly reluctant to be more specific about the actions of a woman they each disliked and distrusted.

Lissan held out an inviting hand, motioning the child to come closer.

"Everyone knows that Morag can't be trusted, even though—mayhap because—she claims to see the future," Hildie blurted out while stepping within arm's reach of her magical hostess. "That's why 'tis so hard for me to understand why near everyone remaining in the keep after the warriors departed this morning crowded around her at once."

Afraid any interruption by spoken words might slow the child's explanation, Lissan merely raised her brows in silent question.

"Rumors, just rumors," Hildie muttered in disgust. "In a place like the keep where so many people live so closely together there's always a steady flow of gossip . . . sometimes even a flood. Doubtless you already know that's true?"

Hildie paused long enough to see her lovely, mystifying friend nod. "But this was different, strange because never before has the source been Morag, who thinks herself so much more important and so far above any other."

Putting aside the uneasiness roused by this odd news for Hildie's sake, Lissan gently tugged the anxiously frowning child down to sit on the pallet beside her. Not until the girl had settled, thin arms wrapped around updrawn knees, did Lissan speak.

"What gossip did Morag find so interesting that the temptation to share it with even her lessers proved too powerful?"

"Morag spoke so low that it was difficult to clearly hear. . . ." Hildie's words trailed away and she took a deep, spirit-reviving breath before driving onward to the bitter end of her report. "But I understood enough to learn that although Morag acknowledges you as truly the White Witch, she claims to have foreseen a future in which you drive Connaught into slavery, see it humbled beneath Munster's might."

Because Morag had earlier announced precisely the same predictions to her, Lissan wasn't surprised to hear them repeated now. She was, however, discouraged to learn that her treacherous foe had already sown the seeds of mistrust and begun nurturing their poisonous vines to spread ever-strengthening tendrils throughout Rory's lands. If suspicion and fear took hold and flourished amid his people, it would destroy any hope of winning the support she must almost certainly have to see Connaught rise the victor from looming battles.

"It's not true . . . is it?" Sensitive to Lissan's bleak expression, worry put a tremble in the wide-eyed Hildie's voice.

"No." Daylight flowing through a door left open burnished Lissan's mane as she gave her head a brief shake. "I would never willingly harm you or any other loyal subject of this kingdom."

Hildie silently pondered these reassurances for long moments before sharing an additional morsel of information. "Morag warned everyone to watch you closely and not to put their trust in anything that you either say or do."

Worse and worse. Lissan bit firmly down on her lip to block a cry of frustration. Yet, on catching a glimpse of Hildie's still-growing apprehension, she willfully forced herself to relax fingers instinctively laced tight together to keep them from fidgeting. Instead she reached out and tenderly brushed back the mop of ebony hair tangled by a madcap ride from the girl's tension-flushed cheeks.

"Don't fret, Hildie." Lissan repeated again her soothing words of comfort while gently combing fingers through dark tangles. "Truly, neither you, your father, nor anyone else among the people of Connaught need fear harm from me."

In an unexpected, contrary response, Hildie fervently shook her head. That action once more set locks of black hair flying, undoing all of Lissan's patient attempts to restore order.

"I don't fear you—" Hildie earnestly explained. "I fear *for* you."

"You needn't." Green eyes met and steadily held a dark gaze. "In the fairy ring you met *my* father, the King of the Tuatha de Danann." A wry smile gently tilted Lissan's lips. "And you experienced his magic when in the twinkling of a star he whisked the two of us and *your* father from there to here."

Hildie sighed, amazed by this explanation for the impossible action she hadn't permitted herself to question. Slowly nodding, Hildie refused to let their visual bond break even when a whispered challenge escaped. "But you also swore that you weren't a fairy princess. . . ."

"I didn't lie, at least not knowingly." Lissan ruefully wrinkled her nose. "I wasn't aware of such a heritage then. And although my father is their king, I'm not truly a fairy princess. I don't believe anyone like me—half mortal and lacking mystical powers— can ever be that."

Confidence growing under the golden beauty's calm response to the same curiosity Morag consistently derided, Hildie probed further, hoping to learn more. "How did you know your father would answer when you sought him in the fairy ring?"

"He promised to respond whenever I call to him from there." Lissan thought she saw a faint shadow of disappointment cross the girl's face and suppressed a fond smile while solemnly adding, "Though my father gave that vow to me, I believe the ground encircled by forever blooming flowers is so sacred to his people that all intruders are closely watched—and heard."

Pleased, Hildie beamed.

Lissan was happy to provide this winsome child too often the subject of Morag's bitterness with confirmation of a truth behind her mama's tales of fairy magic. Along with that reassuring gift of hope, Lissan shared a precious memory of her own mother.

"My mother was mortal, but while at death's door she gave me her most precious possession—a spell-charmed amulet my father had given her."

"Amulet? What was it?" Hildie leaned forward, the glow of curiosity lighting silver sparks like stars in her eyes of midnight-blue.

Reaching inside the front laces of her green gown, Lissan carefully unfastened the amulet pinned there. She cradled in one cupped palm the onyx circlet containing a unicorn intricately carved of ivory and graced with a golden horn. This she held out for the girl to examine.

Hildie's lips parted on another silent gasp. The magical brooch was unquestionably the most beautiful thing she had ever seen.

"It protects the wearer against harm from any human weapon though it cannot save anyone from the forces of nature—not tempest, flood, or fire." Lissan

smiled warmly at the awestruck child. Certain the
story of her impossible arrival in the midst of battle
had already been repeated so often that Hildie must
know it well, Lissan went on to detail precisely what
part this piece had played.

"It's because I was wearing this brooch that Mael's
broadsword passed completely through me and yet
left me uninjured."

The inquisitive child's head tilted to one side
while with quiet words seeking confirmation of
claimed magical powers. "Then, really 'twas for the
sake of its protective quality that your father gave
the lovely amulet to your mother?"

"I have no doubt that's true but it represents only
part of the brooch's abilities." Lissan chose not to
tease Hildie by waiting for her to request a further
explanation. "When holding this amulet firmly between joined palms, one needn't be within the fairy
ring to summon my father. He can be called from
anywhere—although only if the summoner is threatened with dire peril."

Hildie slowly nodded, gaze shifting to stare
blindly through the open door while mentally sorting through all that she'd just learned about the kind
of mystical beings and incredible feats which were
certain to earn Morag's ridicule.

Noting the child's slide into somber contemplation, Lissan decided they'd had quite enough talk on
serious dangers and uncanny, possibly frightening,
abilities. She set out to shift the subject into others
more benign, more consistently pleasant.

"Did you enjoy living here so far from the keep?"
Lissan again tucked loose tendrils of dark hair back
from Hildie's face. "Or would you rather have resided closer to your father?"

Hildie's attention immediately returned to Lissan.
"I'd never met my father before being carried off to

his keep. I begged him to bring me back and leave
me here in my beloved home but he refused, saying
I'm too young to care for myself. . . ." A young forehead furrowed with remembered resentment. "But
I'm not."

"Ah—" Lissan's brows arched as visions of the
morning she'd awakened to find a solemn Hildie
watching her came to mind, along with memories of
how when Rory arrived he'd chided his daughter for
returning yet again. "So, that's why you keep slipping back to this cottage despite your father's
wishes."

Even while gently teasing the girl, Lissan regretfully acknowledged the only character flaw she'd yet
to find in Rory. And ignoring his child until forced
by the death of her mother to accept responsibility
was undeniable justification for serious criticism of
the man she'd come to admire—and too much more.

"I pray you'll forgive my many visits." Hildie's
penitent smile was in itself a heart-melting plea. "I
look forward to being with you." Shifting uneasily,
she confessed a deeper truth. "But were you not
here, still I'd long for this cottage I love . . . as did
my mother and her mother before."

"Your grandmother lived here, too?" Lissan was
startled.

"And her grandmother and her grandmother
and. . . ." Hildie's smile broadened into a grin. "My
family has lived in this cottage for many, many generations. Since the day, my mama said, that it was
built for your namesake, the princess of the fairy
ring, by her human husband."

Lissan felt like a fool, a silly fool. Rory hadn't kept
a succession of mistresses ensconced in Tuatha Cottage. She had been tricked yet could blame only herself. Though deeply distrusting Morag from the
outset, she'd still fallen prey to the woman's calcu-

lated lies. Lissan pressed cool hands against suddenly burning cheeks.

Because of her own folly in believing Morag's deceptions, Lissan realized she could hardly condemn the inhabitants of Ailm Keep for a similar mistake. That being so, what could she possibly do to uproot the baneful weeds of Morag's scheme and win the people's trust? Here was a problem for which even her precious books couldn't provide a solution.

Though feeling herself slipping into a bleak mood, Lissan saw Hildie's anxiety returning and made another attempt to divert the course of conversation onto less treacherous ground.

"Did your father and his brother return safely from yesterday's patrol?" Lissan hadn't seen the child since sending her home after their rescue of Rory and felt certain that this was the logical next question to ask, one hopefully lacking unpleasant undertones.

"They returned in perfect health." Hildie gladly accepted this welcome path away from uncomfortable issues. "The only thing to suffer was my father's mood. And if not for an apparently nasty message even that might have been righted."

Drats! Lissan inwardly groaned. Again she'd failed to establish a simple conversation on commonplace matters. And yet, all too conscious of the dangers against which an ancient seeress had predicted her alter ego would struggle, she couldn't merely ignore this off-hand clue.

"A message from your king?" Exercising skills learned during a succession of London Seasons, Lissan restrained her voice to tones of casual interest.

"Don't know what it said but I do know that it didn't come from King Turlough." In response to the silent query posed by Lissan's raised brows, the child who took pride in her habit of patient observation gladly explained. "After Donal asked, and though the question made Father's frown deepen, he stated that the letter had been sent by the English king."

English king? Though careful to maintain a bland smile, Lissan's heart thumped erratically. Rory had accused her of being a spy for King Henry, which would seem to prove they were foes. That being so, why would King Henry correspond with Lord Rory?

A murky spring of deep misgivings welled up inside Lissan, threatening to overwhelm her in a torrent of perils impossible to defeat.

CHAPTER 13

"**B**ut for what possible reason would the English king send a message to Rory?" Lissan asked of her fairy guardian again as she repeatedly had in the time since Hildie's departure for Ailm Keep.

As had become their evening habit, Maedra sat perched on a hearthside stool next to Lissan. She truly wished for an answer to give her worried friend. But she didn't possess one and consequently had devoted dwindling afternoon hours to murmuring soothing sounds and useless words.

"It makes no sense." After two decades spent pursuing the ideals of sound logic and investigative learning Lissan was still uncomfortable with irrational matters defying either, despite their abundance in recent days. And her inability to find purpose for so simple a thing as a letter added to the frustrated sense of helplessness building inside.

"I would help you if I could," Maedra leaned nearer to quietly confide. "Truly I would even if it meant bending the rules governing contact between our two worlds."

Lissan rewarded her earnest companion with a grateful smile while inwardly acknowledging that the more hours they spent together, the closer they became. This simple fact opened the door to an odd realization.

In her own world Lissan had a great many acquaintances, but she'd never had a friend with whom she shared such rapport as she did with Maedra. Was it because the fairy in her nature responded instinctively to this magical creature? With a private frown Lissan gave close consideration to that question and came to the conclusion that although the power of such a mystical bond was doubtless true, there must be more. . . . Something about this less civilized world, perhaps? It was here, after all, where she had as quickly grown fond of Hildie and even Liam. Far more importantly, despite the briefness of their relationship, it was here where she had almost immediately begun falling irretrievably in love with Rory O'Connor.

Seeing Lissan's vexation over a vain quest for answers sinking into melancholy, Maedra spoke in an attempt to draw the beauty only half human back from the edge of any deeper abyss.

"Because in my realm things of a certainty one way or another are disdained, I've no way of understanding human motives, mortal reasoning. Lacking understanding, 'tis impossible for me to fathom the purpose for conflict between two mortal kings. More so as for the Tuatha de Danann there is only ever one ruler."

With the sharp human logic Lissan had begun to fear permanently blunted by the flood of too many illogical happenings, she recognized a glaring paradox in Maedra's explanation. "But if your breed views endless change as the ultimate state, how can you bear to consistently serve the *same* king?"

"Here again, O honored daughter of King Comlan—" Maedra's delight danced on a shimmer of laughter. "You've proven how special you are by identifying a supreme and precise example of the Tuatha de Danann's true nature . . . ever changing yet always and ever the same. *Both* at the same time."

With a small, pleased grin Lissan modestly shrugged, warmed by the praise. Then while curiously tilting her head in a movement sending the cloud of her hair to fall over one shoulder like a cascade of liquid gold, she posed another question.

"Don't you find it a trial to linger here in a world defined by human reasoning that demands firm control and enforces rigid limitations?"

Maedra unthinkingly imitated Lissan's nervous habit of nibbling a lower lip while wondering if she dared share her deepest dreams with this mortal friend. She could and did tentatively begin.

"Truth be known. . . ."

Lissan was surprised, first by this opening and second by the type of uneasiness from which she'd thought (apparently wrongly) no member of the Tuatha de Danann was likely to suffer. Curiosity roused, she turned to give her full attention to the flustered fairy companion sitting within arm's reach.

"And were circumstances different. . . ." Again Maedra stopped.

Senses sharpened by her own recent admission of doomed love, Lissan glimpsed in Maedra's azure eyes a fleeting vision of the fairy damsel's heart-inspired fantasy. Added to observations already made, this was hint enough for Lissan to understand.

"Circumstances? You mean were Liam to find the courage to court you?"

"Liam is a very brave man." Maedra straightened to immediately defend her human warrior against Lissan's implied insult.

"Of course he is. As an experienced guardsman

Liam doubtless stands strong in warfare." With a
fond smile of gentle sweetness, Lissan sought to
calm her friend's ruffled composure. "But because
he lacks training in its tactics, Liam hovers uncertain
at the edge of the heart's tender battlefield.

"And, although from what I've seen he is as smit-
ten with you as you seem to be with him, I suspect
there's something you don't realize," Lissan earnestly argued. "Liam is so in awe of you that it
weakens his resolve and prevents him from confessing his feelings."

Rather than the bright flash of hope revived that
Lissan had hoped to win, a forlorn smile barely
lifted the corners of Maedra's mouth.

"To what purpose my pursuit of Liam?" Maedra
sadly asked. "What use my longing to spend a human lifetime at his side when an alliance between
us can never be more than an impossible dream?"

"Impossible? Why? Because you believe your di-
verse natures decree that it must be thus?" Lissan
was truly aghast at this suggestion. "How can you
even suggest that this simple fact poses an impass-
able barrier when your king is wed to my mortal
mother?"

Maedra gazed blindly into the flickering flames of
a fire burning low while mournfully responding.
"As was proven by the first Lissan's experience,
there is *always* a price to be paid for a fairy's love of
someone from your world."

"I see," Lissan softly mused, although she didn't.
"Unlike my namesake, you aren't willing to surrender the magic of fairy powers in exchange for a lifetime with your beloved?"

" 'Tis not that," Maedra answered, slowly shaking
her head with anguished regret. "Gladly would I follow her example, gladly . . . were it possible."

"But why is it not possible?" Lissan persisted, as

anxious to encourage Maedra's dream as she had been to offer cheer.

"Were I to take such an action here and now, it would alter the flow of mortal history." Maedra shifted slightly on her stool to gaze directly into Lissan's eyes. "It would make a change so serious that you likely wouldn't exist."

Lissan frowned. This made even less sense than a letter from King Henry to Rory.

"Fairy time is vastly different from that of humans. I too came back through a parade of human centuries to reach this year in your world's past." Maedra tried to explain something no being purely human was likely to understand—but then her companion was half fairy.

"When the Irish abode you knew as Daffy's Cottage was inhabited by your mother's great-aunt Daphenia," Maedra slowly continued, "it was I who served as the elderly woman's protectress—just as I have done for you here in this era."

Whether the result of fairy intuition or human logic, Lissan quickly comprehended the complexities of the situation and yet asked the first question that came to mind. "Then you knew my mother when she and my father first met?"

Maedra nodded, smile flashing. "Aye, a dark beauty Amy was . . . and is once more."

"She *is*?" Lissan repeated, hesitant to pursue details while fearing her fairy guardian had been as firmly cautioned against sharing such information as she'd been commanded to never be seen by anyone purely human.

"As our king's mate—" Maedra promptly eased Lissan's concern. "Queen Amethyst's position will always be at his side."

Lissan was grateful for Maedra's heartening gift of a vision in which her mother sat secure at a be-

loved husband's side now and for countless human
years to come. She longed to reciprocate by giving
hope to Maedra's troubled romance. And yet, as
clear as if just spoken, Lissan heard again her father's warning against teaching people here any part
of what humanity wasn't meant to discover until
centuries had passed. That warning issued before
the bringing of her trunk from London reinforced
Lissan's awareness of the importance of doing nothing to alter time.

Still, Lissan wanted to encourage her friend by
urging her to continue seeking an answer for the
problem. "There must be a way, some action to take
that'll allow you to remain with Liam, without dam-
aging the time stream."

At Lissan's reminder of a future without Liam, the
bright smile inspired by talk of her king and queen
faded from Maedra's lips as rapidly as her spirits
sank under the gloomy prospect's weight.

"If there is a way, I haven't found it despite my
desperate search." Maedra let her attention return to
the flamed-darkened hearth.

"It seems we are both trapped in the shifting snare
of time." Lissan acknowledged a dismal fact. "This
dilemma poses for each of us a baffling puzzle, sep-
arate but similar."

This oddly convoluted statement offered a challenge to Maedra's fairy nature that lured her from
the bleak contemplation of billowing smoke.

"What do you mean?"

"Plainly the unbreakable law forbidding damage
to the currents of time places an invisible wall between you and the man you love," Lissan responded
quietly. "While my precipitous tumble through the
centuries, inexplicable and thus fearsome, created a
wall of suspicion between me and mine. One which,

I've sadly learned, even the sword of truth cannot penetrate."

Rory stepped into his bedchamber and quietly closed the door behind. After a message had again arrived during an evening meal, he'd chosen not to read it while closely observed by too many, opening the way for questions best answered in private—if at all.

Settling into the sturdy chair positioned to one side of a heavily draped bed, Rory first methodically rearranged several down-filled cushions for greater comfort. Not until that was done did he break the seal and carefully unfold this missive from Turlough, his young cousin and king.

Alister has returned. While reading these few words Rory's black brows crashed together in a fierce scowl. Alister, initially an English slave but now a loyal supporter of Connaught, had accepted an honorable commission and with his king's trust had been positioned for an "escape" into Munster. Once inside that opposing kingdom, Alister was instructed to embark on a flexible strategy calling for the use of both his natural friendliness and sharp wits to insinuate himself into the royal court. Rory and his royal cousin had been certain that Alister would be assisted in this chore by spreading a false tale of harsh captivity and professed hatred of all Connaught.

A muscle began to twitch in Rory's clenched jaw. This news of Alister's early return to Turlough could portend many ills.

Dark eyes racing ahead, Rory skimmed over the lengthy report, reading in patches. *To evade our defenses, foes from Munster carried Alister up the coast by boat and dropped him on our northernmost shore . . . with*

*great difficulty made his way to me bringing a message
from Muirtrecht of Munster. . . .*

Rory paused only long enough to thank Providence again for the father who had insisted his sons learn to read and write for themselves rather than trust the uncertain honesty of others. Then he lifted the page nearer, the better to focus on each important word. *Our arrogant enemy claims his forces so superior to those we command that he cedes the weapon of surprise and warns of armies massing all along the border between our two kingdoms. In addition, though it seems proof bloated pride has driven him mad, King Muirtrecht announces that with the dawn following Whitsunday there will be an invasion.*

A soft growl of disgust rumbled from Rory. Because he had long since learned to respect the powerful Muirtrecht's skill in devising battle strategies, he was skeptical of the too revealing message's validity. And, as shown in the last line written by the young man he'd trained to be a king, Rory saw that he was not alone in this suspicion.

I pray you, cousin, to investigate the claim of armies gathering. Too, I earnestly pray you to beware of traps likely laid against logical actions he doubtless expects.

Vellum sheets crackled as Rory refolded them, an action reviving a too vivid memory of when he'd recently done the same with another letter even less welcome. Rory had spent sleepless hours the previous night and most of this day mentally reviewing every phrase, every word, addressed to Lissan in a search for hidden meaning but still had found no purpose for the English king to have dispatched it. Nor, to his sorrow, had he discovered any excuse to absolve her from its indictment for the wrongdoing implied.

Now, with Turlough's plea for aid, Rory could no longer postpone a duty he would yield near any-

thing save honor to avoid . . . and his honor would
be the price for shirking this necessary task. He was
the one who must go and demand answers to difficult questions from the enchanting woman warming Tuatha Cottage with her presence.

Though a daunting prospect even to a powerful
warrior of his iron self-control, Rory knew he must
confront the seemingly vulnerable colleen who had
first mysteriously saved his life and then shared with
him a night of honey-sweet and fiery delights. But
then in the light of day she'd backed away, shamed
by the joining in which he'd found naught but pleasure matched with a rare sense of peace and contentment.

Between this letter and the English king's intercepted message it was ominously clear that strange
matters were afoot. And Rory didn't like it. He
didn't like it at all.

Morag marched from one side of the small chamber
to the other, irritably kicking at floor rushes and
glaring at the door. Impatience simmering, it seemed
as if days had crawled by on inordinately slow feet
while she waited for her husband to come back and
report on his brother's royal letter.

The door creaked open, at last, and Morag's
pointed stare bored into the unhappily returning
Donal.

" 'Struth, Rory's letter was sent from Turlough."
Despite fingers automatically curling into fists,
Donal made no attempt to evade the subject his wife
was plainly determined to pursue until she had ex-
tracted every detail that he'd learned.

"And what did it say?" Morag harshly demanded.
Unwilling to see her sway over Donal lessened by
the yielding of even so much as a single particle the

size of a dust mote, she refused to grant him the space of a moment's hesitation.

"Munster's armies are massing along the border." Donal fought to stand unbowed beneath the freezing power of an icy gaze that further belittled and left him only ever more aware that in Morag's view he was merely a weak reflection of his older sibling. He went on to complete a required but blessedly brief account of the message's contents. "And King Muirtrecht warns that with the dawn following Whitsunday they will attack."

An almost tangible fury instantly engulfed Morag. To tame useless emotions, the better to think clearly, she resumed her relentless march back and forth across the room whose cramped proportions she'd long decried as unworthy for a younger heir to the keep.

Morosely Donal watched his wife's brisk movements, uneasiness growing. Her rage was a fearsome sight.

Morag fumed. Apparently Mael's influence over his king was not so strong as he'd claimed. Couldn't be when Muirtrecht had plainly disregarded a supposedly respected advisor's counsel, turning aside to pursue strategies of his own ... strategies almost certain to wreak havoc on Mael's vigilantly nurtured plans.

Whitsunday? Morag momentarily paused in her march. Given that specific date, foolishly provided by a man she'd thought in possession of sharper wits, she must and would push her schemes forward at an uncomfortably brisk pace. Uncomfortable? Aye, and difficult, too. But what must be, must be.

"This means—" Morag turned toward Donal with a false sweetness that struck terror into her prey. "Where Mael and his men failed, you *will* succeed."

Color drained from Donal's face, leaving it an

alarming shade of ashen grey. Despite a long-standing resentment of Rory, he was horrified by Morag's suggestion—nay, command—that he be personally responsible for his brother's death.

Morag recognized her husband's reluctance and, impatient with his weakness, immediately berated him for daring to pose so foolish a threat to the carefully plotted attainment of her goals—*their* goals. Her rebuke ended with a further demand issued on a particularly sour note.

"And it must be done soon, very soon, elsewise it'll come too late to be of any use—Whitsunday falls only a few days hence."

"But Morag, pause to think logically." The moment these incautious words left his mouth, Donal recognized the serious error in suggesting his wife's thought processes capable of being less. Too shaken to think rationally himself, he foolishly hastened to cover his mistake with an overabundance of more.

"I mean, what am I to do? Wildly brandish my broadsword to challenge my brother in the great hall? Attack him boldly in the courtyard?" Donal lifted battle-scarred hands palm up in an instinctive gesture of supplication for leniency. "Even were I to fall upon him amidst the stable's shadows, everyone would know with whom he had entered."

Morag's lips took on a disdainful tilt. How was it that she'd been foisted off with a mate of such limited intellect? How? She answered her own question. A decade past, her determined craving for vengeance following Rory's rejection had led her to foolishly expect more of his brother.

Further vexed by this self-criticism, Morag nearly growled but with a confidence-restoring truth quickly banked coals threatening to break out in unruly flames. Donal's duller wits and malleability

were more to her taste than a husband who might,
wrongly, expect to rule her.

Donal found himself the focus of his wife's scorn,
as so many times before. Wiping all expression from
his face, he again stood as the stoic pillar of ice he
so often became while subjected to Morag's coldness. And thus Donal remained even after she returned to striding back and forth.

"No," Morag absently mused at last. "Not in the
great hall, courtyard, or stable." Her listener was initially spared her ire by this demand that close consideration be given to a modification of plans. But,
although inattention blunted the sharp edge of Morag's tongue, it was a brief respite too quickly ended
when she turned to meet dark blue eyes filled with
a worry impossible to hide.

"You ride patrol alone with Rory each day."
Morag blandly identified an opportunity so simple,
so obvious, it had nearly been overlooked. "And
who is to say some cohort of his earlier assailant
wouldn't have returned to finish a slain friend's in-
complete task?"

By the air of resignation settling over Donal,
Morag knew the *logic* he'd questioned had prevailed.
He would do as she directed. Mayhap with regret,
but do it Donal would.

Morag turned sharply, an unspoken dismissal of
her husband, to walk toward the chest hosting a ba-
sin and ewer of freshly drawn water. While pulling
pins free to release braids neatly coiled atop her
head, Morag's attention shifted as easily from the
cowed man still hovering behind to ponder her second problem, one she'd already declared a greater
danger than Rory. She slowly loosened thick plaits
by combing her fingers through the dark mass while
reminding herself that Lissan could be removed with
even less opposition.

That fact had been clear since the moment Morag first heard the tale of Lissan's arrival to dine in Ailm Keep. To Morag it seemed the actions she intended had been predestined by the visitor's failure to offer a public dissent after Donal named her the White Witch. The church declared witches an evil presence casting a dark blight to despoil the earth. Christians were admonished to root the wicked creatures out and consign them to flames.

Lips curling into a vicious smile, Morag was pleased that she'd already set into motion a plan to see that command fulfilled and retreated to the tester bed for a surely well deserved rest.

CHAPTER 14

Again Hildie gazed down from her perch amid the gloom-shrouded rafters of a great hall illuminated only by the fire in its central hearth and weak glow of the few tallow candles Morag allotted for use at each trestle table. When first venturing to make this climb, the child hadn't for a moment suspected what an important role it would eventually play.

And again, after Hildie's father and his brother led the keep's warriors in departing on a variety of equally important duties, Morag became the center of attention for those left behind. But today the woman wasted no effort on soft speech, made no pretense of imparting secrets. Instead, with amazing ease Morag began whipping her listeners into an intolerant frenzy that filled Hildie with horror.

"You know, all of you, how often I have been to Tuatha Cottage." Morag's pale and piercing eyes swept around a sea of watching faces. "But I swear that never until my last visit had I ever before seen that peculiar chest with strange words branded deep into its lid with fire."

These words were imbued with such dread-inspiring menace that even the safely concealed child cringed away from their speaker.

· " 'Tis huge and bound by metal strips inscribed with sinister characters indecipherable to mortal man." This announcement's powerful suggestion of unworldly forces was intended to rouse alarm, and Morag was gratified to see by widened eyes and quickly signed crosses that with it she'd succeeded.

Above the hall filling with a quiet gale of hushed voices echoing condemning words, a young heart sank. Hildie had hoped, had foolishly expected, more time to see Morag's vicious slander exposed as an untruth. Apparently that hope was doomed.

"I recognized the chest's evil threat, experienced its wicked lure." Again Morag's intimidating gaze made a slow circuit of her listeners. "It wasn't there before *she* fell from the sky—bringing nothing."

Having listened at a recent mass where an itinerant priest ardently preached the pope's call to join a holy crusade, Hildie recognized the similar fervor infecting Morag's words. And yet, within zealous words Hildie also heard the hollow ring of insincerity.

"So, I ask you, from whence came a thing so monstrously large and assuredly too heavy for any man to carry alone? How could it possibly have appeared in Tuatha Cottage without human aid ... or leastways the knowledge of others residing hereabouts?"

Silence fell, heavy with unspoken fears and dire foreboding. But only a brief span of uneasy moments passed before the ominous tension goaded Padriag, the burly metalsmith, into erupting with a gruff demand for answers.

"Come, follow me to Tuatha Cottage—" With this loud rallying cry Padriag thrust a mighty fist into the air. "We'll drag the witch out, destroy the chest and its vile contents!"

"Aye, come!" A younger, equally aggressive male

was prompt to zealously support the action. "To the cottage and the witch."

Morag took dark, cruel delight in the agitation rapidly escalating and spreading through the crowd. This was precisely the response she'd meant to incite and nearly hissed when a servant of advancing years stepped forward, summoning the attention of his peers.

" 'Struth," said Noel, a man who had earned respect for being wise and fair. "We must open the chest and see what's inside. But we dare not act against its owner till we know for a certainty that 'tis truly evil that's cradled within."

When Noel's sane caution was met and near overwhelmed by a disgruntled chorus of protest, he quickly added, "If the devil's work we find inside, then burn the chest we should. Aye, cleanse it with fire we must!"

"Reduce the chest to purified ashes." The keep's alewife, near as large and certainly as strong as any man present, loudly shouted her support for this course and with even greater heat demanded the pursuit of a further goal. "To that pyre we must also consign the witch in mortal need of cleansing flames."

Morag tamed her satisfaction with the unruly mob into a tight smile. Far less effort than expected had been required to incite such useful fervor, and she was most pleased by this fact boding well for success in attaining her ambitions.

Maedra hovered with rare uncertainty just outside the cottage door. With Lissan's encouragement, she meant to seek Liam out and overcome his awe to learn if, truly, he felt for her any portion of the tender emotion she hosted for him. Despite an uneasiness given rise on finding it necessary to bolster the wavering of a courage usually strong, she moved boldly forward to stand in the lean-to's open end.

Liam wasn't there. Maedra's shoulders sagged while a sense of relief immediately clashed against sharp pangs of disappointment. After spending tense hours the past night in devising a precise strategy to see her through the expected scene, this anticlimax was devastating. More so for the fact that she was unlikely to ever again be brave enough to risk daring another such meeting. It was a dismal admission from a being whose lifespan would encompass more time then any human could easily comprehend.

"Have you need of me?" Liam spoke from directly behind his unexpected visitor.

With the previous night's carefully laid plans already pulverized into worthless dust and now scattered by the sound of his voice, Maedra continued staring into empty shadows but haltingly responded. "I wanted to talk with someone but Lissan's asleep and I didn't wish to awaken her."

Liam smiled, oddly heartened by the uncertainty in this amazing damsel's words, an uncertainty which allowed him to feel less of an inferior creature than usual while in her presence.

"I was preparing to lead my stallion a scant distance into the forest." With hands gently curled over her slender shoulders, Liam turned Maedra to face him. "There's a small brook and lush grasses sprouting there. Come with me?"

Maedra gazed steadily into solemn eyes of an uncertain hue perfect to attract a whimsical fairy, being neither purely brown nor green. She ought refuse to leave this glade, particularly as to go with Liam meant leaving the cottage completely unguarded by either human strength or fairy power. But, she reminded herself, Lissan was not actually asleep and

had urged her into taking action to draw out the
reticent Liam.

Though a pitifully weak justification for doing
what she shouldn't, Maedra couldn't force herself to
forgo this too likely lone opportunity. With a nod of
her gloriously golden head and an equally bright
smile, she accepted the young man's invitation.

Liam was afraid that if he mounted his steed and
offered to safely hold her close while riding to their
destination, strong feelings might lead him to em-
barrass both himself and her. Instead, he held the
reins in one hand and proffered his other forearm to
escort Maedra down a newly blazed path.

With a quiet smile, Lissan reached for an empty water bucket waiting next to the cottage's outgoing
door. As more than adequate time had passed since
Maedra departed on her quest, by now she must
surely have found Liam. Feeling wistful over an ill-
starred love which likely destined her to a lonely
future, Lissan earnestly hoped her friend's romance
would find a happy ending.

Lissan slipped quietly outside, intent on fetching
fresh water from a well on the side of the cottage
opposite from where the lean-to was built. Deeply
inhaling fresh air untainted by smoke from the chim-
neyless hearth, she glanced upward.

Although bands of ragged clouds stretched like
shredded cloth across the pale morning sky, there
seemed no threat of rain. Lissan was determined to
block gloomy thoughts of her own troubled love and
concentrated on positive wishes for Maedra and
Liam while making her way to the well covered by
a steeply pitched roof.

After drawing up a bucket full of cool liquid, Lissan turned to make her way back into the humble
structure that had become her home. Her attention

was caught by a glimpse of unusual colors moving on a distant horizon. Pausing, she peered curiously at the shifting configuration and amazing variety of outlines and hues emerging from the forest's dark silhouette.

People were coming. Not merely one or two but a large group who clearly were also the source of an indistinct, rumbling noise. Shocked, Lissan found herself frozen in place while the initial hint of movement became a crowd of ominous size and once faint sounds proved to be a threatening roar punctuated with words frighteningly clear.

"There stands the witch, bold as you please," shouted a Padraig worked into an unreasoning frenzy and stomping relentlessly toward the wicked creature who must be purified with fire.

Lissan focused on the hulking, red-faced man it seemed must be the mob's leader as the whole halted once he paused a few paces in front of her.

"The devil's spawn she is!"

Lissan's attention shifted to this insult's source, a woman standing beside the leader and of almost as daunting a size. And yet she wasn't nearly as terrifying as the figure Lissan next recognized boldly striding to the forefront.

"Aye, here is the accursed one, the White Witch of legend who is endowed with evil powers that must be exposed. Come—" When Morag dramatically waved the crowd's attention toward the cottage entrance, as if in emphasis, a faint breeze caught the bottom edges of her flowing cape and lifted it in a black billow. "We must go and bare the dark source of the witch's wickedness to the purity of daylight."

Breaking from her trance, Lissan desperately sought to reason with the unruly throng moving like a storm cloud toward the cottage entrance. She attempted to tell them their fears were unfounded, but people worked into a crazed state paid her no mind. Try as she might, Lissan was unable to fight her way through and protect her precious chest.

On his way to the door, the mob's leader found the axe Liam had left buried in a stump after he'd last finished splitting firewood for the cottage's temporary mistress. Wielding this well-honed tool, the burly metalsmith shattered Lissan's sturdy chest with disgusting ease.

Not until this vicious chore was complete did a corridor open for Lissan to approach between walls of condemning glares and hissing disapproval. Feeling like a condemned Moses walking through the Red Sea, Lissan moved forward to gaze down in horror at chunks of splintered wood layered with a snow of pages rudely torn from books scattered across the floor.

"Noel," Morag loudly called out from within arm's reach of Lissan. "You demanded proof of this creature's evil nature. Now you have it and must agree that these strange creations are of a certainty the devil's own handiwork."

Painfully biting her lip, Lissan instantly turned to see one of her most treasured books lying open across Morag's outstretched arms to display photographs of various wheeled vehicles—everything from unicycles and bicycles to the newest in motorcars.

"'Struth," the large woman still standing beside the mob's leader shrilled. "But 'tis surely this as what shows how horrible are such vile powers of darkness that snare peoples' souls to imprison them thusly." She wildly waved a copy of the London *Times*.

Startled, Lissan exercised every ounce of courage she possessed to keep from cringing. She had carefully preserved this issue for the sake of a scientific article written by her oldest brother. Never once had she given a moment's thought to photographs of the Season's reigning beauties which it also contained, photographs this woman plainly found terrifying.

"But the most serious, I fear," Noel said, saddened that it was so, "are these gruesome images and strange characters forming meaningless words."

"Do you know their meaning?" The grey-haired man solemnly gazed toward Lissan while holding out a slender medical text which used anatomical diagrams and current scientific data to theorize future blood transfusions. "And can you prove them no threat to us?"

Again Lissan bit her lower lip so firmly that it hurt. What could she possibly say? Even were she to read and translate the words, there was no earthly way for these people to understand their meaning. Her father's warning of a disaster sure to follow any such scene as this came forcefully to mind. In addition to that, she remembered depressingly well the importance of doing nothing to alter the flow of human history. And that assuredly meant changes which such knowledge as this would almost certainly bring about.

"She dares not speak aloud the devil's words," Morag gleefully chortled. "She dare not for fear of her sinister master's fearsome wrath!"

"Burn her!" screamed a ragged child from the crowd's midst.

"Aye," the youth's mother loudly echoed. "The witch must be burned!"

" 'Struth." Another joined the discordant refrain. "The priests have always held such punishment is required to cleanse the earth of such black sins."

These demands were met with other like sentiments all of which quickly joined to became an increasingly wild chant ever gaining in volume and momentum . . . until a gloating Morag motioned for others to pause and listen to her counsel.

"Burn the witch we will, but in the right place and at the right time." Her satisfaction nearly scalded with an acid that muzzled demands for immediate action which burned on the tongues of her audience. "The right time is with this evening's setting sun. And the right place will be in the courtyard of Ailm Keep."

Morag knew her followers would not welcome any delay but was certain they'd again follow her lead. And for her the pleasure in having the two halves of her scheme come to fruition at near the same moment would be a joy so sweet as to be worth the wait.

Unnoticed by the frenzied mob intent on their prey, a small figure hovering on the throng's outermost fringe turned and quietly slipped away. Hildie's cheeks were blanched white by a trepidation which perversely bolstered her determination.

"Right there." After a long day spent in vigilant patrol, Rory was again on the forest-shadowed path leading toward Ailm Keep and motioned Donal's attention to the site of ambush. "That's where I fell."

While giving this definitive answer to an idle question earlier posed by his brother, Rory's eyes narrowed on the still-visible signs of his attack. Crushed grasses and broken bushes marked the spot where he had painfully dragged himself through thick vegetation bordering the open path to seek even a limited protection amidst its concealing foliage.

"You left such an obvious trail that I'm amazed you survived and returned home all of a piece." The honesty permissible in such a statement allowed Donal's strained nerves a moment's respite. Tension aggravated by the need to guard every word, every inflection, had nearly driven him to the brink—but whether to confession or rash action even Donal didn't know and wished he needn't ever learn.

Though silence fell again Rory failed to notice its uneasy undertones. He was still convinced his injuries had been less than life-threatening and yet knew that he shouldn't have survived, not while other intruders sent on the same quest to see him dead had doubtless lurked near.

His deliverance had unexpectedly been accomplished by Lissan and Hildie. Rory knew this was true despite disgustingly patchy memories left after drifting in and out of full consciousness for an uncertain length of time. Between them they'd somehow accomplished what, a niggling inner voice told him, even his experienced warriors couldn't have done.

Fiery memories of all that had followed his awakening in the cottage filled Rory's mind with images so vivid he could nearly feel the warmth of satin skin, taste the sweet nectar of Lissan's mouth. . . . Rory shook his head to free thoughts of the exquisite colleen's persistent hold on his waking daydreams and night fantasies.

Yet even while forcing his attention back to the chill realities of daily life and its many serious challenges, Lissan dominated. Surely the woman who had saved his life wouldn't at the same time have been involved in a plot to see it end?

Black brows scowled above the eyes nearly as dark gazing blindly into the woodland's gloom. The two letters were the key. One announced the failure of a spy dispatched from Connaught to carry a false tale into Munster, the other purported to have been sent by the English king and addressed to Lissan.

Aye, Rory saw it plainly now. Just as his royal

cousin had sent Alister to fool Munster's King Muirtrecht, the messenger they'd intercepted had as
surely come not from England's King Henry but
from Munster's royal court.

Unseen by the brother riding slightly behind, Rory's honest smile flashed white for the first time
since the moment Lissan had backed away from him
in shame.

Rory's expression was hidden from Donal who
rode behind, grateful for his brother's unusual pre-
occupation. It freed Donal to watch and wait for the
perfect time to take a dreaded but promised action.

It came too soon when Donal realized that he
wouldn't find a more appropriate place than this site
of an earlier assault nor would there be a more propitious moment. Because Rory had, as always, taken
the lead, Donal realized it would be a simple thing
to slip his dagger from its sheath and with a single
stroke see the deed done.

Turning thoughts into actions, Donal was soon
leaning cautiously, quietly forward with deadly
blade firmly clenched in the hand of his upraised
arm. . . .

CHAPTER 15

Riding through a small woodland glade, Hildie glanced anxiously toward the western horizon. The sun hovered barely above its stillness. And, the despairing child acknowledged, its position was too perilously low to lend hope for Lissan's rescue.

When Hildie's pony slowed to a dragging pace, a sense of defeat prevented her from whipping it into resuming their valiant quest's initial brisk pace. She had run the whole way from Tuatha Cottage to the stables at Ailm Keep for the sake of having her pony's strength and speed to aid in the search for her father. But in the end she'd failed.

Under Hildie's urging the diminutive steed had zigzagged from one side to the other of the patrol route usually followed by her father and his brother. An action that accomplished nothing save the smothering of any hope for securing her father's aid and authority to command a halt to the vicious intentions of Morag and her fear-enflamed mob. Hildie was left feeling utterly useless by this defeat of her once-promising plan to help rescue the wondrous friend who for some bewildering reason seemed to lack the magic to save herself.

While rounding a bend in the use-rutted pathway,

Hildie was so lost in morose contemplation of green forest shadows to the left that when her pony's already dragging gait came to an abrupt halt it was a shock. The attention so rudely demanded immediately narrowed on a terrifying sight—the glitter of a deadly blade which Donal held poised above . . .

"Father!" Hildie shrieked as loudly as she possibly could.

In desperate haste, Donal slashed downward, narrowly missing the target who twisted around in answer to a child's call.

Others among her kindred in King Comlan's hall could say whatever they liked about the lesser attributes of human males, but now Maedra knew better . . . leastways where her Liam was concerned. To satisfy a longing to gaze more completely at her sleeping lover, she rose up to rest on an elbow cushioned amidst the dense blades of lush grasses that thinned only where overtaken by moss on the bank of a sweetly murmuring brook.

'Struth, Liam hadn't the golden hair of her race, nor had he either the azure or emerald eyes of her kind. But in Maedra's admittedly biased view he was infinitely more attractive. To her mind Liam was the answer to a fairy's desire for things neither one way nor another. After all, the strands of his thick hair encompassed the myriad shades between the deep umber of bark and the brightness of sun-bleached wheat while his eyes were constantly, subtly changing between the liquid brown of a doe's and the deep green of forest shadows.

Beyond Liam's physical charms, Maedra admired the courage this human had demonstrated even in the face of inexplicable dangers he could nowise understand. It was an admiration strengthened by his unquestionable sense of loyalty and the gentleness he'd demonstrated in his fond dealings with the human girl-child.

Maedra reached out to trail one slender forefinger over the curve of Liam's strong cheek and down his throat to the vulnerable dip at its base. Though their purpose for walking to this lovely little glade had been for the sake of seeing Liam's stallion watered and allowed to graze, they'd quickly lost track of that worthy beast.

Instead the two of them had settled into an easy flow of conversation which led to feelings shared and at length to the bittersweet lesson taught by a tender union of soul as well as body. Aye, bittersweet . . . their loving had tasted of the sweetest ambrosia but a bitter tang lingered in knowing such a union could never truly be hers for more than a few precious, stolen moments. Maedra felt the sorrow of a desolate future beginning to build and firmly bit her lip to still its trembling.

Liam had initially been nudged closer to wakening from satisfaction's warm slumber by a soft caress, but it wasn't till a crystal teardrop fell to his cheek that his eyes flew open.

"Sweet enchantress, why are you crying?" Her woeful expression hurt him like a physical blow. "Is the love of a mere human so disappointing?"

"Oh, no," Maedra instantly denied, leaning forward to brush a kiss across his lips as if to wipe away the taint of hurtful words. "I cry for what I most desperately want but which can never be mine."

Having touched in spirit, an interaction he hadn't dreamed remotely possible, Liam recognized what Maedra meant and immediately sought to show her the error in her thinking.

Gently pulling Maedra down to lie across his chest, Liam nuzzled and whispered into her ear,

"Surely anything is possible when two people love?"

Maedra buried her face beneath Liam's chin while tears streamed from azure eyes. His simple confidence left it too difficult for the fairy she was to justify a detailing for her human love of the many reasons why the hopeless dream of their relationship could never become a reality.

"Sweeting, don't cry." Liam brushed his mouth across the top of her golden head. "Your weeping tears at my heart."

Beneath comforting caresses and repeated tender kisses the desolate sounds slowly lessened. Once calm was restored, Liam gently rolled his ethereal beauty over to lie on her back. Lifting up on his forearms, he gazed down in awe of her beauty and in wonder that she claimed to love him as much as he loved her.

Marveling over so deep a bond between them that he shared her pain, Maedra reached up to brush fingertips over his lips. Liam caught the dainty hand and buried his mouth into its palm which in turn earned Maedra's immediate giggle of delight.

The ensuing game of enticing loveplay soon fanned hungry flames to a fever demanding more. But when Liam's mouth lowered to settle over Maedra's with renewed passionate intent, she inwardly confessed fear of the price for again welcoming the sweet fire of such temptations.

Yielding once more was almost certain to dangerously sap Maedra's already weakened ability to refuse the gift she wanted so badly but which would demand that too high a price be paid by too many others. To forestall this peril, she pushed Liam gently away and seized on an all too true excuse.

"It was morning when we left the cottage," Maedra reminded Liam, staring into eyes passion-darkened to purely brown. "But now the day is growing old. Lissan must be wondering, fretting about what happened to us. Best we hasten back to her side."

Liam rolled to lie facedown in cool sod while with the instantaneous speed of her breed Maedra rose fully dressed. Not wanting to further strain the mood of this companion doubtless as physically frustrated as she was, Maedra silently waited for him to compose himself. But when he rose to don his clothing with the slow actions required for humankind to perform this simple chore, she couldn't prevent her approving eyes from following his every move.

Neither Liam nor Maedra spared a moment's thought to question the stallion's absence before setting off toward the cottage. And it was the fact that no words were spoken throughout their entire return journey that increased an awkward tension stretching between the two who stared blindly into the distance ahead, into gloom on either side, or anywhere but at each other.

The moment Maedra stepped through the doorway and into the cottage, all personal woes were overwhelmed by horror over the waiting scene of wanton destruction. The chest that she knew Lissan treasured lay in ruins while the books which must have been stored inside were tattered and strewn haphazardly across the floor.

"Lissan?" a concerned Liam loudly called out, striding toward the hearth in the room's center. "Lissan, where are you?"

There was no answer and Maedra was immediately struck by guilt rare to a fairy. While quickly joining Liam's search, she berated herself for thinking first of damage to inanimate things rather than fearing for her friend's safety.

Separating to cover more potential locations, Liam went to make certain Lissan hadn't been trapped in the cellar as he had once been while Maedra climbed the flimsy ladder rising to a corner loft.

Maedra hadn't truly expected to find her friend in the loft but was dispirited as she descended to the hall once more. Admitting how unlikely it was for Lissan to be anywhere near, her shoulders slumped beneath the weight of a much greater guilt.

"Lissan isn't in the cellar," Liam announced, clearly worried as he stepped back into a gloomy cottage lacking the light of a well-tended fire.

"Nor here," Maedra responded while moving in the blink of an eye to stand two paces from Liam. "But if I hadn't failed in my duty, she would be."

Liam scowled but couldn't truthfully refute her words and compromised by saying, "'Struth, had we remained where we were posted, we could've guarded Lissan against any evil scheme."

Maedra nodded, choosing not to uselessly insult Liam by pointing out that while he'd only a stave and mortal strength to lend that task, her magical spell of protection was invincible . . . so long as she was near. She hadn't remained close to Lissan and that meant she alone must bear the blame.

With a stern smile meant to reassure, Liam announced, "I will find my errant horse and ride out to retrieve our lost mistress."

"No." Maedra quickly stepped forward to clasp Liam's arm. "Night approaches and too likely the same foes who took Lissan are waiting in the forest to capture anyone foolish enough to follow."

Knowing full well what a pitiful excuse this was, Maedra didn't expect it to restrain Liam from an honor-demanded duty for long. However, by the action Maedra also learned to what lengths she was willing to go to keep her love safe—despite her own intention of rushing off as soon as possible. She would hasten to the place Hildie's earlier warning suggested would be the most likely site of Lissan's dangerous captivity.

"If there are more enemies lurking in the forest," Liam tactfully began, stating logical arguments to support his proposed action. "Then surely 'tis all the more important that I lose no moment in seeing them exposed and defeated."

"Yes, my love." Maedra nodded with feigned meekness, knowing she had little choice but to agree and yet determined to keep him, at least, safely within the circle of her protective powers. "I will go with you but first let me restore this havoc to good order so that Lissan won't be greeted by this disheartening sight when we bring her home."

Maedra's assent, too easily given, left Liam slightly uncomfortable. Though doubting such responses were common for this magical being, he was more seriously concerned about losing time important for a successful rescue while she wasted it on the mundane task of tidying. Liam scowled yet since Maedra had yielded to him on the first matter, he could hardly refuse her this and shrugged a reluctant acceptance.

In the next instant, right in front of Liam's stunned gaze, Maedra took control of unseen forces. With sweeping motions accompanied by unintelligible words of haunting beauty she waved the chest's shattered pieces into floating unsupported. They hovered for brief moments before with a rushing noise rapidly fitting themselves so tightly together that no sign of axe-wreaked destruction remained.

Maedra continued her chore with further gestures and melodious words while the restored chest waited. This time sheets of paper, no longer torn and suddenly wrinkle free, danced through the air. They

came together to be rejoined between their covers—
books whole once again. Volumes thus revived next
seemed to march in unison and to a brisk tempo
arrange themselves neatly inside a chest that looked
brand-new.

With his fear of wasted time proven thoroughly
unnecessary, Liam gladly acknowledged himself a
fool to worry over Maedra's wish to accompany him
on the search for Lissan. She certainly had the right
and he could hardly fear her likely to face a danger
she couldn't easily defeat.

She was in the dungeon. Lissan stood on tiptoe,
striving to peer up through iron grating more than
an arm's length above her head—to no avail. Yes,
this was definitely Ailm Keep's dungeon.

With her love of history Lissan had read a good
deal about dungeons . . . while safe within the cozy
walls of her London library. She'd even visited one
or two while accompanying her mother on cultural
tours, joining the older woman to traipse through
ruined castles and the grand houses which in later
years had been built over a good many.

But nothing, absolutely *nothing* could prepare a
body for being rudely dumped down a hole in the
floor of a keep's bottom level and then abandoned
to the darkness and dank chill of moss-slimed stone
all around. Worse still, she could hear a disgusting
scuttling that she feared must be a whole platoon of
rats. Rats with beady eyes and sharp teeth. . . .

Having been stripped of all she'd been wearing by
the large woman quick to obey Morag's command,
for even meager warmth Lissan was left to pull tattered rags more closely about her shivering form—
whether from fear or cold it hardly mattered. Both
Lissan's disgust and despair deepened with the repeated memory of being as deftly stripped of op-

tions when even her mother's brooch was gleefully appropriated.

Robbed of that precious amulet, Lissan couldn't call for her father, and without his help there was no hope. Discouraged, Lissan sagged against an unpleasantly damp wall. Only Rory had the power to command an end to the planned burning of a witch; and, considering his suspicion of her, she feared that he wouldn't spare her life even were he to return to the keep in time.

Despite fervent wishes it seemed she wasn't destined to change the course of events printed in the history book rioters had surely destroyed. This gloomy thought greatly intensified Lissan's sense of desolation.

"No!" Straightening away from the wall, Lissan shouted the word. Though it was unlikely that anyone would hear or care if they did, she encouraged herself by shouting the word over and over again. She wouldn't give up so easily. The odds were undeniably, overwhelmingly against her. But surely, if the incredible events of recent days had taught her so much as a single lesson, it must be that anything, absolutely *anything*, was possible.

Determined to make the best of a wretched situation, Lissan began to stomp her feet. By the immediate flurry of scurrying noises she knew she'd put her unwelcome rodent companions to flight, at least for now, and that was a start.

"You've got to save her, Papa." Anxiety threatening unwelcome tears, Hildie tightly squeezed her father's hand. "You've got to!"

Rory gave the child a grim smile. Seemed there would be no end to this day's nasty revelations. First, he'd confirmed the massing of hostile troops all too near the border. Then when responding to

Hildie's scream, he'd found himself the target of his
own brother's deadly assault—a soon-fleeing
brother he hadn't had the heart to chase. Now, if
Hildie were to be believed, Lissan was in imminent,
mortal peril.

"Tell me again," Rory quietly demanded. "Tell me
what you saw and heard." Before he could act these
were things he must know.

Frustrated by any waste of precious time, Hildie
irritably snapped, "They mean to burn Lissan with
the setting sun. Look at the sky . . . don't you see it's
nearly sunset now!"

Though needless, Rory glanced into the western
sky. The sun's lower edge rested just above the horizon's dark silhouette. If what Hildie claimed was
true, and he didn't really think the earnest child lied,
they were already too late. With that truth, an abyss
of despair opened in his heart. Not even the fleetest
of stallions could carry him to Ailm Keep before the
sinking sun painted the sky with brilliant hues.

As if she'd eavesdropped on his thoughts, or perhaps they were her own, Rory heard Hildie implore,
"Please, Papa, please come with me and I'll take you
to someone who can instantly carry us both to Ailm
Keep."

Dubious, Rory sadly shook his head. And yet—
suffering his own painful frustration, deeply aware
of an unfamiliar and ghastly sense of helplessness—
he chose to lessen the child's distress by yielding this
small boon. He allowed small fingers to clutch his
and pull him toward mangled shrubbery crushed
during his escape from an earlier assailant.

Hildie ducked beneath low-hanging branches and
stepped over others sent crashing down by past
windstorms all while weaving around and through
thick trees and at the same time pulling her father
steadily up a hillside.

Even as Rory followed the agile child on her wild chase up the slope he realized that this desperate action emphasized a further truth. Although he no longer suspected Lissan was Henry of England's spy, even were she guilty of that and worse, he would give anything, risk anything to rescue his beloved.

Distracted by bleak thoughts, Rory was unprepared when Hildie came to an abrupt halt. He nearly tripped over the girl. Recovering his balance, Rory glanced up. Deep sapphire eyes widened in surprise for finding himself unexpectedly standing on the outer edge of the fairy's ring of magical flowers.

"Come, Papa," Hildie softly begged, again tugging at his hand as she placed first one foot and then another safely on the vibrant floral band's far side. "Step inside with me."

Rory met the wistful child's earnest stare with a wry smile but again yielded to her surely foolish plea, taking equal care not to trample the enchanted circle's beautiful blossoms while joining her there.

As silence stretched, the first ominous streaks of rose-tinged gold began to glow on the western horizon. Rory felt as if sunset's vivid shades were an assault of sharp blows. They were a condemnation of him for wasting precious moments coming here that should have been given a determined attempt to rescue the incredible woman he loved, even if doomed to fail.

To tame his growing rage against the fate that had brought him so wondrous a creature as Lissan only to steal her back so soon, Rory grated out a pointed question. "What are we waiting for?"

"It's who and you will see." Despite the emotional turmoil radiating from her father, Hildie tried to remain confident and promptly dropped to sit cross-legged beneath the young oak.

Rory lowered himself to rest at Hildie's side, earnestly wishing her childish faith in fairy tales and magic had a basis in fact.

"Why have you come?"

The deep and utterly unexpected voice shocked Rory. His head snapped around to meet a gaze as brilliant a green as Lissan's. Their owner stood only a step behind and Rory immediately leapt to his feet to boldly face the other's unblinking stare. But, having no answer to the question, Rory didn't speak.

"It's Lissan," Hildie blurted out, clambering up to hover uncertainly between two powerful males.

"What?" The newcomer's attention dropped to narrow on the young speaker. "What have you to tell me about my daughter?"

Rory's penetrating gaze scrutinized the unearthly being whose sudden arrival, words, and appearance suggested that—like the vulnerable innocence he'd wrongly doubted—Lissan's claim of an otherworldly heritage was equally true.

Intent on her goal, Hildie was oblivious to the undercurrents flowing between her companions. "The wretched Morag whipped the people into a frenzy with wild tales of the devil's wicked spawn and a witch's sinister powers. She has them believing Lissan the soul of all things evil and they mean to burn her at the stake as a witch."

"When?" Comlan thundered, golden brows crashing together like flashes of lightning.

Though shaken by the power of his fury, Hildie would've found the courage to answer had Rory not shielded her by providing the information demanded.

"At sunset in the courtyard of Ailm Keep . . .

CHAPTER 16

Though standing within a ring of undeniably charmed flowers, Rory glared suspiciously at the golden stranger who had ordered him to move nearer and close his eyes. Rory had taken commands from no man since he'd left childhood behind. Not even the young king whom he had trained in the methods of battle and use of royal power would dare such a deed without first consulting him. Except, of course, under such dire circumstances as Alister's return with news of an invasion.

"Come." Comlan's demand was curt as he impatiently motioned for the obedience of a dark lord refusing to be intimidated even by mystical powers this human must surely realize far outreached his own. "We've no moment to waste."

This repeated order struck Rory with renewed horror. How could he risk again being the cause of a foolish delay raising the prospect of failing Lissan when she needed him most? While Rory promptly stepped closer to the amazing visitor as tall as himself, he cast a quick glance toward Hildie who waited on the man's other side with eyes shut tightly.

In the same moment that lashes settled on his

cheeks, Rory could've sworn he felt the slight brush of a cape swirling around him but that sensation was so quickly come and gone he couldn't be certain. It was followed by a faint but instantaneous shift in temperature and the sudden awareness of something more solid than turf beneath his feet. However, even if he'd had the inclination and time to spare for further exploration of these matters, such an intention would've been crushed by the shock of what awaited when his eyes opened in response to a child's horrified cries.

"No-o-o—" Hildie wailed. "No-o-o—" Her pitiful screams were lost in the crazed shouts and cheers of a frenzied mob.

Flying beyond figures madly dancing around a carefully built pyre, Rory's penetrating gaze narrowed on the stake to which Lissan was firmly bound while completely enveloped in flames.

The ghastly sight scattered into obscurity any thought of the impossible feat performed to instantly transport both a man and child from fairy ring to this landing at the first bend of Ailm Keep's entrance stairway. Rory's muscles instantly coiled in preparation for a dash to Lissan's aid, but the unaccountable power of a golden being froze both his intended action and the thunderous command for an immediate halt poised at the tip of his tongue.

Comlan silently motioned for his two human companions to look more closely at the dreadful sight. Despite grim reluctance they instinctively complied . . . just in time to view the unfolding of a further miracle, one every bit as shocking to the king of the Tuatha de Danann as to any mortal present.

Lissan's firmly tied bonds disintegrated into useless ashes while Rory scowled and Hildie gasped, as did a great many others. Comlan slowly shook his head. That his daughter was special he had never doubted and yet what he had just witnessed should, by the rules governing his realm, be impossible for a being only half-fairy to survive.

"There must be more of my fairy nature in Lissan than I thought possible," Comlan softly mused without intending to be heard. "She couldn't elsewise have survived the flames."

When both Rory and Hildie cast him a curious glance, Comlan responded with a wry smile before disappearing as abruptly as he'd arrived on the hilltop.

In the courtyard below Lissan had expected to die in the fire and was amazed by the cool breeze she found at the firestorm's center. Using neatly stacked bundles of kindling as a stairway, she gracefully descended unscathed from the site of her intended murder.

The once-wild crowd, shocked into silence, fell back in terror yet found they couldn't flee once their intended victim began to speak.

"Though Morag would have you believe it true, I am *not* the devil's wicked spawn."

After a quick glance around proved the cunning woman in question had already escaped, Lissan focused on the grey-haired gentleman who she'd learned during the debacle in the cottage was named Noel. Noel, it had seemed, was someone rational enough to demand proof supporting the charges against her.

"Rather," Lissan firmly stated in a voice that would carry to all. "I am a child of the Tuatha de Danann."

Lissan paused, allowing listeners time to grasp the full import of her words. Next she turned and approached the mob's brawny leader, Padraig. Again at his side was the large woman who had left Lissan with rags after taking a "witch's" belongings.

"I have come as the White Witch foretold by a Druid seeress and with me bring an earnest desire to see Connaught rise victorious over Munster's dishonorable ambitions."

The pair facing Lissan immediately nodded while, as one, their sheepish gazes dropped to the trampled dirt at their feet. She turned and started to walk in a slow circuit around the still-blazing pyre. Despite deepening shadows of dusk, by firelight she saw shame and sincere regret on the faces of people still gathered in a motionless ring.

"Though I came to help, I'll not remain where my presence is an abhorrence." Lissan stopped at near the point where she had begun and asked a solemn question. "So with honesty tell me now, will you accept my support or shall I begone?"

Silence fell on the once-crazed mob whose ranks, Lissan was all too aware, had been swollen by a frightening number of guardsmen returning from patrol, but their shamefaced expressions spoke volumes.

"My lady—" It was Noel, the respected leader nearly ignored by the throng during their hours of madness, who stepped forward to speak for the whole. "Pray forgive us for being so easily misled by a truly wicked woman's treachery."

Lissan responded with a gentle smile and soft words. "There is nothing to forgive when it's so clear that the sinister inspiration for the deed came not from your hearts but from another's."

Noel's relieved grin laid a warm wreath of wrinkles around his mouth. "I know I speak for all when I promise that your support is heartily welcomed. And more, we'll pray that you might be willing to remain with us forevermore."

The hearty chorus of agreement quickly filling the courtyard lifted Lissan's spirits to a pinnacle as high in reverse proportion as the depths of the abyss into which they'd earlier fallen.

Comlan knew that in this event's excitement he'd already been forgotten by the two humans he'd whisked to its site. And though he'd purposefully become invisible to all of their kind, he remained long enough to watch as his daughter proved more than capable of dealing with any challenge in this barbaric world—at least for now. Once thus reassured, he gladly returned to his own realm and the beloved Amy waiting for him there.

Not until the crowd began to disperse did Lissan at last answer the call for her attention more powerful for being voiceless. Her emerald gaze glanced up to find an intimidating sight—Rory high on the keep's stairway, powerful legs firmly braced and mighty arms crossed over a broad chest while dark eyes penetrating even at this distance stared at her unblinking.

Had Rory been there the whole time? Under the many uncomfortable implications of that possibility Lissan's heart thumped erratically. Was he disappointed that she had thwarted Morag's intent? Worse, infinitely worse, had it been his plan, too?

In an instant the flash of a potent smile brimming with sincere relief scattered foolish apprehensions like thistledown by a steady breeze. And when Rory held his arms out to her, Lissan raced across the courtyard oblivious to both the pyre she had thought would kill and the penitent good wishes of those who'd put her there. She felt as light as if carried by moonbeams although that silvery orb had yet to rise.

Rory stepped to the ground in time to welcome Lissan into a loving embrace with fervent gratitude for her safety. That this incredible woman had as miraculously descended unharmed from a ferocious vortex of fire as she'd survived a broadsword's deadly blow was assuredly cause enough to marvel. But nearly as amazing was the fact that with her most recent demonstration of magical abilities she'd won the loyalty of a people who never gave it lightly.

Gladly wrapped in Rory's powerful arms, Lissan tilted a bright head back to gaze into his handsome face and inquire, "How long have you been here?"

"Not long enough to prevent that ghastly scene—" Regret darkened sapphire eyes to become near all of black. "Although it was our goal."

Lissan let the mention of "our" pass temporarily unquestioned in order to ask something she viewed more important. "But *how* did you get here?"

"Your father brought us," a small voice piped up. Hildie had followed Rory down the steps but at the considerably slower pace required by a child's shorter legs.

Lissan glanced to the side and found her solemn young friend standing very near. The girl's answer was an explanation yet hardly complete.

"But how did you—" Lissan began again only to be interrupted by an impishly grinning Hildie.

"I led *my* father to the fairy ring and there we waited for *yours* to arrive." Hildie was so pleased with herself for succeeding in this venture that her delight bubbled over into a small giggle. "And, just as you promised, he did."

"Not *my* promise, *his*." Lissan made the correction before with an approving smile adding, "But it was certainly clever of you to put that memory to good use in securing necessary aid."

" 'Struth, very clever," Rory agreed, giving Hildie a wink even as he swept Lissan completely off her feet. "And now I'll thank you kindly to use those sharp wits to consider well the unwelcome impro-

priety of intruding on the privacy I intend to be
shared by only Lissan and myself."

Far from offended by this less than subtle demand
that she leave them alone, Hildie's spirits soared. Occasional giggles escaped as she watched her father
steadily carry his prize up the long stairway, moving
beyond even the great hall's entrance to the outer
portal of his private chambers one level above.

Lissan, initially uneasy at being lifted and cradled
against the devastating man while the focus of attention, glanced upward and was immediately overwhelmed by the power of his midnight gaze.
Wrapped in an intimate embrace and separated by
so scant a distance, reality narrowed dramatically to
include only herself and the man into whose strong
arms she gladly yielded.

Delving into the intriguing mysteries of emerald
depths, Rory tumbled into a sweet, private world of
promised delights. And though continuing to steadily climb, he found himself firmly snared in this beguiling woman's thrall.

After a door was at last opened and Rory ducked
beneath its low frame, tendrils of enchantment eased
sufficiently for Lissan to realize they'd reached his
chosen destination. As Rory lowered her into a chair
already host to several cushions, she inwardly marveled at the strength of this man able to carry her
up so long and steep a flight of steps without any
sign of fatigue, not even a shortness of breath. No
man in Lissan's world, not even her too often sed-
entary brothers, could have done the same.

With a wry smile of self-mockery, Rory cautioned
himself that to sit too near the exquisite beauty
would be to shatter a strategist's most basic tenet—
never willingly be placed in a position of vulnerability. Considering the vines of intoxicating awareness already stretched taut between them, a

temptingly close proximity would almost certainly strangle any hope for a necessary conversation. Wary of the danger in this powerful physical attraction, Rory chose to sit in a matching chair positioned more than an arm's length away from her and immediately began.

"Your promise to the people, despite their mistreatment of you, proves you more than worthy of their admiration and respect—" Rory heard a distinct lack of praise in these words and without a moment wasted on the careful forethought for which he was famed, quickly added, "Sentiments I share."

Under this sincere approval Lissan's cheeks flooded with the heat of a blush once rare but of recent days ever more common. Nonetheless, she met and held the dark intensity of his gaze while making an earnest inquiry.

"Then you too will accept my support in the goal of defeating Munster?"

"Gladly," Rory promptly answered. "But for the sake of avoiding duplicate efforts wasted, I do ask that you share your intentions with me, the better to see our plans smoothly coordinated."

Lissan nodded without hesitation although as yet she had only the vaguest of ideas as to the nature of those intentions. After nibbling her lip for a brief time and gazing at the single candle apparently lit earlier in anticipation of the lord's return, she asked a vital question of her own.

"Before I can devise and then share firm intentions with you, there are things I must know. Are we certain in exactly what form the danger from Munster will arrive? And do we know from precisely which direction it will come?"

Rory instantly brushed aside the last tenuous threads of the foolish web woven in his mind by previous suspicions and incredulous distrust. This action freed him to give Lissan a full account of all that he knew on the matter.

"King Muirtrecht of Munster sent a warning—part of which I verified earlier today." Rory went on to first tell of armies massing just beyond Connaught's borders, then continued to speak of Alister and explain the role played by that onetime slave in seeing a threatening message delivered.

While Lissan pondered these revelations, Rory calmly shared another . . . one that concerned her. "Just as we sent an imposter into Munster, they sent one to us for much the same purpose."

Distracted by important facts already learned, Lissan was only half listening but absently nodded.

Although the urge to drop the issue here was strong, Rory forced himself to go on. "Munster's infiltrator carried a letter purporting to be from King Henry of England . . . and addressed to you."

"Me?" Lissan gasped, delicate brows arching to meet golden curls fallen forward on her brow. This news made very clear how difficult it must have been for Rory to risk trusting her.

"I've never met the man!" Lissan rushed to reassure her partner in a newly formed alliance. "Nor, I can swear, has he ever in his life heard of me."

"Of that I have no doubt," Rory flatly stated. "However, to my shame I must admit it was my own stubborn cynicism which too long prevented me from realizing that by saving my life you'd proven the letter a sham even before it was intercepted."

"Yes, you should've known—" Lissan's teasing grin robbed stern words of their sting. "Just as I ought to have recognized Morag's spite in lies told to turn me against you . . . tales of trollops habitually kept for your convenience in Tuatha Cottage."

"What?" The disclosure startled a bark of laughter

from Rory. "That home has been inhabited by Hildie's family for many generations."

"Yes." Lissan solemnly nodded while only the corners of her lips tilted slightly upward in a rueful smile. "So the child later told me."

With their relationship growing more comfortable—though she didn't know whether because or despite of the never-faltering bond between them—Lissan dared to ask Rory another more personal question. One she'd asked before. "Is Hildie your daughter?"

Rory's warm smile slid into cynicism but a cynicism neither directed toward her nor bearing a cruel edge. "Hildie looks very like me, a fortunate fact which protects her from unjustified attacks."

This wasn't exactly an answer but Lissan chose to patiently wait.

"Aye," Rory repeated, holding emerald eyes with his penetrating gaze. "She looks like me . . . but like her father, too."

Lissan's brow furrowed for only a moment before the obvious explanation mocked her folly in not earlier recognizing Donal as Hildie's true father.

"My brother—coddled far, far too long—takes what he wants with no thought given to the consequences others must pay." Rory shook his head in slow disdain. "Hildie's mother was generous with warm fairy tales but shared with the girl nothing of her father."

Rory paused long enough to organize facts into pithy statements. "Of course, any who saw the girl came to their own conclusions and gossip spread. Then, when she was left all alone in the world by her mother's death, Hildie's neighbors deemed it only proper to deliver the child to my keep."

Lissan listened intently, eyes widened by a story as intriguing as any fairy tale she could remember.

"They waited until the great hall was filled for the evening meal before leading Hildie to stand below the dais while introducing her as my daughter. Though I knew she was not my child, I also knew whose she must be just as clearly as everyone else would were I to publicly deny her mine."

Lissan saw what a quandary Rory had found himself in through no fault of his own and could easily guess at the frustration and doubtless irritation he'd suffered in dealing with the impossible situation.

"Although a hardened warrior—" Rory concluded his account of Hildie's arrival in his life. "I discovered that I wasn't heartless enough to abandon the young innocent to Morag's far from tender mercies."

By the close of Rory's amazing account, Lissan's admiration for him increased severalfold.

Rory, after having talked openly of his family, turned his attention to Lissan's. "As Hildie told you, during the course of this day's events, I met your father." Smiling ruefully, he added, "With the experience I came to accept that he truly is the King of the Tuatha de Danann and can only pray you'll forgive me for finding it too implausible before?"

"Easily." Lissan gave Rory a sweet smile. "Though you found it difficult to believe, consider how nearly impossible that same task was for me. After living two decades in a safe and prosaic world, I tumbled through time and survived a broadsword's blow only to be given the shocking, never remotely suspected news of my half-fairy blood!"

Candlelight rippled over black hair as Rory slowly shook his head. "I wouldn't have believed it."

"Nor did I, at first," Lissan immediately agreed. "And it would've been just as well had I never known considering that I am only half fairy—a split-blood—and lack their magical powers."

"Lack their powers?" Rory gently scowled at Lissan. "Hah! When you stepped free of the fire unharmed, your father said there is more of him in you than even he had thought possible."

A small pleased smile curled Lissan's lips. Though she hadn't had time to pause and wonder about her escape from the flames her father said only a true fairy could survive, Lissan was warmed by the thought that her link to his heritage was so strong.

Of a sudden Lissan realized that by telling Rory she had no fairy powers, he might doubt her ability to help in his fight to protect Connaught. Or, worse, he might demand the kind of detailed explanations for her actions that currently she neither could nor (even if she knew) would dare provide.

To tilt the subject away from perilous ground, Lissan quickly added, "At first I kept thinking I would wake up—but never did."

Until this moment, Rory hadn't paused to consider how unpleasant his world might seem to someone from a place in the future likely as filled with wonders as her father's Fairy Realm must be. How could Lissan bear to linger here? With that question Rory was immediately struck by a painful prospect too certain to materialize. She would return to her own, leave him here grieving over his foredoomed love lost.

"When does your father intend to escort you back to your London home?" Rory held his voice utterly emotionless as he bit out the despicable question whose answer he so little wanted to hear that he quickly asked another. "Will you linger long enough to fulfill your promise and help Connaught defeat Munster?"

Lissan cringed, face instantly drained of color. Because Rory calmly assumed she would leave, it was clear that he cared little whether or no she remained in his world. It felt as if the broadsword blow once escaped had now struck in earnest—not a clean slice but ragged and excruciatingly painful. Silent tears like liquid crystal escaped through tightly clenched lashes.

The sight of Lissan's pain devastated Rory. He jumped up to kneel before her chair and pull her urgently into his arms, raining comforting kisses over soaked lashes, damp cheeks, and trembling lips.

"We're too late," Liam groaned while Maedra buried her face against his chest. Too late, even though they'd located his horse with all possible haste and then spurred the poor animal into galloping the whole way to the foot of Ailm Keep's motte. From there, with the ethereal Maedra shielded inside the voluminous folds of Liam's dark cloak, they had quickly made their way into the courtyard.

It was dusk, that mysterious time of fading light between sunset and full darkness, and from their present viewpoint amid shadows just inside the stable's doorway the sad truth of the bitter price paid for their failure to arrive sooner was clear. Its irrefutable evidence lay in a smoldering pyre reduced to glowing coals across which lay remnants of the stout stake to which Lissan must have been bound.

With the acute senses of fairykind, Maedra knew precisely what depth of guilt Liam was suffering and ached for him although his distress mirrored her own. Had they not yielded to selfish desires this morn, they could've prevented a terrible wrong.

Maedra nestled more closely against Liam. Her remorse was deepened by awareness that had she not foolishly shirked the hours of practice necessary to hone skills, this tragedy could have been avoided. Though perfectly able to carry someone into or out of any structure in the blink of an eye, she couldn't transport even herself alone any great distance. A being as powerful as King Comlan could whisk them both from cottage to keep in less time than required for a shooting star to cross the night sky. With practice, she might have been able to do the same.

"Liam, have you just arrived?" Approaching from the rear of the stable, an older guardsman gruffly called out to the back of a young man he could nearly swear hadn't been part of the sunset debacle . . . and yet how could that be when the lad had been posted at Tuatha Cottage?

Disconcerted when the female in his arms simply vanished, Liam turned to find his questioner's gaze filled with an alarming suspicion.

"I . . . I . . . ." Flustered at having no real idea of precisely what circumstances he'd stumbled into, Liam fought to stammer out an excuse he hoped would sound plausible despite having no vague notion for what the excuse was intended to cover. "That is, Lord Rory stopped in at the cottage this morn and ordered me to check the bridge, its supports and surroundings, then come to bring him my report."

The man nodded a head of thinning hair. That Liam hadn't been present and likely hadn't yet heard an account of the shameful event explained his bewilderment. Still, the lad had best be warned.

"Considering all that's happened, your time at the cottage must surely be at an end. That being so, I counsel you to seek out the guard captain for a reassignment as soon as possible." The man bent nearer, as if meaning to share a secret although the volume of his voice did not lessen. "Rumor has it that an invasion is imminent."

Liam gravely nodded and watched the other man stride from the stable.

The instant Liam's inquisitor disappeared, Maedra reappeared. "I've walked through the pyre's coals and can swear that neither Lissan nor any other human perished there."

"Of course not."

Maedra and Liam turned in unison to meet Hildie's impish grin, bright even in the twilight dimness of an unlighted stable.

"Lissan simply walked free, untouched by the flames."

Maedra's eyes widened for an instant before a brilliant smile bloomed on soft lips. "Of course! Lissan *is* King Comlan's daughter."

Having yet to meet the king of the Faerie Realm, Liam had no basis from which to truly comprehend this statement. However, after all that he'd seen and learned in Maedra's company, he would no longer assume anything was impossible.

"Where is Lissan now?" Maedra asked of Hildie.

"With my father in private chambers above the hall."

With a grin at least as impish as ever Hildie's own, Maedra swirled the cloak she wore around its owner. The pair of them disappeared.

Now she'd done it. . . . Hildie grimaced, gazing up to where tiny gleams of light escaped through the shutters of a single small window high, very high on the keep's wall.

"Lissan . . . Lissan. . . ."

This call from so near, which should've been impossible without his permission to enter, effectively pulled Rory back from the exquisite colleen trembling in his arms. Over his shoulder he sent a freez-

ing glance like a bolt of black ice to unwelcome
intruders.

While it had no effect at all on Maedra, the man
at her side was instantly flooded with an embarrassed crimson so bright that he nearly glowed.

Lissan peeked around a broad back purposely positioned to shield her from prying eyes. On seeing
who their uninvited visitors were, she recognized
just as clearly how the pair had managed to make
so abrupt and poorly timed an appearance.

"Who are you?" Rory demanded. "And what are
you doing in my *private* chambers?"

"This is my friend Maedra," Lissan smoothly answered, taking the lead for the sake of calming an
impending confrontation before it could escalate.

"But why is she here?" With the question Rory's
harsh glare returned to Lissan only to immediately
soften on the vision of a temptingly rumpled beauty
whose lips were a deep rose and still slightly swollen from the passion of his kisses.

Lissan lightly trailed her fingertips over Rory's
brow, smoothing his frown away while quietly explaining. "When first I arrived, just as you assigned
Liam to guard me, my father soon sent Maedra to
ensure the same goal."

Rory responded with a faint growl—plainly
meant for the sole purpose of indicating that her explanation of the woman's presence in Connaught
was inadequate to account for why she was in precisely this place.

Knowing it was fortunate since she'd no answer
to give, Lissan was grateful when Liam spoke up for
the first time.

"First person I met on reaching the keep tonight
hastened to share a distressing rumor." Terribly uncomfortable with having so rudely intruded on his
lord, Liam stammered out the only excuse that came

quick to mind. "He said that people are whispering about an imminent invasion."

" 'Tis true." Rory saw no reason to avoid the subject when he must soon summon his warriors and plan strategies to meet the threat. He rose to his feet and turned to face his young guardsman. "Troops are massing all along Munster's border while King Muirtrecht has sent warning of his intent to lead an invading force."

"But it makes no sense—" Liam frowned in bewilderment. "Why does he warn when the act robs him of surprise's weapon?"

"Our King Turlough thinks it proof that bloated pride has driven the King of Munster mad. But by my acquaintance with and knowledge of Muirtrecht's methods I've come to believe the warning's purpose carefully conceived.

"Muirtrecht assuredly knows that we've long expected his attack and have erected defenses to meet it. Thus, any attempt he makes at surprise cannot succeed as an effective weapon." Rory's faint smile was grim. "On the reverse side, Muirtrecht might rightfully believe the strategy of boldly announcing his intent to launch an assault with the sunrise following Whitsunday sufficient to rouse more useful emotions in his foes. And either terror of an invader so confident or the unjustified relaxation of defenses against someone so foolish might prove weapons of more value than an unlikely surprise."

Liam solemnly nodded understanding and agreement with the assumptions of his lord, a great tactician himself.

Whitsunday? Lissan silently gasped. This she hadn't earlier heard even though the fact was of critical importance since that date loomed perilously near. There was no time to be lost.

Lissan immediately stood up, absently smoothing

the tattered skirt of pitiful castoffs still worn. An immediate return to the cottage was imperative. There the rescue of all that could be saved from the mob's attempted destruction of her trunk and its contents must begin at once.

Her best hope for finding means from the future to help her friends surely lay in those books. She refused to be daunted by the prospect of too many hours of serious labor required to restore any small measure of order to the chaos. But order she must have before she could begin the true search for methods to aid Rory in seeing Connaught not only survive Munster's threatened invasion but defeat their foes. And order she *would* have.

CHAPTER 17

"Enter," Mael irritably called out in answer to a knock on the door of his private solar and glared at the offending portal as if daring it to open the way for further ill-tidings. More he didn't need! Not while already feeling unfairly abused by far too many unreasonable expectations, the inadequacies of his subordinates, and the sudden, unaccountable irrationality of his king.

Morag stepped boldly into the chamber, refusing to let her manner betray a recent, critical defeat.

"Oh, it's *you.*" Mael nearly spat out the unwelcoming words. "I should've expected your arrival after your husband slunk into my hall like a pitiful sewer rat evicted from the moat."

"Donal's here?" The flatness of Morag's voice made the words more a disagreeable statement than question.

Morag had slipped safely away from Ailm Keep at the first sign that her golden-haired prey would escape a carefully plotted death. Aye, she'd gotten safely away—but at a cost. Being early gone, Morag had no way to know the outcome of Donal's assigned task. The lack of that information left hope that at least his part of the plan would succeed. And had Rory indeed been dispatched, her lost ground could've been recovered.

Now all was lost. Morag's already thin lips further compressed while a black scowl descended over grey eyes gone to storm-cloud darkness. Donal's presence here in Munster made that fact disgustingly clear.

Ever one to take joy in another's misfortunes, more so those of this overbearing creature, Mael's vicious grin deepened. "For someone who claims magical powers, you have a most appalling history of failure."

That was twice! Storm-cloud eyes suddenly flashed with lightning bolts of rage. Twice now this wretched cur had dared denigrate her powers. Soon—not this instant while in need of his hospitality but very soon—she would teach him a painful lesson in the stupidity of doubting her unearthly abilities.

Though night lay full upon them, Lissan hesitated with her hand on Tuatha Cottage's entrance latch while Liam and Maedra hovered at her back. A too vivid memory of the depressing chaos left behind when unwillingly hauled away by an angry mob led her to dread the renewed sight.

Reaching from behind, Maedra placed her hand over Lissan's and pushed the door open.

Stunned emerald eyes widened—not because of the expected revival of an unpleasant shock but in response to the delightful discovery visible by the glow of a banked fire. For near the first time since her adventure in this world began, Lissan found herself blessed with a welcome surprise.

Rushing forward and sinking to her knees, Lissan leaned forward to rest one cheek against a trunk not merely miraculously restored but now in rather better condition than when she'd last seen it whole. Very well aware that no human could've performed this miracle, Lissan turned and sent Maedra a tender smile of sweet gratitude.

"There's more," Liam hastened to announce, beaming with pride for his Maedra's wondrous abilities. "Look inside."

Too impatient to wait for Lissan to act, he stepped forward and lifted the heavy chest's arched lid.

Lissan sighed in pure delight. Her treasured books also were again as whole as their once-shattered case. This amazing fact gave her confidence in the possibility of attaining important goals.

"By this gift you've not only restored these *things*—" Lissan offered quiet gratitude to Maedra. "But you've rejuvenated my hopes for putting the knowledge these books contain to good use in aiding Connaught's defeat of Munster."

Though Maedra had acted merely to lessen her friend's troubles, she was happy to think that the action might also help Liam who would doubtless take part in any struggle between the two mortal kingdoms.

Lissan's attention returned to the chest. She began sorting through the books inside, pulling out those most likely to be of practical use in her quest, and carefully stacking them along the pallet's edge.

After settling on the straw mattress, Lissan was soon surrounded by volumes thumbed through and then gently scattered across a blanket-covered surface. Neither books on abstract mathematics nor medical texts were promising sources for tactics useful in warfare. The same was true of bound scientific papers on odd and mostly worthless chemical compounds. Absorbed in research, she didn't notice when her companions disappeared.

Ever conscious of unbreakable parameters that

forbade altering the flow of time, Lissan grew discouraged while considering—and rejecting—an increasingly desperate list of ideas. She daren't try to explain the mechanics of dirigibles hundreds of years before the principles of lighter-than-air flight could possibly be understood; couldn't formulate dynamite without a fully equipped lab; couldn't even show her confederates how to make simpler bombs. . . . Or could she?

A slow smile spread across soft lips. Were the required materials available? Potassium nitrate, charcoal, and sulfur. Yes, these elements could be obtained—with a little help. It was true that she could neither teach nor leave such technology in their hands. However, she'd already proven her unusual abilities by surviving a broadsword's blow and fire. Surely after viewing such amazing events both her allies and their foes would believe that the sudden, loud eruption of fire and smoke were merely a further example of her mysterious powers.

Now with this specific goal in mind, Lissan refocused attention on her books. After rapidly leafing through the pages of several she located precisely what she was looking for: a recipe listing the correct proportions of ingredients for the making of gunpowder. Black powder was the oldest of explosives but unknown in 1115.

Though pleased with her find, Lissan realized that before devising a strategy for the explosive's actual use, it would be prudent to concoct a small bomb. She could practice with it to be certain everything would work as planned.

Lissan scrambled to her feet, intending a search for Liam and Maedra whose help she'd ask to identify the best and nearest sources of required elements. However, since Liam, before leaving, had prodded the hearth's fire to renewed life, her hasty movements were cast into long, wavering shadows across the wall by the flickering flames behind. The unexpected, eerie sight startled Lissan into an abrupt halt.

It was the middle of the night and her friends deserved their well-earned rest. Lissan was weary herself and, although Whitsunday loomed near, the first steps toward fulfilling her promise and overcoming Munster's challenge could wait for morning.

Despite the extremely late hour in which Lissan had repacked the chest with books before dousing her candle to welcome sleep, she was awake before the full glory of dawn painted an eastern sky.

Lissan reached for the pegs from which hung a severely limited wardrobe further reduced by the taking of the gown stripped from her the day past. That thought was an unpleasant reminder of a more distressing event. However, it wasn't until she moved aside the tattered gown in which she'd been "burned" that the ache of a greater loss struck.

The brooch once her mother's had also been taken and was too precious to easily surrender. She must find the woman and ask for its return. Only if that failed would she take the matter to Rory.

Lissan gave her head a sharp shake. She was vexed with herself for allowing anything to divert attention from the critical task at hand. Even looking for the woman holding a treasured amulet would have to wait. Matters far more important than personal belongings had to be given priority.

Lissan donned the brown homespun gown Rory had brought on her first morning spent in this cottage. It was dowdy and too large but practical. With a busy schedule of uncertain tasks that must be accomplished today, practical might be the wisest choice. It was a decision reinforced by the fact that she had only one other option: the white dimity dress highly impractical for the waiting task despite having survived a broadsword's blow untouched.

"Come," Lissan called out in answer to the faint tapping on the cottage door that began just as she finished settling excess cloth over the braided belt riding on her hips.

"Good morrow, mistress," Liam said as the door swung open. "Have you had sufficient time with your books to know what you would have of us?"

"Yes, I have found my answer." Lissan nodded, gratitude for this wholehearted and easily given support blooming in her tender smile. "It's one whose purpose can't possibly be accomplished without aid I'd greatly appreciate."

"Then where do we begin?" Liam enthusiastically asked while Maedra hovered behind, barely seen save for her moonglow aura.

"There are three elements that I will need in goodly quantities." Lissan's hopes for success rose in response to his cheerfulness.

"What are they?" Maedra asked, moving to stand at Liam's side.

Though casting her fairy friend a quick smile, Lissan didn't answer directly. Rather she turned to question Liam. "Please tell me whether there are limestone caves on your coastline."

After a quiet moment's thought, Liam responded. "Several small ones but none of any great size."

"Small will do." Lissan quickly nodded. "So long as they're large enough for someone to enter."

"No one of my size," the young man regretfully admitted. "Nor, I fear, even yours."

Lissan immediately looked to Maedra who could surely whisk herself inside any small space.

"I would gladly do anything to help you ... if I could." The other female shifted uneasily. "But you must know I can't—" she gazed anxiously into emerald eyes. "You must remember what I earlier explained about fairy limitations in your world?"

Again Lissan nodded but more slowly while her smile faded along with sinking hopes.

"As one from among the Tuatha de Danann," Maedra unhappily restated, "I can never intervene in matters destined to affect human battles."

"Hildie could climb down into the caves," Liam announced, triumphantly slicing through the women's gloom. " 'Tis an agile little thing she be."

Lissan was uncomfortably aware that the more people from this time who became involved in her actions, the greater the danger of history being changed by facts learned before their time. However, since the child already knew about Lissan's background . . .

"Before we go off in search of Hildie"—Lissan meant to rectify her error in not beginning this endeavor by effectively organizing the use of time with choices likely to prove fruitful—"there's another task we should first set in motion, one able to continue untended while we move on to fill other needs."

Curious, Liam silently nodded.

"Clear an area of the garden." Lissan knew how difficult this chore would be for Liam and earnestly wished it wasn't necessary but . . . "Leave only a wide circle of bare earth."

Regret darkened Liam's eyes to doe-brown. He had labored over the gardens since the first day of his assignment here. Under his long hours of steady toil, the fields were very nearly restored to productivity and the notion of destroying his handiwork was most unpleasant.

Despite her empathy, Lissan ruefully continued. "Once that's done, throw logs from the woodpile into the center. Toss, don't neatly pile them."

Lissan's two companions looked bewildered, and she wished it were possible to help them understand. However, if she gave an explanation for even this simple method of securing charcoal in great measure, she'd likely be expected to explain the more complex actions yet to be undertaken in the creation of gunpowder. And she absolutely could not divulge scientific facts that must wait for later generations to comprehend.

Despite the certainty that her next directions would confuse them further, Lissan stoically ordered, "Dig a ditch around the pile, shoveling dirt atop logs and leaving an opening only large enough for a fire to be lit."

Liam and Maedra exchanged a glance which made it perfectly clear they suspected their friend had truly gone witless.

Fearing the pair's doubts would mislead them into failing her in this critical challenge, Lissan urged them to begin immediately by announcing that she was ready to get the task under way.

By the time a brilliant sun neared its zenith the chore was all but finished—at the cost of blistered hands and aching backs. Even Maedra joined in the physical toil although, without restraints imposed upon her in the human world, she could've seen the deed done with the flick of her hand.

The two women stepped back to eye their work— a steep, unnatural hill. As they watched, Liam bent forward and from an iron kettle poured glowing coals taken from the cottage's hearth through a small opening in the side of the mound.

"What are you doing?" By speaking from behind, Hildie startled the three intent on their handiwork. "And why?" Deep blue eyes peered suspiciously at the strange formation that definitely hadn't been there the previous day.

Elated by the completion of this one chore at least, Lissan's bright laughter danced on the day's still air. "You ask too many questions."

"Aye," Liam agreed, adding in mock disgust, "That this elfling does and always has."

"And I'll pester you again and again," Hildie jestingly threatened with a fierce scowl, "until you give me the answers."

"Oh, no!" Lissan's hands immediately flew up as if to ward off some hideous, ravening beast while at the same time offering answers to appease its hungry demands. "This is a charcoal pit and the first step in my plan to aid your father's goal of repelling Munster's invasion."

Hildie nodded knowingly, despite a faint, skeptical glitter in her eyes.

By the child's reaction Lissan realized that in order to succeed in her goal she would have to share some few details, though not the whole, with her closest allies. It was easily decided that in addition to Liam and Maedra, she would trust Hildie. And, most importantly, once certain her scheme could work, she would collaborate with Rory on timelines.

"I'm glad you've come," Lissan announced to Hildie with a sincere smile. "Your arrival saves us from a journey to the keep to find you."

"Why?" Hildie asked. She earnestly wanted to help but couldn't help shifting uneasily from one foot to the other. "What would you have of me?"

Lissan gazed steadily into solemn eyes of darkest blue. "Liam tells me you are likely my only hope to see another step complete."

" 'Tis true, elfling," an equally serious Liam added when Hildie glanced toward him. "The lime caves

on the coast above Beasham have openings too small
for any of us to climb through.

"Oh." Hildie was relieved. Having worried that
their sober words portended some nebulous, fright-
ful request, she was pleased that for once her small
size would enable her to do something others could
not. "I've been exploring there before."

Lissan was glad to hear Hildie's claim of experience. It eased her concern that the caves might be
too small even for this child.

"I will happily do what you ask but—" Hildie
posed the next logical question. "Why do you want
me to crawl through those dark caverns?"

Lissan's soft smile was an acknowledgment of her
young friend's willingness. "I need the crystals
you'll find inside—crystals either clear or milky
white."

"Is that all?" Hildie shrugged, mildly disappointed. She couldn't see what possible value such
common and plentiful rocks might be, but for Lissan
she would fetch as many as were wanted.

Liam cut across chatter of dubious value to remind Lissan of an important fact. "If we're going to
accomplish what you've asked before daylight's
gone, we must leave immediately."

"Yes," Lissan promptly agreed. "But first I must
have your oaths that never, *never* will what we do
be shared with another living mortal." Her serious
gaze moved steadily from one startled ally to another. "Do I have your word on this matter?"

"By the Holy Cross," Liam immediately responded while steadily meeting emerald eyes.

Hildie echoed his answer precisely but Maedra
merely nodded.

To Maedra the oath seemed an unnecessary action
when as fairy she was already forbidden to share
secrets with humans. But then, Maedra realized, Lis-

san might feel there was reason for fear considering the Tuatha de Danann rules that had been broken by virtue of her relationship with Liam. Besides, it was all too certain that King Comlan's daughter must have learned from him how a fairy was required to answer any question directly posed by a human.

A quarter moon provided more than adequate light for the small party returning triumphantly to Tuatha Cottage with saddlebags full of the crystals they'd gone out to fetch. Fortunately, that morning Hildie had ridden not her small pony but the placid mare also always hers to take. That choice made it possible for Lissan to ride pillion with the girl on the journey to coastal lime caves. Maedra had shared Liam's stallion—explaining again that though she could do nothing to interfere in the course of human history, she had been commissioned to guard over Lissan and to do so must remain nearby. After all, only see what had happened after she failed in that duty the previous day.

As the cottage door swung open, Liam made a wry jest that won bright grins and gentle laughter. But all were instantly washed away as effectively as dust by a sudden cloudburst.

"Where, pray tell, have you been?" demanded an angry Rory standing with fists firmly planted on hips and glaring at the returning four while appropriately silhouetted against the roaring blaze he'd stoked to great heights in the hearth.

Liam loudly gulped and Maedra fell behind his shielding back but Hildie defiantly met her father's temper unflinching. Yet even the child left to Lissan the responsibility for braving an answer.

"As I promised both you and your people," Lissan began, stepping fully into the room, "I have been

making arrangements to lend support in the defeat
of Munster's assault.''

"Arrangements you deemed rightly shared with
these three—'' He waved dismissively at the trio still
hovering framed in the open doorway. "But not
with me, the lord of this area and commander of its
defenses?''

Smiling soothingly, Lissan moved forward to
stand a mere pace from her irritated interrogator
while in dulcet tones providing a perfectly logical
reason for her actions.

"With so great a task looming ever nearer, I was
certain you had an abundance of important challenges to overcome and more urgent demands for
your time.'' Heart already aching with apprehension
for her love's safety in the coming struggle, Lissan
spoke the undeniable truth. "To save you wasted
effort, I thought to lay my plans and make certain
of their effectiveness before bringing them to you.''

Rory was mollified by intentions so sensible and
regretted his unfair attack. The sight of Lissan's courageously lifted chin further deepened in him an uncomfortable sense of guilt seldom experienced before
she arrived in his life—but a small price and willingly paid for the joy of her company.

At the sight of two becoming deeply absorbed in
their own world, Liam motioned Maedra and Hildie
to join him in backing away. Once outside, he quietly shut the cottage door, closing the pair in privacy.

Lissan recognized the strong man's regret for his
unwarranted reaction to her absence in serious eyes
gone all of black and instinctively sought to comfort
his distress by making a belated offer.

"But now that you're here, perhaps you can spare
a few moments for me to explain what I intend in
Connaught's defense?''

Though seeing the exquisite colleen's wish to smooth his discomfort, Rory wanted to show his trust for her and slowly shook his dark head to decline.

"When I arrived here and found you gone, I feared that under the traitorous Morag's influence an advance party from Munster might have crept across the border to abduct you again. But now that I know you've safely returned unharmed, 'tis true that many important details await in Ailm Keep to be decided and I'd best waste no time to see them settled."

"I appreciate your concern for me." Lissan gazed upward the scant distance to dark velvet eyes that immediately caught her in their thrall.

Rory was as thoroughly snared by the moonspun web of her enchantment, and his jaw went tight. Though cursing himself for a weak-minded fool, he took terrible pleasure in her eyes' unshielded revelation of growing hunger while slipping his hand beneath the weight of a single thick braid of golden hair to gently cup the back of her neck. His mouth gradually descended to move gently, enticingly across hers.

Strength stolen by that sweet meeting of lips, Lissan trembled as without thought hers parted beneath his tender assault, inviting the further sweet invasion he'd taught her before.

A low groan broke from Rory's throat as he pulled her pliant body tight to the whole length of his form and accepted her offer, deepening their kiss into a devastating intimacy.

Exalting in his strength, Lissan arched even nearer shuddering with wild excitement while her hands moved restlessly over muscular biceps, broad shoulders, and strong neck—impatient with the cloth barrier between her touch and his skin.

Knowing it was time to pull back—now while he could, Rory struggled to end an embrace which in this hour and this place was purely wrong. Yet in leaning away, he erred in gazing down into the winsome face of one more beautiful in her passion than any female he'd ever known, one he dangerously craved. Yielding to an enticement too intense, Rory reclaimed the ambrosia of her mouth in a kiss even wilder, hotter, and more unbelievably sweet.

The sound of a moan rising up from the depths of Lissan's passion shook Rory from his desperate hunger with a sharp reminder of guilt for the wrongful taking that must not be repeated. In one corner of his mind, sanity shouted a bleak warning: She would return to her own time, leave him behind. And another experience of sweetest delights could only intensify the forever lingering pain of loss.

Lissan bit her lip in anguish as the man whose face had gone to ice-coated stone abruptly turned and left without further word. Already certain Rory had little care whether she went or remained in his world, she believed the seeming ease with which he walked away was surely a further demonstration that he felt no more for her than a passing physical interest.

CHAPTER 18

"Is this what you meant?" Hildie asked, glancing earnestly up at Lissan from her position kneeling on the edge of a square of linen cloth laid over an area of floor swept clear of rushes.

Lissan had been watching Liam check for the continued safety of their still-smoldering charcoal mound from the cottage's open door. She had taken precautions to prevent unintentionally teaching what must not be shared by arranging for the production of charcoal in far greater amounts than useful for her purposes.

This tactic, she hoped, would confuse a recipe in truth simple. And such confusion must surely help prevent her explosives from being easily reconstituted by someone later trying to either wheedle or force the information from Liam or Hildie. These trusted two were the only other humans she dared allow any part in the making of her black powder, and those relatively minor roles. She had far rather have performed *all* the tasks herself but with so much to be done in so little time . . . Lissan tamped down her concerns with the poor comfort that her choices were pitifully few. She most certainly could not share the recipe, and thus must mix it herself

while the charcoal pit demanded more strength than
even she possessed, leaving only Hildie to help with
this final chore.

Lissan's morning had been spent working in the
cottage performing the most dangerous task alone.
First, she'd separately pulverized saltpeter crystals,
pieces of sulfur, and lumps of charcoal earlier taken
from the still burning mound. Once armed with
three bowls containing the powder of these elements, as precisely as possible without modern
equipment she carefully mixed the correct proportions—seventy-five percent of the first, ten percent
of the second, and fifteen percent of the last—to
form the compound she sought.

Fervently wishing it were unnecessary to involve
Hildie in this mission, Lissan answered the child's
call by stepping back inside. "Yes," she said, smiling
approvingly while gazing down at the long, twined,
and oddly moistened threads which Hildie had
painstakingly rolled across an equally long strip of
black powder. "That's just what needs to be done."

While Lissan mixed the mysterious weapon, at her
direction Liam and Hildie had first unraveled homespun sacks, then twined thick threads together, and
like overlong wicks dipped them—but in lard rather
than tallow. Lissan knew but couldn't explain to her
friends that the oil in lard was much more conducive
for turning wicks into fuses.

"Before I start on the next, I'll have to move this
one," Hildie quietly stated, looking with pride over
the product of her curious chore. "What shall I do
with the first?"

This was a question Lissan had given considerable
thought. "Roll it into a ball—*loosely*."

Hildie promptly nodded and obediently lifted one
end to begin the process. Lissan, however, was anxious to prevent the accidents possible where even a

small amount of this volatile explosive was present and again restated important safety precautions.

"Please handle them cautiously while placing them in the cloth-lined basket I prepared." Lissan's solemn tone and steady gaze emphasized the seriousness of her words. "Take care to see that a cushion of cloth lies between so that no two rub together."

"My lady—" a tentative voice hesitantly called from the still-open doorway, winning the immediate attention of the two inside.

Turning toward the sound, Lissan found the portal filled by the same large woman who on the day of her burning had stripped her of clothing . . . and taken the amulet now resting on an outstretched palm.

" 'Tis such a pretty piece," Ina awkwardly said, moving a step closer with her offering. "I knew I ought no' be lettin' another day pass without I sees it given back to you."

"It was my mother's." Lissan nodded and the late afternoon sunlight falling through a doorway no longer blocked by the visitor's bulk glowed on golden hair. "And is most precious to me."

Lissan accepted the lovely brooch with a smile of sweet gratitude and lost no time in fastening it to the brown bodice of her simple homespun gown. Glancing up from the welcome task, she noticed where precisely her guest's steady gaze rested—the fuse Hildie was obediently coiling into a loose ball.

"If you mean to return to Ailm Keep," Lissan hastily intruded, calling her visitor's attention back, "I hope you'll permit me to journey there with you. I have business with your lord."

" 'Struth, to Ailm Keep I go." Caught staring, the flustered woman immediately answered. "And a welcome companion you'd be. I am Ina, the keep's alewife, and prays I that in me return of your brooch and this gown, 'tis worthy of your trust I've proven and willin' to journey with me you'll be."

Lissan was disconcerted. Focused on her amulet, she'd failed to notice that the dress taken in that same hour was neatly draped over her visitor's arm. But more important than that simple lack, Lissan was struck with guilt by Ina's pleasure in a dubious honor when the purpose behind this proposed joint trip was merely to hustle an uninvited visitor away with all possible speed.

And yet, Lissan comforted herself, she hadn't lied. Tomorrow was Whitsunday, which meant that the moment really had arrived for first sharing what she could of her plans with Rory and then with him coordinating their implementation.

Lissan accepted the returned gown and moved to hang it on the peg from which she first collected her cloak. With this action she also managed to surreptitiously scoop up a small leather bag and attach it to her belt beneath the cloak's loose folds. Then, before setting off with Ina, she feigned a casualness she was far from feeling to wish both Hildie and Liam good fortune in finishing their "chores."

It was at Liam's suggestion that Lissan rode his stallion into a twilight forest on the path to Ailm Keep. From the present companion she'd found strident in their first unpleasant meeting flowed an endless stream of amicable chatter.

However, Lissan felt an uneasiness building even before the cottage disappeared from backward glances. Not for her own safety. She knew that Maedra, after her absence when the mob forced their way into Tuatha Cottage, as protectress was doubtless near although unseen. No, Lissan's stress centered on a prospect both longed for and dreaded—

seeing again the devastating man who'd abandoned her so abruptly the night past.

"Aye," Ina rattled on, "and sure it be tha' there is noon here as would blame Lord Rory for bein' shut of his fool brother."

These scornful words caught Lissan's preoccupied thoughts. She glanced toward the speaker so involved in her subject that she'd hadn't noticed her companion's distraction.

"As for the blatherin' fool's wife, 'tis a sorry fac' what wicked thing Morag be." The heavy woman gave her head a disgusted shake. Then casting a knowing glance to her magical listener with meaningful pauses, she added, "Now all we needs fear is ta where the wretched pair has gotten off . . . when they means ta return . . . and what mischief they intends."

Because Lissan's full attention had initially been demanded by the challenge in finding a way to help Rory, next by the difficulties of procuring necessary elements, and then by mixing black powder, she knew nothing about the "wretched pair's" absence. Even now her immediate response to this information centered on questioning a fact she'd wondered about since seeing the brothers together when Rory first took her to share a meal in his keep.

"Why is there so much animosity between your lord and his brother?" Lissan hoped her talkative companion wouldn't suddenly develop a conscience about gossiping—it seemed unlikely.

"Aye, well—" Ina sent the lady a speaking look of disdain for the query. "You had as well ask as why some flowers be red and others be yellow."

Putting aside the fact that this certainly wasn't the time for a botanical lesson, Lissan refused to be so easily fobbed off. "I can't believe there's no certain source for such strong currents of emotion."

"I'm no' sayin' there isn't." Ina defensivelly
puffed up and instantly responded. "We of the keep
know it be a certain fact tha' blame lies in two simple
words . . . both amongst the church's seven deadly
sins: covetousness and envy."

"Covetousness . . . envy." Lissan's musing repetition wasn't a question but Ina treated it as one.

"Oh, aye." Ina earnestly nodded. "Donal has envied his brother's position, coveted his every possession since afore the day their da died, leaving
puir Lord Rory to raise a ne'er grateful brother."

Lissan's head tilted to one side while she pondered this statement.

" 'Course, muddied the waters considerable, it
did, when Donal wed and proudly brought ta the
keep a woman tha' talebearers soon tattled his
brother had rejected. Seems since tha' day, both he
and she ha' done all they might ta make Lord Rory's
days no' but a misery. . . ." Ina paused ominously.
"And there's many o' us who thinks as how they
means far worse."

While Ina veered off course and into a diatribe
against the whole of Munster's looming threat, Lissan's thoughts settled on her love's unhappy family
relationships. Though Ina had shared suspicions of
Donal and Morag as if it were a secret known by
few, Lissan had already come to the same conclusions. The question now was how to protect Rory
not merely against Munster but also against his own.

When their journey came to an end Lissan felt as
if they'd only just begun, although the heavy shroud
of night had long since settled across the earth.
Moonlight filtered through a billowing ground fog
that suddenly parted on the site where Ailm Keep
thrust into the black sky. Her gaze moved up over
sturdy stone to where gleams of firelight escaped
from tightly shuttered windows high, high above.

The keep's inhabitants greeted their White Witch with a far more pleasing welcome than on the visit during which she'd been relegated to its dungeon. Once inside and standing at the back of the great hall, she gazed over rows of trestle tables to the dais beyond—and met a steady gaze devastating even at this distance.

Lissan was disconcerted at being unable to distinguish whether his eyes held a lingering anger or a powerful lure. Perhaps both? While she hovered, praying her knees wouldn't buckle and leave her looking either a trembling pigeonheart or too easy prey for his charms, Rory motioned a guardsman to escort his unexpected guest to the high table.

"Welcome." Rory's deep voice rumbled as into the chair beside him settled the beauty who'd suddenly appeared as if she were the materialization of thoughts never far from her.

"I wanted to visit you at the cottage today but . . ." With a rueful downward tilt to his lips, Rory echoed words she had said to him less than a whole day past. "I have important challenges to overcome and urgent demands for my full and immediate attention."

Lissan felt the warmth of a relieved blush brighten her cheeks. Pleased to learn that, despite his cold departure the previous night, Rory had wanted to see her again, she immediately responded with a tender smile of unequaled sweetness.

"Toward our common goal, as promised," Lissan quietly said of the reason for this visit. "I've come with a report of my scheme to aid you in defeating a soon-arriving danger."

"Come." Rory nodded, pushing back an already emptied trencher before rising to his feet. "Join me again in my private solar."

Memories of intimate pleasures shared when last

in that room rekindled in Lissan fires banked by the
untimely appearance of well-meaning friends. In
that instant she decided, if given the opportunity,
she would set aside the maidenly virtues she'd been
taught to hold dear and seek what he had so recently
refused to give. After all, since the night to follow
must be devoted to preparations for the struggle to
come, this night was too likely her last opportunity
for sweet delights shared with the man she loved.

"Are you hungry?" For a second time Rory repeated this question to the exquisite beauty gazing
blindly up at him.

Embarrassment further brightened the color in
Lissan's cheeks as she realized what a complete
ninny she must seem, mutely gazing at him like the
kind of besotted fool she'd always viewed with disdain.

"Yes," Lissan firmly stated. "I am." Preoccupied
with careful preparations, she'd spared little time to
eat. In fact, she couldn't remember having consumed
a single bite this entire day.

Rory immediately issued orders that a platter containing portions from the evening meal's variety of
dishes be delivered to his solar. Next he formally
proffered his forearm to aid Lissan in rising and escort her above.

Lissan instantly rested dainty fingertips atop the
velvet of his scarlet tunic's sleeve, but as she stood
her attention was caught by an earthen mug whose
ale Rory must have drained.

"Might I have that mug?" she politely requested.

"You won't need it," Rory answered. "The platter
will arrive with a goblet of fine wine for you."

Holding a dark gaze with the steady purpose in
her emerald eyes, Lissan gave an infinitesimal shake
to golden hair. "Please, might I have that mug as
well?"

Giving a slight shrug and dubious grimace, Rory responded by using his free hand to lift the mug and with it motion toward the interior staircase leading to his private chambers.

Once there with cloak hung from an empty peg, as on her previous visit, Lissan was directed to sit in the chair lent comfort by several cushions. From there with silent admiration she watched as the powerful man clearly possessed of inner strengths carefully leashed lowered himself into a matching seat.

Rory didn't speak. But through the gloom of a chamber lit only by the flames in a small fireplace built into the stone wall's width and the flickering of a single candle, he stared at Lissan with an intensity that was an effective demand for the promised report.

"I cannot share the secret of how it was made and pray you will not ask," Lissan began while freeing the small leather bag she'd covertly attached to her belt when leaving the cottage. "But I've brought something whose force I would like to demonstrate for you."

Dark brows arched in wordless question above piercing eyes focused on the weapon so tiny as to fit into a sack little bigger than any hunting falcon's hood.

Sensing his disappointment, Lissan was anxious to prove the worth of her contribution but was delayed by a gentle rapping on the door that heralded the arrival of a commanded meal.

Silence reigned while a sturdy platter was placed on the flat-topped chest at Lissan's elbow. On it rested two types of meat covered in curious sauces, a bowl of steaming pea soup, and thick slices of wheaten bread along with a wedge of cheese and dried fruit. And, as promised, to drink there was a

doubtless precious glass goblet filled with a dark
ruby wine.

Once the servant had withdrawn and while Lissan
ate, Rory shared an updated account of enemy
movements, troops increasing in numbers and thus
in strength beyond the border. Truly interested, Lissan listened. Yet, the greater portion of her attention
narrowed on a small puzzle she ought to have already solved. How could she light black powder
without blowing off her own hand? The speed with
which she'd begun the meal—nearly inhaling the
food—slowed drastically as she traded the easing of
hunger for time necessary to find an answer.

Before she returned a bowl scraped clean (how
was it that the peas she despised in London seemed
not so repulsive here?) to a near-empty tray, she had
what she sought and triumphantly turned toward
Rory.

"If you'll hand me the mug I requested, I'll demonstrate how valuable to your effort my meager contribution may be."

Rory remained dubious but willingly complied.
Closely he watched the beguiling colleen cradle a
crockery vessel in the crook of her left arm while
lightly tucking into it one of the small cloth squares
left for use in baths daily brought to him here. She
next moved to open the shutters of this chamber's
single window with her free hand.

Once barriers to the chill air of a spring night were
spread wide, Lissan settled Rory's mug on the portal's ledge and pulled out the small cloth to neatly
fold and lay it nearby. Then, repeatedly dipping
thumb and two fingers into her leather bag, she
withdrew small amounts of powder, every particle
of which was dropped into the vessel. After returning to her cloak, she pulled from it a single thick
strand of wool. One end of this she draped into the

mug while leaving the other end to dangle a brief distance below the inside windowsill. Next she carefully placed the folded cloth almost but not completely across the mug's open top.

The beauty's peculiar actions increased Rory's curiosity. Though he saw nothing remotely sensible in anything yet done, he could hardly question a being able to survive the deadly perils she had. Still, when Lissan took a burning splinter from the fire and with it lit the dangling end of a thread, he was hardpressed not to laugh.

"Duck!" With that wild demand Lissan threw herself across the room. She landed in a startled Rory's arms, burying her face into the crook between his shoulder and neck just as a resounding boom and the noise of shattered pottery filled air as instantly suffused with grey smoke.

Rory's powerful arms automatically sheltered the woman tightly in a protective embrace but his piercing eyes were narrowed by a fierce scowl as he glared toward the window-source of alarm.

"Consider your surprise at even this small sample of what can be done." Lissan pulled back but only a handsbreadth away. "Then imagine what response will be won by an abundance of larger explosions greeting foes who come to invade."

Rory's head fell back and the velvet thunder of his laughter rolled out to echo in a room appropriately filled with stormy mists.

"Shock alone will put a great many of the craven fools to flight." He leaned forward and took Lissan's small hands into his much larger ones. "But how do you propose to set these traps?"

"Stealthily," Lissan promptly answered. "Unseen in the darkness tomorrow night we must see a multitude of more sizable charges laid out to wait concealed until foolish invaders approach."

"This truly can be done?" Rory posed the serious question that must be asked.

Lissan nodded. "If you'll command your supporters to precisely follow my instructions. They must be warned that should there be even the slightest deviation, the action will almost certainly demand an instantaneous and deadly price."

"They would obey my command in any case," Rory said, gazing down into her earnest face, "but when performed at your behest, their attention to the tiniest of details will increase fourfold."

Rory was enchanted by the tint of color these words brushed across her cheeks and bent to caress their satiny warmth with his lips. Reminding himself again of the pain he courted in falling to such sweet temptation, he pulled a whisper away. His good intent was singed to ashes by green eyes gone so dark they threatened to swallow him whole.

Lissan lay against Rory's broad chest in complete trust, silently renewing her earlier vow to seek what he had denied her last night—a final taste of love's feast of sensual delights and sweet memories to live on throughout the lonely life certain to follow her exile from his.

Meaning to subdue the fire in his blood, Rory tucked Lissan's face back under his chin—to little avail as her heady wildflower scent rose while her generous curves melted against him.

From beneath her ear, pressed against the rich velvet of his scarlet tunic, she could hear the pounding of Rory's heart. Its cadence was almost as rapid as her own. An emerald gaze rose to study a tightly clenched jaw and with trembling fingers she stroked over its rigid tension.

Rory shuddered. Lissan's touch broke his fierce effort to keep from looking down at the exquisite temptation he'd little hope of resisting. Gazing into

her beguiling face, open and trusting, he wondered
if she had any notion of what a seductive vision of
willing surrender she presented.

Dazed by the singeing heat of silver fires blazing
in the depths of midnight eyes, Lissan remembered
the feel of his hard mouth on hers and ached for its
return. A moan rose from her depths. The sound
was more than Rory could withstand. He bent his
head to take lifted and silently pleading lips in a
succession of slow, brief, tormenting kisses.

Clinging to powerful shoulders, Lissan helplessly
shifted to brush lush curves across muscles she felt
ripple in answer to her desperate movements. With
the reins to his self-control thus knocked completely
from his hold, Rory wrapped both arms more firmly
about this tender colleen and crushed her even
nearer.

For feverish moments Rory gave Lissan the unrestrained ardor of his devouring mouth. But still it
was not enough for either of them. He urged her
head to fall back against one mighty arm while his
lips dropped to follow the line of an arched throat
laid bare and vulnerable. With his free hand he
struggled to dispense with her plain gown's front
lacing. Once it was sufficiently loosened, he tugged
homespun down and groaned his response to the
prize set free—breasts high, firm, tip-tilted, and lacking even the minimal protection of the delicate un-
dergarb worn when last she'd lain so intimately in
his arms.

Lissan knew she should cover her nudity, should
feel shame, but lost in Rory's thrall could not. Longing for the return of another sweet anguish, her lips
parted on an unsteady breath as she arched upward
toward the caress urgently sought.

The deep sound rising from Rory's throat was
muffled by the sudden giving of what she sought,

of what he also hungered for too strongly to forgo—
the taste of her velvety skin.

Lissan cried out, shivering under the burning
pleasure of his mouth on her breasts, a painful joy
that both satisfied an initial need and roused another
much deeper. She wound her fingers in black
strands, holding him tightly to aching flesh and
trembling with a hunger she feared too deep to survive.

"This is the worst of folly!" Rory suddenly, relentlessly pulled from the too welcome cradle of Lissan's arms. He must stop now before stealing even
more of his love's innocence and with that wrong
create additional memories of delicious torment able
only to increase the anguish of a desolate future.

In those words like rough velvet Lissan thought
she heard the final death knell to her desperate hope
for a last experience of love's sweetest expression.

"I know you don't share the emotions I feel for
you, but if you must exile me from your world, first
grant me one more portion of passion's feast."

Rory went utterly still, expression frozen into forbidding lines, but Lissan refused to easily yield an
ardently sought boon. "Please give me this one
night, this precious memory of love to exist on for a
lifetime alone."

"I could never, would never send you away—"
Rory swept Lissan near while answering an earnest
plea that had shaken the foundations of his world
and thrown wide the gates to a paradise he'd
thought forever beyond reach. "Such a deed would
demand the plucking out of my own heart."

In a soul-binding kiss Rory reclaimed sensuous
lips turned cherry-bright by their earlier play while
Lissan marveled at his confession of a love returned,
welcomed it as the greatest joy and the one she
would treasure for all her days.

When Rory again pulled from Lissan's tender arms and rose to his feet, the aching loss that filled green eyes passion-glazed nearly sent him again into enticingly extended arms. Yet with a half-smile of incredible potency he held back. He fully intended to see them both consumed again by flames of desire but meant to first see them ensconced elsewhere in far greater comfort.

"Patience, my love—" The tender sincerity in Rory's endearment melted Lissan's last fear of rejection. "I mean only to see you installed where you rightfully belong—in the lord's chamber . . . and bed."

Lissan made to get up but Rory forestalled her willing compliance by lifting her with the great strength she found so amazing. After carrying her to his bedchamber, Rory allowed her body to slide down the hardening contours of his—proof of his exciting intentions—and quickly finished the half-done task of ridding her of unwelcome cloth barriers.

Pleasurably aware of Rory's height and breadth, Lissan remained motionless while with one smooth movement he stripped off the impediment of his tunic. Emerald eyes widened, stunned anew by the magnificent and frightening view of his hard torso. Breath caught in her throat as he reached out to draw her back into his embrace. Lissan wanted nothing more from life than to feel its heat and swayed toward the burning strength of his body.

Rory was as anxious to revel in the sweet-silk touch of full curves and yet curled gentle hands over slender shoulders to hold her a breath away while a tormenting need grew and heightened their senses. Only at an agonizingly gradual pace did he ease soft flesh nearer until she lay completely against him.

The wild pleasure of her bare skin brushing the heat of his wide chest left Lissan trembling. Heavy

lashes drifted down on a moan as she buried her
lips into the curve between broad shoulder and
neck. Surrendering to temptation, she allowed an
honest curiosity to lead her along the path he'd
taught by example. Slowly she moved her mouth in
a trail of teasing caresses across the planes of the
massive chest rising and falling heavily. Sensing in
him a potent hunger growing to awesome dimen-
sions to match her own, she grew bolder in her explorations.

Rory willingly lay vulnerable to his fairy-witch's
explorations, restraining an urgent need to crush her
to his aching body despite the tormenting provoca-
tion . . . until she found a flat, masculine nipple.

A low growl rumbled from Rory's throat. He
could bear no more. Lissan gazed up from between
the thick lashes of eyes grown heavy with passion.
He lowered his head for a devastating kiss so overwhelming that she'd no thought to spare as he lifted
and laid her across the wide comfort of his bed.

Even if she'd wanted to, and she didn't, Lissan
couldn't have looked away while Rory divested
himself of the last remaining obstacle to their joining.
Thus with unhidden admiration she boldly watched
his awesome display of magnificent muscles high-
lighted by candlelight and shadow.

When Rory lay down and took her into his embrace, Lissan wrapped her arms around him, twined
fingers into cool black strands, and savored the tex-
tures of his hard back. While his lips trailed sweet
torment over breasts that swelled to meet them, Lissan tumbled into the welcome darkness of wild
wanting so deep it seemed certain she must drown
in bottomless realms.

In the sensuous body writhing against his own
painfully taut form Rory felt the end to his tenuous
control slipping away. Sliding one leg between

silken thighs, he shifted to lie full atop her slender length and rise on his forearms to watch the desire-rosed face framed in a golden halo of bright curls while pressing intimately nearer.

Caught in a tumult of raging passions, Lissan couldn't bear the gradual, tormenting pace of his movements. Desperate to be carried deeper into the firestorm, to be consumed by the blaze waiting at its core, she clasped his hips nearer and wrapped soft limbs about him.

Rory yielded to erotic enticements too potent to deny and rocked them both deeper into the ever-hotter conflagration. When he went still at the eye of the storm, Lissan surged upward with a feverish cry of yearning. The shocking pleasure of her action seemed to light the fuse to an explosion of unfathomable ecstasy more powerful, more intimately shattering, than any black powder blast.

An uncounted time later, a replete Rory drifted on clouds of smoldering passion while resting a cheek against the golden head nestled on his shoulder. He slowly stroked Lissan's passion-tangled hair and a satisfied smile curved firm lips.

Delighting in the warmth and power he exuded even now, Lissan buried her face against his throat to whisper, "No matter what comes after, that you love me now is enough to see me through all the days to come."

"Nay," Rory immediately answered, rising on an elbow to gaze down into green crystal eyes. "Never enough—we both will always crave more and must survive to share that future together."

"Yes-s-s . . ." Despite looming danger, Lissan was elated by this repeated declaration of a shared love she'd believed could never be hers. And that elation joined with the sweet relief of having a firm decision for her father to inspire an absurd but pleasing thought which freed a bubble of bright laughter. "As is the end to every good fairy tale, we shall live *happily ever after*."

Heavy lashes narrowed dark eyes to mere slits while Rory sent Lissan a wary glance. He tried to stifle the unwelcome suspicion that she was mocking his earnest proclamation of love (a vow of the sort he'd never spoken before) but . . .

Realizing that she had erred in not speaking more plainly, Lissan hastened to clarify words he'd obviously misinterpreted.

"It's a familiar saying in my world and simply means that a happy future is our destiny."

Lissan tilted a golden head back and gazed up at him with such open emotion that Rory felt humbled by so precious a gift. Threading fingers through her hair, he urged her mouth to his and coals of passion merely banked quickly warmed to a sweet fire demanding more.

With renewed love play they both sought to block the ominous reality that dangerous challenges waited like fire-breathing dragons to be slain before their bright future could truly be claimed.

"Haymert—" Mael snarled at a young guardsman hovering uneasily in the private solar's doorway. "Did you find my wretched guardsman?"

"Aye, my lord." Haymert's voice trembled. "Fergil hastens to your presence even now."

"Fergil should've been here before." The spite behind Mael's snarl was in no way lessened by the perverse pleasure he took in seeing Haymert's uncertain gaze drop beneath his steady glare. "The man should never leave my keep but that I send him forth."

"Aye, my lord," Haymert stammered again, refusing to meet the colorless eyes of his impatient master and instead focusing on the rushes servants had wrongly allowed to bunch in piles. With great relief, he gladly escaped when the subject of Lord Mael's ire brushed past to enter the chamber.

"I was summoned to the palisade gate to meet King Muirtrecht's messenger." Fergil launched into speech even before he had crossed the room to face the lord who'd paused in his irritable pacing. "And I accepted this from him on your behalf."

Although this excuse for Fergil's absence was valid, it deepened Mael's frown. He snatched the folded parchment from the other's outstretched hand and broke its seal with little care.

" 'Tis only a reminder that the invasion is to begin with the first streaks of dawn's light little more than a full day into the future." The bright heat of Mael's growing vexation matched the brilliant shade of his hair. "Tch, as if I am like to forget a tactic so foolish."

"But why?" Fergil asked simply.

"Why does our king plan something so witless?" Mael resumed his habitual stomping from one side of the chamber to the other. "Or why does he bother to remind me of his demands?"

Fergil shrugged uncomfortably as if to rid himself of a distressing weight.

"Humph." Mael's growl of contempt was distinctive. "I think he's gone daft, deeming himself the High King of all Ireland and invincible as that."

Since the red-haired lord had stopped directly in front of him to make this assertion, Fergil meekly nodded.

"And he reminds me, not because he thinks I might have forgotten, but rather to earlier rid the path toward Connaught's defeat of its only barrier by permanently removing Rory O'Connor." Mael jabbed Fergil's chest with his fist. "The self-same assignment in which *you* failed me."

"But you know—" Fergil immediately began blustering valid reasons though they hadn't been before and wouldn't now be found acceptable excuses.

"What I know," Mael broke in, "is that you've failed in previous attempts but on pain of your own death *must* not again! No matter what else transpires in the coming battle, you *will* see O'Connor dead!"

CHAPTER 19

Lissan slowly became aware of an unfamiliar comfort. It wasn't merely the lack of a straw pallet's lumps or prickly straws poking through its ticking. Nor was it solely the unusual warmth protecting her from morning air ever chill before a hearthfire could be prodded into renewed heat.

Braced on a forearm resting in the comfort of his bed's feather-filled mattress, for long moments Rory gazed down on a sweet vision of tender beauty. Then he dipped his head to nuzzle her ear and whisper, "Wake up, sweeting."

Even before Lissan could force sleep-heavy lashes to rise, a gentle smile curled lips still slightly swollen from their night's delicious play. Memories of events during recent hours and words of love exchanged softened emerald eyes which soon visually caressed the stunning lord so near.

"I fear we're woefully late for the morning meal." Rory grimaced ruefully although without a trace of sincere regret.

"No one waiting there could've missed you as sorely as I would have lamented the loss of a single instant of our time together." With a passion-tangled glory of golden curls surrounding her face and cloaking slender shoulders, Lissan gazed up at her lover in open admiration: superbly masculine, handsome, and—most remarkably—hers!

" 'Struth." Warmed with pleasure by the honest emotion in Lissan's words, Rory trailed gentle fingertips over the curve of her cheek and she trembled. "We've devoted their lost time to an infinitely more delightful cause."

Lissan turned her face to first kiss and then nip at his palm.

Rory was charmed by her playfulness yet felt unhappily compelled to point out facts considerably less enjoyable. "With the forewarned hour of invasion looming and so much to first be done, I fear we must go down to join our supporters."

Leaning forward again, he brushed a gentle kiss on the corner of her lips. "The duty is a cheerless distraction from far more welcome deeds, a duty made bearable only by the comforting promise of shared years ahead."

Rory chose not to dim these glad moments for Lissan by voicing the fear that silently warned their future of happiness might be limited to a span no longer than a single day more.

Lissan nodded immediate agreement with Rory's rationale for this necessary action. Still, though warmed by his use of the term "*our* supporters," she was suddenly struck by the chill of an uncomfortable realization. By her descent to the hall below at their lord's side the bawdy suspicions of his people would be confirmed. And there was little doubt but that the previous evening they had drawn their own conclusions after watching her accompany him alone to his private chambers . . . and not later return.

But it didn't make her what Morag had warned: Rory's temporary trollop! No, he wanted to share his

life with her. Casting the devastating man a sidelong
glance, with a faint smile of self-mockery, Lissan admitted that even if such scorn was the cost for time
with her beloved, she would willingly have paid the
price.

Rory was concerned by the shifting emotions
crossing an expressive face and rubbed away the
frown threatening to pucker delicate brows while offering a heartfelt reassurance.

"Once we're seated at the high table and are the
focus of attention, I'll announce the bond we've
pledged and command that planning begin for a
feast to celebrate not only Connaught's defeat of
Munster—but our nuptials as well."

With this fresh confirmation of the commitment
she'd sorely feared could never be hers, joy bubbled
up in Lissan like the waters of a hot spring. Beaming,
she reached up to tangle her fingers into Rory's
sleep-disordered black strands, urging his surrender
to her enticing arms.

"Fie, temptress. We must go down." Despite this
quiet, sane reminder of a waiting obligation, Rory
yielded to Lissan's embrace.

Rory's honest intent to restore the measure of willpower necessary to focus on duty was driven beyond reach by the feel of lush curves crushed
intimately near. Still, he rested his chin on the gilded
silk of her hair with faint hope that a refusal to gaze
directly into a piquant face might lessen the hunger.
It didn't. Not when, though focusing on a pattern
woven into the ceiling of his heavily draped bed, he
saw only lips berry-bright and just as sweet, fathomless eyes of emerald, and the golden halo framing
an exquisite face.

"Soon . . . but not now." Lissan nuzzled her face
against Rory, laying a rain of teasing kisses like a
path of fire across his shoulder, throat, and chin.

"Soon," Rory agreed and, losing will to fight, gladly welcomed powerful temptations whose delights he already knew were worth any price.

Mouths joined in an aching demand that fostered a near-consuming hunger, Rory urged silken curves to conform to the hard angles of his body. Lissan willingly gave herself up to the flames sweeping her into a firestorm of sweet love returned.

In the aftermath of consuming desire, the pair again floated on lingering mists of satisfaction. Lissan lay with her cheek supported by a pillow of hard muscle and firm skin while drowsing in warm awareness of the happy ending granted her private fairy tale by Rory's wish to marry her. But too quickly the haze was parted by the cool breeze of conscience whispering that only a selfish heart would welcome a deed likely to increase danger for those whose well-being her alter ego, the White Witch, was meant to help. And the almost immediate announcement of wedding plans would assuredly be a distraction for people she must lead in dangerous tasks.

"Rory—" Lissan hesitantly began, "I look forward to the proud day when I become your wife." She rose far enough to gaze earnestly into his midnight eyes. "And the prospect of telling others of our joy is wonderful . . . but I think sharing news of our union would be best made after the battle is won."

"Do you?" Dark brows arched for an instant before his potent smile flashed. "I agree, it might behoove us to keep the focus on the challenge ahead, wait until we've won . . . perhaps until we have your father's approval?" He thought the latter likely of as much import to her as the former.

"No." Lissan immediately shook her head. "My father will approve of whatever decision I make." And despite his unshielded desire for her to take a different path, she had no doubt that her remarkable father would approve.

Rory had long been confident that his judgment of others was seldom wrong. And to him the King of the Faerie Realm hardly seemed the sort to accept any commitment made by a daughter without his approval. Thus, Rory remained skeptical yet hid his uneasiness from Lissan since talk of the struggle ahead had already clouded green crystal eyes.

Although Rory's handsome face was utterly devoid of emotion, by their growing closeness of spirit, Lissan sensed his doubts. But then how could she expect this man from an era during which women were viewed as chattel to understand the relationship between a father and daughter in 1900? The small, amused smile inspired by this question was soon tamed by the solemn nibbling of her lower lip that came with recognition of another fact coming into focus.

Considering that their viewpoints and values were separated not by mere generations but by centuries, there would obviously be obstacles to overcome in sharing their lives. But, she gladly acknowledged, these difficulties would save her from the boring predictability of the respectable life her sisters had planned for her to take up in London Society. And beyond that, far beyond that, she would gladly fight to smooth out any impediment threatening her future with Rory.

Worried by the troubled spirit suggested by widely varying and rapidly changing emotions chasing across Lissan's exquisite face, Rory sought to soothe her distress with news of a different sort. "My cousin King Turlough will arrive by noontide."

As Rory had expected, this statement set Lissan hastily into motion but still they barely arrived in the great hall before a sentry posted above the palisade gate came to report the royal party's approach.

With no meal immediately pending, the hall's trestle tables had been disassembled and their components moved to lean against stone walls behind lines of benches. As the king was ceremoniously announced, Rory strode forward to meet the young monarch halfway.

"My liege." In formal greeting Rory sank down on one knee with fist pressed to heart and dark head bowed.

"Rise, cousin—" Turlough instantly reached out to clasp Rory's shoulder. "It always seems that I should bow to you as all that I know, you taught me; all that I possess is mine because you showed me how to hold it secure."

Black hair brushed broad shoulders as Rory shook his head while rising to give the younger man an affectionate hug. "And I taught you, sire, to not only accept but demand fealty sworn by *all* who owe it."

Still standing by the hearth where Rory had left her, Lissan studied the young sovereign who looked to be little older than Liam. She could hardly hold Turlough's few years against him, not when it was a fact suggesting that they were separated in age by only one or two years. Besides, she was pleased to see in what esteem and affection the young man held his cousin Rory. Because they agreed on this subject, at least, Lissan was sure they could be friends.

"Lissan, come meet my king." Rory called for the the plainly preoccupied woman's attention.

Cheeks burning with the much-rued blush become too familiar, Lissan felt woefully ill-prepared to meet someone obviously important to Rory. Her sleep-tangled hair was poorly combed and untamed by braids she'd learned were the expected style for well-born females. Worse, she was garbed in a brown and dowdy homespun dress worn for two consecutive days and badly wrinkled.

Rory could see how rightfully enchanted his cousin was by the vision of loveliness slowly gliding forward—honey-sweet smile and blush-tinted cheeks framed in a glory of gilded curls.

"You are the White Witch?" Though Turlough was plainly curious, the tone of his voice held an odd mixture of awe and disbelief.

Lissan's smile deepened, but uncertain how much of the truth Rory wanted revealed to Turlough, she left the providing of answers to him.

"I see her as an angel come in the guise of the White Witch to help us poor mortals of Connaught defeat invaders from Munster."

At this extravagant claim from a man to whom such flowery phrases were uncommon, Turlough's eyes widened. However, after another glance toward the ethereal colleen, he decided the description nearer to fact than fantasy and contented himself with a succinct, single-word query. "How?"

Rory gave Turlough no verbal explanation but rather moved to fetch an unused mug from among several left on one end of the high table. When he returned and handed it to Lissan, she acknowledged his wordless request for a repeated demonstration of her weapon's force with a slight nod.

Uncomfortably aware of being the center of the crowd's attention, Lissan was glad she'd taken time to reaffix the leather bag to her belt before descending to the hall. Lissan decided that since this room was so much larger than Rory's bedchamber, she ought to use more of the black powder and nearly doubled the amount dropped into the vessel. Fortunately, as a precaution, she motioned everyone to press as far away from the vessel as possible before lighting and dashing away from another improvised fuse.

Lissan learned as much as her audience did about the force and volatility of the explosive she'd produced. Compared to the first, this blast was considerably louder, sparks and shards of pottery flew a great deal farther, and smoke clogged the air of even this large chamber. Indeed, if the keep's walls hadn't been of stone, she felt certain they would have shaken.

To Rory's delight, observers stood in awe of such power, grateful that the lovely White Witch was their ally. With her as foe, arrogant invaders were destined to fail.

"Aye, then we agree?" Mael's bright hair gleamed as he nodded toward the woman who was his ever more hostile conspirator. " 'Tis best that Donal accompany me and my warriors to the bridge where his brother will doubtless make a stand as its defender—Turlough won't deny him that right."

Morag chose not to waste breath agreeing with so obvious a decision. Taking the bridge was a critical first step for any plan to conquer Connaught. It was a pivotal site on the border, the only one affording easy access for an invading force of any worthwhile size. Elsewhere the border was marked by either swift-flowing rivers or treacherous mountain pathways, neither of which could be crossed by a multitude of warriors with the speed necessary for a successful invasion.

"Once facing Rory O'Connor from the span's Munster side," Mael continued when it became annoyingly clear that Morag meant not to answer. "I will point out that his brother is with me and waiting to assume leadership of Connaught—as a subordinate kingdom subject to High King Muirtrecht's control."

Though seated at the same small table in Mael's private solar, Donal sat back to watch through narrowed eyes while the pair discussed him as if he were no more than a lifeless puppet. In the past decade of wedded life he had nearly grown impervious to his wife's contemptuous dismissal of his wishes, his aspirations. But now watching her collude with Mael was like watching her gladly negotiate with the devil—trading his soul for the fulfillment of her ambitions.

"But what if Rory survives the invasion?" Only this mortal threat to her goal was serious enough to force Morag into seeking the counsel of Mael. By harsh experience she'd learned the wisdom of limiting further dealings with him and meant to sever their uneasy bond . . . after she'd won what was sought. "He is not so easily killed."

"You would know." With sour glee Mael ridiculed Morag's unkept promises to see the deed done. "But 'tis certain success will follow steps I've taken to ensure that Lord Rory O'Connor will not live out the morrow."

Connaught's armies gathered at Tuatha Cottage in the area where once had been a garden tended by Liam but now hosted the smoldering remains of a charcoal mound. It was the perfect staging area for their defense—close to both the bridge, certain site of the invaders' most intense assault, and the place where waited their White Witch's cache of mysterious black powder.

The afternoon had been devoted to gathering pottery vessels donated by the people of keep, village, and countryside for use with a magical weapon. At

Lissan's direction, these contributions were brought
to her at Tuatha Cottage.

Lissan's emerald gaze slowly scanned the cottage's single room and found daunting the sight of
every available surface covered with vessels in a
wide variety of sizes and shapes. The prospect of her
task to determine the proper amount of black powder and length of fuse for each was formidable—
particularly when any error would likely bring harm
to the very people she wished to protect.

Along with a lecture on the vital importance of
following her directions precisely, Lissan demonstrated how a hole of exactly the right depth must
be dug in the earth to contain each vessel. She taught
them the way to use loose dirt in refilling any gap
around the outside of the container up to a point
just below its rim, explaining as she did so that this
would prevent enemies from noticing and investi-
gating oddly placed pottery. Although inwardly
hoping against hope that the entire confrontation
would be over so quickly this wouldn't be an issue,
she knew that being prepared for any eventuality
was the better part of valor.

Next she showed how to place one end of what
her warrior-students jestingly termed an overlong
"wick" in the vessel and then roll out the remainder
to its end a safe distance away. Along with this display Lissan emphasized the need for another critical
action: to lie flat after lighting the fuse and cover
one's head with both arms.

As the finish to a long day neared, an exhausted
Hildie slept soundly on a friend's pallet inside Tuatha Cottage while just beyond the door Lissan stood
with Rory to watch as the gloom of descending dusk
met rising ground mists. The world seemed to become a uniform grey through which moved indistinct shadows—warriors off to carefully do precisely

what their lord and his magical companion had commanded.

King Turlough and his personal guardsmen had already set off to lead divisions of a sizable force in slow patrol all along the border. There with the first glimmer of dawn terrifying surprises would be waiting unseen in areas most vulnerable to the crossing of invaders. But the vast majority of Lissan's black-powder weapons would, of course, be placed around the bridge's Connaught end since it was there that Rory would stand as commander of its defense.

"But Rory," Lissan argued, trying to convince him she should be permitted to watch from the conceal-ment of woodland shadows bordering that site. "After having seen me survive both Mael's broadsword and Morag's fire, what manner of danger do you fear the battle ahead might pose for me?"

Holding his gaze unblinking, Lissan tilted her chin upward in a fine show of easy courage that she hoped would hide her actual uncertainty over just how protected she truly was.

Rory scowled. That Lissan's logic was sound did nothing to lessen alarm raised by the thought of her threatened by the wide variety of hazards for which someone with so little experience of his world's vi-olent side couldn't possibly be prepared.

Now dark eyes held an emerald gaze in a steady bond while Rory tried to reason with his valiant love. "Nothing prevented you from being captured and hauled away by Mael's minions."

Lissan promptly nodded while without breaking their visual link giving a quick retort. "And to the rescue came my father, Liam—and you."

"I wish that were true." Even amid a twilight haze the white flash of Rory's mocking smile was clearly seen. "But, unaware of your capture, I didn't set out to rescue you."

"Yet carry me to safety you did." With her fast retorts Lissan had proved herself as stubborn and unwilling to cede the point as Rory.

"But if you're there—" As a last argument, Rory offered one he thought her most likely to accept. "My concern for your safety may be a dangerous distraction when I most need to maintain a clear mind and quick reflexes."

If not alone, then amidst dense mists nearly so, Lissan nestled against the strong man unaccustomed to yielding a woman her way. "I will stay hidden in the shadows. You won't even know I'm there."

"Hah," Rory muttered in soft disbelief but didn't flatly deny her the proposed action.

Lissan knew that, even had Rory refused, he realized nothing could prevent her from taking the proposed action with unspoken hope of warding off any possible harm to him. With the horrible image of Rory wounded came a much brighter thought. She *could* protect him from physical injury.

"In my time old tales are still repeated that tell of knights wearing their lady's favor into battle for good fortune."

"Hah." This repeated soft growl made Rory's disdain for such romantic foolishness clear.

The unpromising response reminded Lissan that in this year the royal Eleanor, patron of the troubadour's *Courts of Love*, hadn't yet been born. Still, she doggedly continued.

"I pray that for love of me, you'll wear my favor." Without waiting for a response, she pinned to his tunic the brooch removed from her own bodice.

At the sight of elegant hands affixing the lovely piece all the scorn Rory had heaped on his peers for

surrendering to a woman's nonsensical wishes came
back to mock him.

"Please wear it." Desperation crept into Lissan's
voice. "I swear it will keep you safe for me."

"Of course I'll wear it, sweeting." Rory's voice
was a deep burr of unshielded emotion muffled
when he bent his head to claim her mouth.

Acknowledging the need for postponing even
sweeter delights, Rory lifted his head to murmur, "If
you insist on coming to the bridge with me, then
allow me to get your cloak. The air will lose all
warmth before the dawn and the excitement we've
arranged to accompany its arrival."

"Thank you, my love, but there's something more
I would like to fetch so let me go inside for just a
moment and I'll soon return."

Before Rory could respond, Lissan had slipped
away, and although she was gone longer than the
promised moment he didn't mind.

Once Lissan was snugly wrapped in her cloak and
seated before Rory on his stallion, they steadily
made their way to the proposed site where she knew
a great many others waited unseen.

For Lissan the remaining hours of night passed
with agonizing slowness. She fervently wished it
were possible for her to supervise the placement of
every crockery bomb. It wasn't. Though difficult, her
trust must be given to those she'd trained. All Lissan
could do now was pray that they'd return unharmed—leastways by the weapon she had provided.

When finally the sky grew marginally brighter,
Rory deposited Lissan amidst a thick clump of flow-
ering bushes heavy with pale blossoms before has-
tening back to await the battle forewarned.

Lissan was caught between apprehension and impatience. She glanced into the eastern horizon, then
peered toward the bridge for a glimpse of Rory. At

last as dark purple brightened to rose a battle cry soared from the bridged valley's far side. Though hardly unexpected, the ominous sight of ground seeming to come alive with a swarm of warriors sent a shiver of cold panic through Lissan.

"You are a fool, O'Connor, to leave this bridge so poorly guarded," Mael chortled. Despite Donal's unexpected disappearance, he was confident that nothing could halt his powerful army and jabbed his broadsword into the sky. Its blade caught and reflected the vivid shades of sunrise as he swung it halfway down to motion his troops forward.

The bridge was instantly crowded with warriors, each anxious to prove himself a great warrior by being among the first to crush Connaught.

They were halted in an instant by the loud report of an unnatural thunder accompanied by a shocking flash so brilliant it vied with any streak of lightning ever seen. As the men stood stunned beneath this terrifying, unearthly defense spewing a shower of dirt and glittering sparks out in all directions, a second explosion from the bridge's Connaught end sent those on the span scrambling over one another to escape. The rapid echo of other loud bursts heard from varying distances added desperation to their fight to be first in retreat.

Almost simultaneously and much nearer, a third, fourth, and fifth went off. Pandemonium swept out from the crowded span to roll over the whole of Munster's troops in an ever-widening tidal wave of panic.

Mael watched in stunned horror as the vast majority of an army larger than any he'd ever dreamed of leading turned and fled like cowards. But he didn't. No, while his king and a hardy few remained steadfast behind, Mael positioned his steed so that he directly faced the enemy on the deep valley's far side.

"You cannot win," Mael shouted, peering at his foe through the lingering smoke settling over a deserted span. "Munster *will* take Connaught."

To Mael's surprise, before Rory could respond, onto the bridge's first plank stepped a female in white—the same one who had survived his broadsword's mightiest blow unscathed.

"No, you will *not* triumph over Connaught. Not now. Not ever." Although quaking inside, Lissan was certain only apparent confidence in this bold claim would win the day. Toward that end she'd donned her dimity gown and now forced a bright smile.

"Surely, by what I've done to see your invasion end here in utter failure, you must realize that your puny strength is as nothing compared to the feats I am able to perform."

Mael silently fumed. The interfering female was wrong. His plan had not utterly failed! And once Rory had been permanently removed he was near certain that the woman would depart.

A glimpse of movement on the cliff face below the span's opposite end lent sufficient hope for Mael to rein his horse into turning. Proudly he led his badly decimated force in riding away. He had another conflict to wage; another example of treachery and deceit waiting retribution in his own keep.

The warriors of Connaught were elated by a battle won without a single blow struck or drop of blood spilled and quick to celebrate. However, pleasure for this satisfactory end to a dreaded threat lulled them into a dangerous inattention while other lesser perils yet remained.

Unnoticed, up from the cliff face below the bridge's outset swung one determined to end the life of a man too often proven impossible to kill. Then, just as the growing warmth of a morning blessed with unexpected peace was shaken by a low growl, from woodland shadows came a loud and desperate warning.

"Ro-o-rrr-y, be-e-w-w-a-rre!"

Rory spun about to find the glitter of a enemy's sharp blade hazardously near. In the next instant he was knocked completely to the ground by the solid force of a man launching himself from the forest gloom on one side.

As he struggled to sit upright, Rory's irritation with the second assailant was scattered by the sight of Donal lying in an awkward heap, blood gushing from where a dagger protruded from his neck. Only vaguely aware that two of his guardsmen held a struggling captive between them, Rory scrambled to kneel at Donal's side.

"Why?" Rory's single-word question surpassed mere query of brotherly resentment or even of loyalty and honor.

"For all my sins . . . love my brother. . . ." These simple statements seemed to have required too much of Donal as he struggled for the breath to say more. "Wronged you . . . forgive. . . ." These words were carried on the faintest of whispers and were Donal's last.

Watching in horror, Lissan had gasped as the same man who'd once captured her swung up from the cliff edge where the bridge began. When, with deadly dagger raised high, the man had dashed immediately toward a broad, vulnerable back, she'd had but an instant to hope her amulet's protective powers would prove as effective for Rory as for her. Instead it had been shown unnecessary as in that moment Donal threw himself in harm's way to save the life of his too long resented brother.

Lissan moved to gracefully sink down at her hurting love's side and leaned forward to gently close Donal's unseeing eyes.

Mael was in a fury. Having lingered just inside the woodland's edge long enough to see Ferlich fail and Donal die in Rory's place, he had mercilessly spurred his stallion into racing toward his home. At its door he swung down and stomped inside.

Unpleasantly surprised by so quick a return, Morag rose from her seat on the hearth's outer edge. Before she could take more than a single step toward the great hall's entrance, Mael burst into the room.

"You are a fake and a fool!" Mael raged while jerking a boar-crested helmet from his head and recklessly throwing it into a dark corner.

Morag straightened, chin rising against this abrupt assault from one who, though never a friend, in the norm delighted in quieter, more subtle, and thus prolonged insults.

"Would that you truly possessed even so little as a tenth of the powers which the White Witch wielded this morn." Mael jabbed at the open space between them with his unsheathed sword. "If that were so, we *might* leastways have seen Rory O'Connor's interference put to a halt."

Morag's lips twisted into a humorless smile. It seemed her erstwhile ally had failed in his oath to see the lord of Ailm Keep dead. 'Struth, it was unfortunate. And yet she couldn't mourn the man's inability to keep an obviously too proud vow.

Recognizing the course of the woman's thoughts by the sneer on her face, Mael took pleasure in demolishing her plans as thoroughly.

"Rory lives, 'tis true." As Mael nodded, fiery hair reflected his flaring temper. "But Fergil did succeed in killing one O'Connor."

When his prey exhibited no more than a slight interest, Mael realized that she'd taken unjustified comfort in the fact that in Connaught O'Connor was a common surname shared by many. He wasted no moment to drive his vicious point home.

"Rory's life was saved by the brother who sacrificed his own instead."

Color drained from Morag until she seemed frozen into a block of cold marble.

"Aye," Mael gleefully added. "Because you hadn't the power you claimed able to forestall the White Witch's defenses, you will never be the Lady of Ailm Keep . . . far less the Queen of Connaught."

An icy cold rage filled Morag. She had sworn the wretched Mael would see her power and see it he would! Adopting an ominously vacant stare while folding arms across her waist and tucking hands beneath elbows, she glided forward.

Made more than uneasy by her expressionless response, Mael fell one step back from the steadily advancing woman and then another.

Morag neither slowed nor hastened until within arm's reach of the cowering man. Then her hands flew out, a dagger in each. She threw herself upon the shocked man while on either side of his neck sinking a weapon to its hilt.

And yet even as strange foe pounced, Mael reflexively swung his broadsword up and drove it into the back of her dark head.

Two bodies fell lifeless to the rush-bestrewn floor.

Lissan had begged leave from Rory and his king to return home to rest, bathe, and return refreshed for the evening's celebration. After pausing for just a moment inside Tuatha Cottage's closed door, she hastened to unlock her trunk, lift its heavy lid, and withdraw the thick volume of history. With unaccustomed awkwardness, she fumbled through its pages in search of Chapter Four, infamous Chapter Four. . . .

Her heart was pounding erratically before Lissan recognized the reason for her failure to immediately locate her goal—the boldface title once trumpeting Connaught's defeat and enslavement now read: The Importance of Connaught's Defeat of Munster's Invasion.

Quickly a smiling Lissan scanned columns succinctly outlining political strife, but on reading the end of the last she flashed a brilliant grin: ". . . and it was with this decisive victory—accomplished by mysterious bursts of fire reputed to be of supernatural origins—that the King of Connaught began in earnest to claim the high-kingship of all Ireland."

CHAPTER 20

Though night again settled its color-stealing blanket over the countryside beyond Ailm Keep's palisade, the courtyard was a cheery sight, bright with merrymaking and camaraderie. Roaring bonfires sent flames dancing high into the dark sky above long lines of trestle tables laden with a great feast of celebration while barrels of ale and casks of wine awaited.

"Join me in a toast of gratitude." King Turlough reached for a glittering, gem-encrusted vessel as he rose from the head table running crosswise to rows of others and called for his subjects' attention. Once the silence was complete and every eye was turned toward him, Turlough lifted the golden chalice above his head and continued.

"Toast with me the one who worked her white magic on our behalf, repelling a massive invasion and putting our foes to flight without a single blow struck."

Every person within hearing distance save one stood to hold high a variety of drinking vessels from the high table's fine goblets to the household serfs' crockery mugs.

"To Lissan, our White Witch."

As the king's hand on her shoulder had restrained her, Lissan was the only one still seated, and on hearing the admiration in these words she felt an embarrassing tide of color rising. Too aware of the handsome young king standing on one side and her incredible Rory so close on the other, she unsuccessfully tried to quell the blush by gazing out over the sea of faces below. Her goal was thwarted by the gratitude and admiration she encountered and which instead merely deepened the rosy glow of her cheeks.

As heads tilted back to drink the toast, Lissan was relieved to find Liam seated near the top of a lower table. She gladly focused on the prompt flash of his broad grin with hope for better suppressing the much-rued, self-conscious tint. However, it wasn't Liam's smile which successfully won that goal but the surprise in discovering Maedra at his side. Her friend had suppressed the moonglow aura to permit a more natural mortal appearance and yet undeniably remained the incredibly lovely Maedra.

Unnoticed by Lissan, Rory was motioning for the attention of those gathered which prevented them from resuming their seats.

"Even before the signal for invasion delivered with the dawn of this day," Rory announced, "our White Witch bestowed upon me a gift of great value—the gift of life."

A hushed murmur of curiosity passed through Rory's listeners but was instantly stilled as their lord explained. "With Hildie, Lissan rescued me from the intruders Lord Mael of Munster dispatched to see me dead. Aye, first I was rescued and then Lissan saw my health restored with a haste that could only have been accomplished by magic."

Lissan silently gasped. She'd believed Rory so thoroughly robbed of right senses by his wounds that he hadn't realized how serious they were. But if Rory remembered this, did he remember the inordinately long time she'd devoted to applying potions to his bruises? Despite the intimate relationship between them now, it was disconcerting to think he might and again her cheeks flooded with bright color.

While Lissan gazed determinedly down at tightly entwined fingers, Rory glanced around the crowd to be certain they understood the importance of what he'd shared.

"And a further gift she has given me," Rory firmly stated. "A gift even more precious—love." With the last word Rory drew Lissan to her feet and held her soft form close to his side while proposing a toast of his own.

"So, drink now to the one who as my wife, Lady Lissan of Ailm Keep, will soon be your lady in truth."

The cheer immediately echoing Rory's announcement left no question about the people's approval of their lord's choice for bride. While drinking vessels were drained with this second toast, Lissan ignored the bright heat of her cheeks. Then as Turlough extended his arm to Rory and the two men clasped forearms in a congratulatory gesture, she made no attempt to restrain a beaming smile and gladly met the many pleased nods and broad grins of those again taking their seats or returning to their duties.

When the meal began, Lissan sat proudly at her soon-to-be-mate's side as a parade of savory dishes was served and both ale and wine freely flowed. The steady call of a youthful but brilliant smile eventually summoned Lissan's attention to the young figure seated on Rory's far side.

By the radiant expression on Hildie's too often solemn face it was plain that she heartily approved of

the coming nuptials. Indeed, the mischievous gleam
in dark eyes suggested that the girl believed herself
partly responsible for bringing them together. And
while the girl soundlessly mouthed the words "so
happy," Lissan was more than willing to give her
credit for something that would be near impossible
to truly explain.

"When do you plan to wed, cousin?" Turlough
logically inquired, meeting Rory's gaze over the top
of Lissan's head.

"Since the threatened invasion demanded our full
attention, Lissan and I haven't had the opportunity
to discuss that question. But given my choice, it will
happen as soon as arrangements can be made."

"Lady Lissan." Turlough let his attention shift to
the emerald gaze of the woman between him and
Rory. "Have you a reason for delaying the cere-
mony?"

Suspecting the king's purpose for asking, Lissan's
heart pounded in growing excitement as she shook
her head. With the motion unrestrained golden hair
glowed as bright as the bonfires whose light it reflected.

"Good." Turlough grinned at Lissan for an instant
before looking back toward Rory. "Then, cousin,
why wait for some later time? A priest always jour-
neys with my entourage and is well able to see the
rite performed tonight."

"Ooh, Papa, tonight," Hildie bubbled from Rory's
left. "Tonight, please?"

"Aye, tonight," Liam called out. Seated nearby,
he'd heard the king's words and, lent a dram of false
courage by combination of abundant ale and Maedra's willingness to remain near even in this public
gathering, boldly encouraged his lord.

Others had heard the king's suggestion and
picked up Liam's refrain, urging their lord to take

prompt action in seeing the union confirmed by God and man.

Rory waited to receive Lissan's nearly impercep- tible nod. Then light from the waxen candles clus- tered upon a silver platter gleamed on black hair as he firmly nodded agreement to the action proposed by his royal cousin.

From there matters were very quickly arranged. The priest not only agreed to hear vows exchanged at the village church's door, as was the custom, but also to say mass from there for the sake of allowing the entire company to witness the full wedding serv- ice.

A chaplet of spring blossoms was hastily provided for the bride still wearing her peculiar white gown from another time and place. Emerald eyes brim- ming with love, Lissan gazed up at the stunningly handsome man who by some miracle of fate meant to swear himself hers.

Welcoming the prospect of exchanging vows be- neath a dark star-strewn sky and amidst so many well-wishers, Lissan felt blessed with more peace and happiness than ever anywhere, anytime before in her life. Furthermore, though the keep was hardly a fairy-tale castle and the future was certain to hold many challenges, she was confident that this was merely the first step in their *happily ever after* love story.

Once the rites and mass were complete, an audi- ence feeling twice blessed by victory and a new lady for Ailm Keep joyously returned to food, wine, and ale that would be plentiful throughout the night. Al- though a lute, pipes, and timbrels began a spritely tune for dancing, Rory swept Lissan completely off her feet. Despite the gentle banter of their onlookers, he again carried his bride up the stairway to his bed's sweet comfort and fiery pleasures.

Liam stood behind Maedra, arms wrapped around her waist while she gazed up with melancholy eyes toward the bridal couple so clearly in love and warmed by the public celebration of their commitment. Resting one cheek atop the gold silk of her hair and arms tightening in anguish, Liam wordlessly shared Maedra's pain that their equally true love could never be allowed approval or even acceptance.

"Nay." Maedra abruptly turned within the circle of Liam's embrace and despite eyes brimming with crystal tears gave an oath. "I *will* speak with King Comlan, reason with him. And he *will* understand and agree to our union. He *must!*"

One quiet evening, a fortnight after the wedding, an unexpected visitor abruptly appeared in Ailm Keep amidst the lord's private solar.

"Father—" Lissan jumped to her feet, nearly oversetting the chess table between her and Rory. Though she'd been lost amid mists of happiness in recent days, more than one pang of guilt had struck to remind her of a promised response too long delayed. "I'm sorry."

Rory's face went to stone. He was sorry, too. Not that they'd wed but that in the haste urged by his king he'd forgotten their agreement to first seek the approval of Lissan's father.

"I failed in my promise to share my decision with you as soon as it was made," Lissan said penitently.

"Aye, that you did." Comlan nodded solemnly but soon grinned. "However, Maedra told me of your marriage and by that I knew you would not be returning to your siblings in London."

"Then why have you come?" Lissan asked, moving nearer to her father.

"Anxious to host a small celebration, Maedra and

your mother too are asking that you, your husband, and stepdaughter come now for a visit."

Having heard him use such excuses for what he wanted to do many times in the past, Lissan discounted the grudging tone of this invitation and glanced nervously at her wary husband.

"Please, Rory," Lissan gently appealed. "I would dearly love to see my mother again."

Wanting always to give her whatever she wanted, Rory knew he was lost and, despite a lingering discomfort with his unearthly father-in-law, agreed.

Lissan looked back to their visitor and unexpectedly offered to bargain for what she'd already admitted to wanting. "We will come, if I may bring one more guest."

Comlan's brows arched. He was not accustomed to others either questioning his decisions or daring to ask for more than he offered. But then, like her mother, this daughter had a willful mind of her own.

"Who?" Comlan succinctly asked.

"A friend, Liam." Lissan had recognized the importance of his addition by Maedra's part in arranging this visit. "He's the young man who like Maedra guarded me during my stay in Tuatha Cottage."

"Very well." Comlan's eyes narrowed but he nodded permission while adding, "If you'll summon him and your stepdaughter to join us immediately."

"I will call them," Rory said as he rose to his feet, choosing to be ignored no longer.

Once an excited Hildie and an uneasy Liam stood close beside their lord and lady, the King of the Tuatha de Danann ordered them to close their eyes. The moment all had obeyed, they found themselves in an incredible place so bright it seemed the sun itself had been trapped within.

Lissan was almost immediately engulfed in a fervent embrace. After pulling back, she directly met the gaze of her mother's young self. It was shocking but a shock quickly overcome by pure delight.

"Oh, Mama, you are here and safe?" With these words she gave the woman another quick hug.

Amy gently laughed in response to her daughter's statement. "As I have been safe since the day I met your father inside his sister's ring of flowers—the one you loved so much."

"I love it even more now." Lissan grinned and turned to tug Rory nearer. "It delivered me to my Rory, although a sudden action neither of us understood or appreciated at the time."

Amy's curiosity demanded an explanation for her daughter's strange statement.

By the puzzlement she'd aroused, Lissan realized her father had shared with his wife nothing of their daughter's adventure. Likely he'd made that choice because it would be unnecessary were she returned to London. But whatever the reason, it left her to explain a great deal.

While Amy fell into close conversation with Lissan and Rory, Comlan gave his attention to the dark child who'd summoned him from the fairy ring to rescue a daughter from being burned as a witch.

"And your mother's name was?" Comlan softly inquired.

"Cleva." Hildie gazed solemnly up at the wondrous figure so close.

Comlan was equally solemn in asking, "It was she who said that you are descended from my sister, the Lissan of the fairy ring?"

Hildie's dark eyes widened but she promptly nodded.

"Did you know there's a way to know if 'tis true?" With a forefinger, Comlan gently lifted the child's chin to directly meet his penetrating eyes.

" 'Struth?" Breath audibly caught in Hildie's

throat. Desperately wanting to know and yet afraid to be disappointed, she scraped together the courage to squeak out a single word. "How?"

"When a fairy's power is shed," Comlan said, impressed by the clearly frightened child's bravery, "it leaves a mark behind. Throughout time every descendant of like gender will bear that same mark."

Hildie bit her lip hard, hoping . . . hoping . . . hoping. . . .

"My sister had a small shape on the back of her neck like a lopsided heart," Comlan softly stated.

Instantly, Hildie swept hair forward and bent her head to reveal her nape and the small shape of a lopsided heart that it bore.

"You are my niece, my human niece." Comlan lifted the child to give her a warm and fatherly embrace of welcome.

While her queen chatted with Liam's lord and lady, Maedra recognized an opportunity she dared not lose. Clutching Liam's hand and pulling him along with her, she nervously approached Comlan to seek an all-important discussion.

"My king," Maedra softly called.

Before turning to answer his subject, Comlan motioned for one of his warriors, both trustworthy and amusing, to come and entertain the child. Suspecting the relationship would be proven, he'd earlier given Kieron his commands.

While Kieron led Hildie off to join a merry dance, Maedra waited in growing trepidation, and the moment her king turned toward her, she launched into a well-rehearsed speech.

"I know the rules controlling interaction between our realm and the human world and would never want to risk Queen Amethyst, your children, or anyone else by changing the course of time. . . ."

"But?" Comlan urged Maedra to the point he had

seen coming since nearly the day he'd dispatched her to Tuatha Cottage.

"Lissan's decision to remain with Lord Rory will not change time," Maedra reasoned. "And it won't if I remain in that time, too." She saw golden brows descending over emerald eyes and hastily added, "I'll appear only in human guise but without either shedding my powers or using them during the span of a human lifetime."

Comlan's frown was in no way lessened by her arguments.

Fearing failure loomed, Maedra took a deep breath and immediately continued with a dangerous rationale. "*You* did the same without causing harm." Her king's expression seemed implacable but still she went onward. "I will give whatever oath, pay whatever price I must for that privilege."

"*Why* do you want to linger in the mortal world? Why when you have so much more here in my realm?" Comlan knew from experience that the answer to this meant the difference between success or failure in maintaining a human guise.

Maedra abruptly realized she'd been foolish not to expect this question. To quickly give an answer, she pulled from her memory the one she'd given Liam when he'd asked much the same.

"In our realm things remain ever the same with few challenges we cannot overcome. In Liam's world all things are new and the game of human life, though deadly, is a fresh vista to be explored." Even as she spoke, Maedra heard in this hollow argument the undeniable ring of a mere façade. Fearing defeat by her own lack of preparation, she stared morosely down at the lush carpeting beneath her feet.

To Comlan this talk of games and exploring fresh vistas seemed proof that Maedra's reasons were superficial which meant she would fail in her goal and

that failure opened the potential for drastic consequences. He was about to deny her plea when unexpectedly the speaker who hadn't glanced up to
face his disapproval went on.

"But the true reason, the most important reason,
is that I love Liam. Aye, 'tis why I want to stay with
him and would want to even if every hour was gray
and cold, even if every day repeated the drudgery
of the last. Together none of that would matter to
me whereas to be here without Liam would mean
becoming a shell with no heart at all."

Comlan smiled. This was a sentiment he recognized, one he'd shared before spending a lifetime
with Amethyst in her world.

"You'll let her stay with us, won't you, Father?"
Lissan had led her companions to stand within arm's
reach of his back.

Comlan answered his daughter without turning
his attention from Maedra. "How could I refuse one
of my subjects the right to experience joys I claimed
for myself?"

Liam had stood silent, overawed by his surroundings throughout Maedra's plea, but when the golden
being who was her king agreed to her plea, he gave
a loud whoop and swept his beloved into a tight
embrace.

These actions inspired a great deal of hearty
laughter and shouted congratulations that soon
drew the couple into a lively dance.

Hildie curiously watched as Lissan and Rory
joined this realm's king and queen at the edge of the
floor where she'd earlier danced while Kieron
watched the amazing dark child so unlike any in his
world in so many ways.

King Comlan had told Kieron about the girl likely
descended from his sister and asked him to accept
the post of guardian and friend. Made reluctant by

the prospect of too much time given a boring human, he would've refused the royal commission if he could. But now that he'd seen and talked with his charge, the duty seemed not so utterly bleak.

"Hildie." Kieron quietly called for the child's attention. When unusual eyes of deepest blue turned to him, he offered what was likely to be the best link to aid him in protecting the child. "I have a gift for you, a very special pet."

"Pet?" Hildie's dark eyes suddenly glowed with silver sparks. She had always wanted a pet of her very own but Morag refused to have another animal cluttering a place already host to too many hunting dogs.

"What kind?" She looked suspiciously at the golden and intimidatingly handsome man unaccountably willing to waste his time with her. Her eyes quickly dropped from others an impossible shade of aqua and anxiously glanced around. "Where is it?"

"Here," Kieron answered and as he spoke a small fox suddenly appeared in his arms.

"A fox?" Hildie was torn between surprise and delight with the dainty creature of auburn fur and black-tipped tail.

"Not only is she tame," Kieron explained as he lowered the animal into the child's welcoming arms, "but she has a very special talent. If ever you have need of my help, send her to fetch me and she will."

Already in a place of wonders and impossible realities, Hildie didn't for a moment question his claim although she couldn't imagine bothering this awe-inspiring being with her petty woes. Instead she merely asked, "What's her name?"

Kieron gave her a gentle smile. "You'll have to give her one after you're both back in Ailm Keep."

Even as he spoke, Kieron's attention was caught

by King Comlan motioning him to bring Hildie up to join others of her party gathered around an open space for the evening's entertainment.

As apparently was common in this realm, Lissan shared Rory's large and comfortably padded chair. She decided it was a lovely custom and happily leaned against her love's strength. With challenges met and near everyone she loved close and happy in their futures, contentment filled her. Soon a head of golden curls rested on a broad shoulder, allowing Lissan to gaze up into a potent smile of unconcealed love.

Against the backdrop of an elegant Cornwall mansion before World War II and a vast continent-spanning canvas during the turbulent war years, Rosamunde Pilcher's most eagerly-awaited novel is the story of an extraordinary young woman's coming of age, coming to grips with love and sadness, and in every sense of the term, coming home...

Rosamunde Pilcher

The #1 *New York Times* Bestselling Author of *The Shell Seekers* and *September*

COMING HOME

"Rosamunde Pilcher's most satisfying story since *The Shell Seekers*."

—*Chicago Tribune*

"Captivating...The best sort of book to come home to...Readers will undoubtedly hope Pilcher comes home to the typewriter again soon."

—*New York Daily News*